NO LONGER PROPERTY OF
SEATTLE PUBLIC LIBRARY

Advance Praise for

THE OTHER NEW GIRL

"Overall, this is a deftly constructed coming-of-age story with well-drawn characters and the narrative momentum of a thriller. Gschwandtner (*Carla's Secret*, 2013, etc.) is a gifted storyteller who ably balances the past and present throughout the novel and never puts a foot wrong. . . . A potent exploration of youth, innocence, and the abuse of authority."

—*Kirkus Reviews*

"'We swim in the soup we've made,' the protagonist of LB Gschwandtner's compulsively readable novel, *The Other New Girl*, observes. The ingredients of this dark and disturbing coming-of-age novel include adolescent cruelty, religious hypocrisy, and the sadder-but-wiser perspective of the adult who dares to look back. Gschwandtner asks the question 'Do we ever really get over high school?' Like me, other readers may ponder that question for themselves as they race through this harrowing and heartbreaking tale of the aftereffects of power misused. I was riveted."

—Wally Lamb, author of six *New York Times* best-selling novels, *including The Hour I First Believed* and *She's Come Undone*, and was twice selected for Oprah's Book Club

"A coming-of-age story, woven with the pace of a thriller. The protagonist is wonderfully relatable, her wise but somewhat salty outlook appeals to the outsider in us all. The prose is fresh while we reminisce with the characters; we learn from them as they reveal their navigation of adolescent rites of passage, Quaker philosophy, bullying, and young love. A nuanced and satisfying read."

—Eileen Dougharty, story

"LB Gschwandtner has created a complex tale of loyalty and betrayal, of youthful alliances and conflicts, and the incredible tension between doing the right thing, and protecting one's sense of self. Susannah Greenwood is not the newer girl; Moll Grimes is. And their relationship, the way this story builds in a setting fraught with the moral and strict demands of both their peers, the stringent Dean, Miss Bleaker, and their own hearts, makes for a fine, moving story."

—Robert Bausch, author of *Far as The Eye Can See* and
The Legend of Jesse Smoke

"This is the work of a master storyteller who introduces the reader to well-drawn characters, and brings the narrator's moral dilemma to a stunning climax."

—Lary Bloom, nonfiction writer, writing teacher,
and co-founder of Writing at the Mark Twain House

"Unlike many books that tease with the promise of what's to come, LB gives it to us up front. Her story takes place in a co-ed Quaker boarding school where students are often left to flounder before coming up for a gulp of the narrator's rarified air. The girls' dean, Miss Bleaker, knows all and sees all—or does she?"

—Suzanne Levine, poet, author of *Haberdasher's Daughter* and
Eric Hoffer Award finalist

THE
OTHER
NEW
GIRL

THE
OTHER
NEW
GIRL

A Novel

By

LB Gschwandtner

SHE WRITES PRESS

Copyright © 2017 L B Gschwandtner

All rights reserved. No part of this publication may be reproduced, distributed, or transmitted in any form or by any means, including photocopying, recording, digital scanning, or other electronic or mechanical methods, without the prior written permission of the publisher, except in the case of brief quotations embodied in critical reviews and certain other noncommercial uses permitted by copyright law. For permission requests, please address She Writes Press.

Published 2017
Printed in the United States of America
ISBN: 978-1-63152-306-9 pbk
ISBN: 978-1-63152-307-6 ebk
Library of Congress Control Number: 2017941522

This is a work of fiction. Names, characters, places, brands, media, and incidents are either the product of the author's imagination or are used fictitiously. The author acknowledges the trademarked status and trademark owners of various products referenced in this work of fiction, which have been used without permission. The publication/use of these trademarks is not authorized, associated with, or sponsored by the trademark owners.

Book Design by Stacey Aaronson

For information, address:
She Writes Press
1563 Solano Ave #546
Berkeley, CA 94707

She Writes Press is a division of SparkPoint Studio, LLC.

The past is never dead. It's not even past.

—William Faulkner

PROLOGUE

I ENTERED FOXHALL SCHOOL IN THE TENTH GRADE. IT WAS a coed Quaker school at a time when coeducation outside of public school was uncommon enough that only a few private schools offered it. Quakers had always treated women as equals—sort of. The school was founded for boys and girls from Quaker farming families in Pennsylvania; a state founded by William Penn, himself a Quaker, or Friend as the denomination was known, for The Religious Society of Friends.

Starting as a sophomore set me apart from the first day. There was only one other new sophomore girl that year. Her name was Moll Grimes. Everyone else had established their cliques and chosen roommates the year before so we were odd girls out from the start. I was stuck in a small, single room on the second floor of Fox, which served as the dorm for most of the girls, as well as housing the school offices on the ground floor, along with the dining hall, and assembly room above it.

The view from my window looked out onto a wide, gently sloping lawn that gradually became the long fields where girls practiced field hockey and lacrosse. Beyond those fields there was a flat grassy area at the end of which was the outdoor theatre, a grass stage about six feet higher than the field, where outdoor graduation was held every June, weather permitting. Behind that grass stage, flanked by huge old oaks, the Foxhall woods spread out and curved around, meeting the Nonnahanny River beyond, on whose banks I would come as close to losing my virginity as possible without technically altering my maidenly status. I was fifteen and arrived at Foxhall both happy and unhappy to be there.

ONE

Hello Again

TWO WEEKS BEFORE HER DUE DATE, I GOT THIS FRANTIC TEXT from my daughter: *com rite away labr strtd.* So at the last minute I wangled a flight standby from D.C. to San Francisco then took a cab straight to the hospital. Everything was going about as expected, but the baby just could not make the final push and that's when the grueling wait dragged on while hour after hour an increasing dread hung over the birthing room.

After twenty-three hours, I wanted to scream at all those hospital workers in soft-soled shoes solicitously padding around, "For God's sake wheel her to the OR and get the baby out. Can't you see she's in agony?"

But my daughter had insisted on natural childbirth and refused to give up. Being an invited guest I kept silent, even when I held her husband in my arms to keep him from slumping to the floor while he sobbed into my shoulder. After it was all over, a bloodstain the size of a VW Beetle covered the floor under her bed. I never want to go through anything like that again. They named the baby James Joseph after both his grandfathers and we immediately dubbed him JJ.

Finally, with little JJ safely cradled in my exhausted daughter's arms I left, dragging my paltry carry-on, and headed for a nearby hotel. Outside, morning fog hovered over the city creating a powdery gray dawn but it was turning blustery with glints of sunlight just breaking through, a ghostly sort of indecisive morning where passersby appeared out of the mist. And as I walked down one of those steep San Francisco hills there was Daria McQueen, an apparition heading straight toward me, her face half hidden behind a fluttery print scarf. When a burst of wind blew it sideways, wrapping it across her neck like a small sail taking a hard tack, we made eye contact and both of us stopped abruptly. I hadn't seen her or heard anything about her in forty-five years. And then, suddenly there she was.

Even after all the time that had passed, I could tell it was Daria right away but was surprised when she recognized me, too. Later I would have to sort through how I felt about seeing her again and I guess that's why I'm telling this story. But in the moment, what with the night I'd had, I was dazed, not sure how to react. I had never fully come to terms with the event we'd both lived through so many decades before. This chance meeting went way back, to everything that had happened when I first met Daria at Foxhall School.

"Greenwood, is it you?" She peered intently at me in that searching way I remembered.

She'd asked that same question once before, long ago, and the memory of it had stayed with me, popping up in my mind now and again. Daria always called me by my last name back then and it stuck like a tack. For the entire first year, no one called me Susannah, or my mother's pet name for me—Suzi. I learned early on that everyone always fell into line behind Daria. She had some kind of power over us. So, to her,

Greenwood it still was, although I'd been married for decades and no one had called me Greenwood since I left Foxhall School.

My teen years had been a mix of wonderful discovery and terrible insecurity. That first semester, when I was a new kid at Foxhall, left me even now wondering if I had done the right thing. Because really, sometimes it's just not clear where the line falls between right and wrong. The decisions that can change the course of a life are like a maze with all possible exits leading to endless paths of uncertainty.

And now, there was Daria again. At sixteen, she was the girl who seemed to have everything we thought worth having. Beauty, brains, a sharp wit, a girl you hoped would like and accept you because just being around her meant you were accepted . . . somehow special.

Even though I hadn't thought of myself as Greenwood since those battered years at prep school, I answered, "Yes. It's me," and raised a hand to shield my own face from the wind. Then I said, "Daria. How are you?" because I didn't know what else to say but, after all that time, probably I did want to know. Anyway it was what you said to someone you hadn't seen in a long time, even if just seeing that person disrupted your equilibrium and suddenly made you feel like a child who was not sure how she was supposed to behave around adults. There was nothing I wanted less on that glorious morning than to be pulled backward to a time when I didn't yet know who I really was or what I would become. I had no idea how resilient I was, nor, at the time, even knew what that word meant.

"Not a simple question to answer," she said. So like Daria

to keep you guessing. People don't change. Some soften. Some harden. But we all come with our pieces pre-arranged. That's not to say bad decisions don't lead to bad outcomes and good ones can't make you relatively happy. Still, we are who we are. Looking back at the choice I made at fifteen, would I do the same today? Probably, but I can't say for sure. That river swept past me long ago and all the possibilities of those years were gone.

Daria suggested we catch up at a Starbucks on the corner. There was always a Starbucks at a nearby corner these days, no matter where you were, even out there where it could just as well have been a Peet's or a Philz, because coffee was common in San Francisco now the way head shops were when Daria and I were young, back in the sixties, the decade of our coming of age. So off we went, propelled by the wind but also by the passage of time that begged to have its blanks filled in like those little ovals on an SAT test.

We ordered—a skinny mocha for her, a chai latte for me—and sat at a small table on not too uncomfortable wood chairs. We dropped our bags and jackets and then, well, it seemed neither of us knew where to start. It would have been an awkward moment except that Daria started to giggle like a girl.

"You know," she said, "I never really believed you told us the whole story."

So there it was. Right at the start. "About what?" I asked but I knew what she meant. It was as if we had leaped back in time, back to Foxhall School and that suspicious, aggrieved time when we didn't fully trust anyone, especially ourselves. I suppose I was testing her, or myself, wary of being too eager to reveal anything that might hurt. But she'd been on my side back then. She hadn't even been upset by what happened. Everyone else had been in shock. But not Daria. She was just as detached as a runway model strutting her stuff.

"About Moll and Miss Bleaker." She said it matter-of-factly, as if she'd been waiting all these years for me to divulge the truth. Before I could consider an answer, she went on.

"Did we ever find out why she was named Moll and not just plain Molly? I mean what a name for a girl. Sounds like some old, black-and-white, B-movie gangster girl." She giggled again.

She's nervous, I thought, and then dismissed it because it seemed inconceivable that anything could ever have made Daria nervous.

"She told me it was a combination of both her grandmother's names," I explained. Why did I remember that? It's mystifying what your mind holds onto as you age. "Mona and Lillian. But I remember telling her that calling herself Molly would make her fit in better. Seems utterly stupid now."

Back then we all operated inside our own little spaces with invisible walls. We only knew what anyone allowed us to know or what we admitted to or shared. We were close in an artificial way because there we were, stuck at Foxhall School, a microcosm with its distinct reality. Over the decades, I'd had to unlearn the unspoken rules that guided us at Foxhall. I'd had to relinquish the cynical elitist attitude I learned there. It was not what the school taught us. In fact, just the opposite. But it was what the situation required. Or at least what we imagined we needed for armor.

"Well maybe that was afterward," she said. "But before,

you know, before we even knew who she was, when her name was Moll and she was a nameless, gray girl who melted into the background, you know? I mean you were the only one who ever talked to her. We all called her 'the other new girl.'"

I remembered it all. I never spoke up back then, to tell them not to call her that. Never told them it was cruel not to use her name, even behind her back, because people always found out in some way. If they didn't hear it, they sensed it and that could be even crueler than knowing something for sure. A suspicion could eat away at a young girl. Especially if she was not pretty like the others, and she didn't fit in anywhere.

"I think I became a better person because of Moll. Over the long run anyway," I said.

When she said nothing I asked, "How much of it do you remember?"

"I'm not sure," she sipped at her skinny mocha and it seemed to me she was being evasive about her memories. Or it was possible she really didn't remember. Maybe both.

"Enough. Or maybe not enough. It was all so long ago. It shouldn't really matter anymore. So much else has happened," she said.

It mattered to me. All those years later. I wondered, too, what in her life made her think what happened with Moll was trivial.

"But I mean, really, do you remember what it was all about? The details of it."

She smiled and tilted her head in just the way she used to when she was about to deliver a zinger that made you feel about two inches tall.

"Sex, power, religion. What else is there?"

"What about love?" I must have sounded like a naïve child. And at my age. Well, maybe it was better to get more naïve as you age. Cynicism could weigh you down. I'd learned that at least.

"I wouldn't know," she said. "And I think your old friend Moll wouldn't either. Her reasons would be different from mine, I'd bet. She certainly wanted love. Everyone wants love and some people will do anything to get it. And some people who deny they want it, will do anything to keep others from having it."

She meant Miss Bleaker. I was sure of that. "We were cruel back then." I really meant she could be cruel but I didn't want to say that. And, besides, cruelty was a system that fed on our need to be accepted and we could all be cruel in the teen years.

"I don't know about you and the others but I certainly was." So she said it for me anyway, and I did not disagree. "I've paid my dues, though. Maybe not enough to make up for all that . . ." she stumbled over the word and then added, "mess."

I was cruel, too, I thought. But not the way she meant. Yes, I did talk to Moll. And yes, I did step outside of our little circle of cool girls. But I did not stop what happened and then someone was dead and someone else was lost forever. Where does blame reside? I don't know the answer to that. Daria called it "that mess." As if you could dismiss life and death as a simple mess.

TWO

The Makeup Room

I MET DARIA MCQUEEN IN THE FIRST WEEK AT FOXHALL. She was hard to miss and impossible to ignore in that sequestered community.

Going "away" to boarding school—prep school it was called by those who felt it necessary to designate exactly what rung one belonged on in the social strata—was looked upon by the girls I was leaving behind at my all-girl day school as something of an oddity. We were in eighth grade, a temporary way station between childhood and high school when girls were figuring out what was important to them. Clothes, boys, makeup, in any combination. Why would you want to go away to boarding school, they wondered. At our girls' day school we wore gray uniforms and, when I told the girls I'd be going away to a Quaker school, they asked, "Are you allowed to have zippers in your clothes?"

"That's Puritans," I explained but it didn't stop there. They wanted to know about buttons and if I had to wear black all the time and why would I subject myself to that when I could stay at home and wear whatever I wanted. It would have been useless to point at our uniforms, since the minute the girls were off school grounds they'd change clothes, apply makeup liberally, and meet up with boys. They also wanted to know about Quakers being against procreation. I would sigh and say those were Shakers, not Quakers, but the distinction seemed lost to them and after a while I gave up. When I told them it was a coed school they said, "Oh, well, that's okay then." In those days, only Quaker prep schools were coed except for one progressive school up in Vermont, which my parents considered with suspicion as possibly socialist. Heavens.

Sometimes girls back home went away to "prep"—always to sister schools associated with some elite boys prep school— but none had ever gone to a Quaker school before so I was a trailblazer and an oddity they looked upon with skepticism and confusion. Not a good combination in eighth grade, so I was not unhappy to leave. In truth, I was not doing well at the girls' school and my home life was a mess. My parents wanted to get me into what they called "a better situation." Translation . . . I'd better do well at the Quaker school that was billed as a caring, supportive, and family-like environment, or else. This did not address the messy home life for which I was not responsible but that never seemed to come up in any of the conversations around the dinner table about my so-called lackluster grades or behavioral infractions. When I look back now at my school reports, all of which my mother saved, I am amazed that my grades were actually quite good with one glaring lapse in algebra, which to this day makes no sense to me. And my teachers seemed to like me, according to their comments. But nothing I ever did satisfied my mother. So the impression left was of a slacker who was not living up to her potential. How one pre-measures potential was always puzzling.

At Foxhall I took the place of a girl named Ursula who'd been expelled at the end of her freshman year for sneaking a local boy into her room late one night and getting drunk with him. Or maybe they were already drunk before she let him climb the tree outside her room and come in through her open window. It had happened in the spring, the four girls who took me under their collective wing told me on my eighth day at Foxhall.

I'd arrived at Foxhall in a tentative state, my parents having driven me all the way from Connecticut arguing about something trivial that I tried not to listen to by reading in the back seat, which only made me feel queasy. My mother was starting to act weird again and when that happened she would pick on me. My father would defend me and they would go at it, leaving me caught in the middle and left out at the same time. By the time we'd unloaded my stuff and said good-bye so they could get back before dark, I was glad to be on my own, angry that they'd left me to whatever fate was waiting, and terrified I'd be shunned for being new. So when four junior girls took me under their collective wing, I didn't ask questions or try to figure out why. I was happy to be absorbed into their clan, relieved to belong somewhere, especially if it meant being designated a cool girl.

We had all stayed up past lights out and gone to the makeup room behind the auditorium stage. The room was only supposed to be used for dress rehearsals or during plays but girls sometimes snuck in there after lights out to study or just to do what teenage girls do late at night—talk about boys, other girls, hopes and wishes. Once there, we would gaze at ourselves in the long mirror above the makeup table that ran the entire length of the back wall and point out our facial flaws.

Brady's hair was thick and unmanageable. My eyebrows were too low. Poor Jan's mouth curved to one side, especially when she smiled. Faith had not enough of a chin and her palms had a skin condition that flared up when she was stressed. It was nonsense, of course, because we were all pretty. But at our age none of us was thrilled with the images we saw gazing back at us, as if that mirror had been borrowed from a fun house and told only a distortion of truth. All except for Daria. She was gorgeous and everyone, including Daria, knew it. No mirror could dispute it, and the rest of us could only sigh and think how easy it was to be Daria, as if beauty was a key that would open any door.

I was in a kind of confused state during those first days at Foxhall. Plucked out of my familiar pond at home, out of the only bedroom I'd ever known, the house where I'd grown up, the school I'd been driven to since fourth grade, even the uniform I wore, that I'd gotten used to hating but that allowed me to dress five days a week without thinking about what to wear and what everyone else was wearing and what was acceptable and what I would look like and what the others might say about me or think of me. And boys. Now there were boys everywhere I went. At meals. In the halls. In classes. At the library. On the playing fields. They watched us and hooted at us and talked to us and followed us. I didn't have any idea what to wear, how to act, what to say. Whatever these girls wanted from me, I would be a willing participant. If only they would like me, accept me, make me a member.

In the makeup room, they told me about the expelled

girl, Ursula, whose room I'd been assigned. She'd been on the "outside" as they termed it. I understood right away that simply including me in the retelling brought me "inside" and that was a major coup for me. It was also made clear that since I was the new girl, I had a lot to prove and that night set the wheels in motion. Just to be spirited up to the makeup room after lights out was a sign that I was being tested for membership in their club. I learned later that Daria had set it up, told the others to get me alone and find out what I was made of, if I was worthy of inclusion and how far I'd go to prove it.

The boy Ursula let through her open window was cute, they said with knowing nods and raised eyebrows. A townie whose father ran the local farm store, a successful enterprise as far as a local business could be looked upon by us preppies as worthy. In those days, farms still surrounded Foxhall. The land hadn't been plowed under and gouged out by developers. So he wasn't the kind of poor that would have made him untouchable. Still, he was not one of the boys from Foxhall. Those were the boys we were supposed to date and eventually marry—or boys just like them maybe not from a Quaker school, but from other, more traditional schools.

But, they told me, she shouldn't have done it. At least not that way. The girls were not so much offended that she'd taken up with the cute townie, who was nineteen and rumored to be "experienced," a code word for sexually adept. No, they were more put off by the way she'd done it.

She should have waited for the weekend and gotten a pass to town and met him on the sly. Maybe under the railroad trestle. Or in that big culvert where the Nonnahanny stream ran quietly enough, if there hadn't been any rain, to walk inside and sit down on the corrugated metal with the huge old sycamore standing guard at one open end of the tall tube. No one would have seen them in there and they could have gotten drunk and done whatever they wanted. No one would have known. They were still trying to figure out why she'd taken the risk of bringing him into her room.

"I don't think she expected to get caught," said Jan.

"Of course she didn't expect it," Brady made a face at Jan. "Who would? Especially on that day."

"Well, it was pretty odd letting him climb the tree and opening the window," Jan argued. "She was just stupid."

Daria ran her fingers through her curls and sighed. "I know, the night before graduation. I mean she was a junior so it wasn't her graduating. But still . . . she wanted them to find her. I'm sure of it. She almost waved a red cape at them."

"At who?" I asked and was sorry the minute the words were out.

They all turned to look at me and I could tell by their smirks that I should have kept quiet.

"Who do you think?" asked Jan.

I shrugged and looked down at the makeup table in front of me but I could feel them all watching me.

"Them," said Brady. "The Foxhall behavior squad. The system. The deans. All of them. She hated them. Daria's right. She wanted to get caught. She wanted to get out of here and go back to public school to finish up. She wanted to get her license, to drive and go where she wanted, and not have to get permission to go to town or sign out or any of the stuff we have to do here. She didn't want to be a chicken cooped up in a cage anymore."

Later, I came to understand it. She wanted freedom. She wanted to get caught so she wouldn't have to quit the school on her own. This way, she'd be free to move on and the mark against her would only matter to her parents. She'd feel liberation to their shame. It was a bargain she'd made with herself. And the boy could go back to town and talk about the hoity-toity girl he'd screwed right in her own dorm room because in those days, getting drunk was a euphemism for sex. It was three months shy of 1960, the tail end of the quiet, self-satisfied fifties, on the cusp of the sexual revolution, the Vietnam War, The Beatles, pot, Bob Dylan and protest songs, and turning on, tuning in, and dropping out with a little help from your friends. We were supposed to be innocent. We had no idea what was ahead of us. We were supposed to follow the rules. We were supposed to be preparing for college, responsibility, taking our place among the elites of our country. We weren't supposed to be in the makeup room. We were supposed to be in bed, asleep, alone.

I was so eager to fit in that I would have done almost anything for these girls. I had no idea yet just how deep the pit of acceptance could be. These girls were at war with the rules, but only in a clandestine way. There was a code to follow and when it was broken, they united to protect both the structure provided by the rules and the ways in which a girl could get around them. They were juniors, one year ahead of me, well versed in the Foxhall culture.

We were all away from home, isolated out in the country at a school with more rules than our parents had ever laid down. It was a long time ago now. The world has changed.

We didn't have cell phones or iPads. There was no texting or sexting or free Wi-Fi. There was one pay phone down the hall from the school office, and you could only use it for emergencies or on Saturday between nine in the morning and five in the evening. To receive a call on your hall, it came through the switchboard operated by an ancient woman we all called Mrs. W., although what her name really was, I never knew. She sat in her cubicle across from the deans' office with a panel of wires and plugs that connected her to every phone in the school. She logged all the calls with name of caller, time of call, and who the call was for, all written in a neat script on a giant logbook she kept at her side. The whole thing could have come from the pages of a Dickens novel. It was that nineteenth century.

"You have to carry on the tradition," Brady told me in a quiet voice.

"That's right," said Jan. "It's up to you now. Especially since they gave you her room."

She meant Ursula's room. I didn't say anything.

"Daria had an idea," said Brady. "She said if you agree, then we'll help you . . ." she seemed to be searching for the right word. "Get settled in here at Foxhall," she finally said.

"It can be tough starting out new in the second year, when everyone else already knows the ropes from last year," Faith broke in. She seemed genuinely interested in helping me through the transition. I would come to understand that Faith may have been one of the cool girls, but she was also deeply concerned about doing the right thing. That was the right thing as she saw it and not as the rulebook dictated. She had her own way of living her Quaker faith. Not like Daria's way. And I learned quickly that being Quaker didn't mean there was a mold that fit everyone.

"Thee can count on us," she added.

It was the first time I'd heard anyone speak in that way Quakers had of addressing their families and close friends and was further evidence that I was accepted.

I must have looked at her with some skepticism because she added, "I don't agree with what they did to Ursula. Yes, she broke a big rule, but expulsion was way over the top. It was cruel." Over time I would also come to understand the Quaker idea of passive resistance, of challenging the system from within, of taking a stand for what you think is right, just, moral.

"So, you see, we have to do something," Brady said. "It's an act of civil disobedience. Emersonian in its simplicity."

"And Daria has the perfect idea," said Jan. She grinned at me.

"What would I have to do?"

Brady leaned in as if we were conspirators in some war game. "It's easy. Just sleep through the whole thing. Or say you did. No matter what happens, they can't prove anything. And all you could possibly get is a demerit. Because without proof or you confessing, there's not much else that could happen."

"But what would I . . ."

Brady interrupted me. "We'll do everything. When we come through your room, you just pretend to sleep through it and leave the rest to us. The less you know the better."

So there I was, my fate decided. I nodded my agreement and was glad to be accepted into their circle, glad to have this group of girls shepherd me through my start at a new school, to be addressed by Faith in the familiar "thee," glad to have an easy assignment to seal my entry into the club.

During the three-day orientation before the actual school year started, new students were handed a thick booklet of rules. You were expected to memorize and follow them exactly. No ambiguities there. Rules were not to be broken and, should anyone break a rule, punishments would be meted out. These were spelled out at the end of the booklet in a section all its own. Reasons for expulsion were extensively covered. When people talk about the past as a more innocent time, less complicated, more personal, easier, simpler, they fail to mention that the human heart never changes and human behavior was as corrupt before as it is today and has been, ever since human history was first recorded. Just read the Bible or look at the ruins of any civilization and you'll see people behaving pretty much the way they do now, except with cruder tools. They had rules, too. That's the way it was at Foxhall. Acceptable behavior may have been codified in a booklet handed out at orientation, but that didn't prevent unacceptable behavior from creeping under the radar. In fact, I would argue it nourished and helped it grow.

That was the way I looked at it now. Back then, at fifteen, I was an integral part of the system, engulfed by the cool girls at the end of my first week. They were the girls who set the tone, made the unspoken rules, created the alternate codes of daily operation. Not that anything about that was recorded or written in a booklet. But we all knew what was what. I discovered, that night in the makeup room long after lights out, that I was the replacement for the expelled girl who had broken with the code and let a townie into her room where she'd been caught with her bra around her waist and the boy, his pants down around his ankles, on top of her, bed springs creaking and the smell of cheap scotch in the spring air that wafted in through the second floor window.

After the event, the girls' dean, Miss Bleaker, directed the grounds crew to cut the branches of the dogwood tree that had allowed this breach of the rulebook. From that day forward, all trees in front of windows around the base of Fox, where most of the girls lived, were denuded of branches above ten feet so that no one could ever again climb into a second floor window.

Someone—no one admitted to it but there were rumors— carved the boy's initials, W. T., into the side of the dogwood trunk that faced the building. And, in September, a week into my first term at Foxhall, a ritual of remembrance began. Brady, Faith, Jan, and Daria stole an hour before dinner to collect dandelion flowers before the chill of fall killed them off, wove them into circles and, late at night when everyone else was asleep, snuck into my room and tossed them from the window where they landed on the dogwood's truncated branches, wilted necklaces clinging like wreaths draped on a gravestone.

When the time came I did what was expected and feigned sleep through this initiation rite. And that was how I became embroiled with Miss Bleaker twelve days into my first year at Foxhall.

THREE

Margaret Bleaker

"TAKE A SEAT." MISS BLEAKER MOTIONED ME TO A straight-backed chair opposite her plain, brown desk. Standing to the right of it, she looked down at me. She seemed to be something other than flesh and bone and hair, like a statue that had escaped its base and begun to move zombie-like among the living. Anyway, she was intimidating, and I tried to avoid looking directly at her so instead I studied the room.

The top of her desk was empty of the sorts of trinkets you'd expect to find in a dean's office. No pictures of family members or a beloved dog, no potted plants or dishes of jellybeans to offer a treat to visiting girls, nor any other sign—except for her presence—indicated that anyone did anything in this office. There was a small bookshelf against one wall containing only The Foxhall Handbook of Rules. I thought it looked lonely, positioned there with no companions, its cover facing the room. One thing was certain. You couldn't ignore it.

As if her tall, rather gaunt frame and black hair pulled back into a tight bun weren't intimidating enough, she didn't smile and hardly moved except to point with one index finger at the seat I was to "take." In the scant week I'd been at Foxhall School, I'd heard stories about other girls who'd been ordered to appear before Miss Bleaker. She had the reputation of being completely unforgiving and this alone served her well whenever a girl was summoned to her monastically appointed office. But those other girls hadn't lived with my mother for fifteen years. Unlike me, they had no idea how to counter an attack or sneak around authority, even lie when necessary to avoid conflict or consequences. The emotionally unstable atmosphere of my family life had turned me into a kind of survivor, like someone who'd experienced the battlefield and returned home, not wanting to talk about it, but on guard, wary of what might happen at any moment, and prepared to hit the deck and then, when the danger had passed, to go back to the business of life as if nothing was amiss. Plenty was wrong. I just refused to show it.

She cleared her throat and moved ever so slightly back half a step, then looked down at me as if by simply staring she could shake whatever nerve I might have out of me and watch it scuttle crab-like down the hall.

"Miss," she looked down at a small slip of paper in her hand, "Greenwood." Not all the teachers called us by our last names but this was Miss Bleaker, and the girls had told me the name suited her, that she was undoubtedly the bleakest person on campus. She always kept distance between herself and the Foxhall girls. We were to respect her the way we were to respect police officers or judges. We were not to question their authority and we were always to remember that they had the power and we had to fall in line. I hadn't yet gotten to the point of recognizing the irony of a school professing to question authority in the greater world while standing up for the disenfranchised and downtrodden, yet expecting slavish devotion to the rules imposed from above on its students.

She stared at me and I wondered if I was supposed to say something and if so, what? But she only paused a few seconds before resuming.

"I've been watching you," she almost whispered it.

I thought if she'd been watching me how was it she needed my name written down to remember it? But I kept still.

"You've been here a week and you've gone through orientation so I can assume you know the rules." Here she pointed a thin finger at the bookcase for emphasis. "Now, because this happened just after the first week of school, I might be persuaded to overlook a demerit and punish you with only a week of kitchen duty cleaning plates. But now," she backed up and moved to her chair on the other side of the desk where she slowly lowered herself and folded her hands so that she almost looked as if she were about to pray. I thought she would have made a good nun. At least what I thought would have made a good nun, never having been in close proximity to one myself. I had only seen her wear the most austere black dresses which each looked pretty much like the others. Her shoes were the sensible sort. She was unadorned by jewelry or hair combs or makeup, save a slash of red lipstick that seemed to be applied more to identify her as female than to enhance any particular feature.

"Now, however," she went on, "I find I can't be lenient as that would send the wrong message. So I shall have to mete out the maximum for such an offense."

Still no word on the offense itself.

"Do you have anything to say for yourself?"

I blinked at her. I hadn't expected this question so I blurted out, "What offense are you talking about?"

Quick as a spider, she pounced. "Are there other offenses that perhaps you have committed? It would help your case to clear the air right now. Otherwise . . . "

She left the word hanging in the air like a balloon. My hands had turned clammy and for all my bravado in the beginning, by then I was beginning to weaken. I knew my tough crust had a thin shell and that underneath I'd been damaged by the emotional trauma that had been perpetrated on and around me since childhood. I might put up a brave front but inside I questioned myself more deeply than anyone could imagine. When I didn't say anything else, she sighed deeply, as if I'd hurt her to the core.

"You girls don't understand how important it is to follow the rules. Without rules, we'd all be just wandering in a desert of chaos. You girls will learn that later in life. But now, it's up to me and your teachers to instill in you the value of following the rules at all times. What happened in the past was a tragedy for one girl and her life will never be the same. Her example is a lesson for all of you. We must overcome the past and the impulses that led to such behavior. That is our mission at Foxhall. And we cannot allow you girls to make a mockery of that."

"But Miss Bleaker, I had nothing to do with that. And anyway it happened last year and I wasn't even here yet." I tried to sound sincere and full of empathy for Bleaker's oh-so-difficult situation.

"I'm well aware of that, Miss Greenwood. I'm asking about what happened just last night." She unfolded her hands and reached in front of her. I heard a drawer slide open and she carefully lifted out a wilted circle of dandelions linked together by their stems and held it dangling limply from her fingers.

Oh, the dandelion rings on the tree outside my window. A long minute ticked away while I stared at that dandelion ring and she stared at me.

"Well?" she finally broke the silence.

"I don't know anything about that," I told her. "What is it?" I tried to maintain a "who me?" attitude.

"Miss Greenwood, this is not a joking matter. These . . ." she seemed to search for the exact word to show her disdain, "symbols are neither funny nor acceptable. And since they appeared in the tree beneath your window, I must assume you are responsible and that means the punishment will be yours to bear alone." She sighed again as if the burden of our collective subversion was too heavy for her to shoulder. And then she continued. "I have told you girls again and again, told you and warned you, that holding hands leads to babies. That is why I patrol these halls, these dances, this school. To protect you girls from the fate that would befall you should you forget that simple dictum." Again she sighed, this time with less depth. And then finally finished her diatribe. "Of course, if you tell me who else is behind this affront to decency, your punishment will be minor."

"Miss Bleaker, I swear I have no idea what you're talking about. I'm a very sound sleeper and maybe someone snuck into my room while I was asleep."

I didn't know it then but news that someone was being interrogated had spread like a rampant flu through Fox Dorm and word was out that this someone was in Bleaker's lair, ratting out the offending girls and soon others were to follow. The longer Bleaker's door stayed shut, the more outrageous the stories got everywhere in Fox and even across campus to the boys' dorms, where whispers of conspiracy, tattling, repercussions and expulsions to follow rang up and down the halls. Finally the gossip culminated in a tale that whoever had ratted out the girls, Daria was the one who would be expelled and that the rat would come to Daria's room in Fox to tell the extended tale and fess up her perfidy to the awaiting tribunal of upper class girls.

Such was a small community that quasi-news traveled faster than solid fact and this fable had taken on its own life and grown wings. It could be hard to tell where gossip ended and information began. The intertwining could be like muscle and ligament, inextricably attached each to the other. I could look back on it now and still not see clearly how the chain of events linked together in more than a general way. As it turned out, that autumn of my sophomore year at Foxhall School would turn deadly, but on that day in Bleaker's office, no one had any idea how events would spin out of control like a tornado, sucking all of us, innocent or not, into its vortex.

FOUR

Study Hall

THAT WAS HOW I ENDED UP RELEGATED TO STUDY HALL FOR the entire first semester—September until Christmas break—of my first year at Foxhall. Study Hall. The jail of prep school, the very last place you wanted to be stuck, even for one week. I'd read about it in the book of rules. While everyone else spent the two hours between social time after supper and the forty-five minutes before lights out in their rooms or their friends' rooms or at the library, anyone assigned to study hall was required to spend that time locked away in one designated classroom with other malcontents or academically below-par performers. Since it was the beginning of the year, there would be only a few of us. It also meant I would be confined to study hall on Sunday afternoons after lunch from one to four—three long hours of staring at Caesar's account of consolidating power, in Latin, or figuring out quadratic equations, a loathsome task under normal circumstances. It looked like the start of what would be a singularly lonely semester.

Innocent of the turmoil brewing while I faced the Bleaker treatment, when finally freed from her grip, I wandered the halls for a while just feeling waves of relief. That elapsed time further fueled the rumor mill until I finally found my way up to the third floor and walked toward Daria's room, because of all the people who I could have faced right then, it was strangely Daria who I thought would be the most supportive of the way I'd held my ground and refused to give up the others to save my own neck. Also I wanted to show her I was worthy of inclusion.

When I opened the door, there they were, seated on Daria's bed like a row of starlings on a telephone line. I was surprised because I'd just come to see Daria alone, and wondered why they were all in her room. The expressions on their faces ran from suspicious to guarded to shocked and, within seconds of opening the door, they shifted to disbelief and then a kind of collective sneer as Daria's voice greeted me.

"Greenwood." She said it like a reprimand. "Is it you?"

Is what me? What is she talking about?

"Is what me?" It must have sounded insincere but I was too perplexed to realize it at the time.

"Is it you?" she repeated. "Are you the rat? Should I expect Bleaker to call me in now?"

"What are you talking about?" I shook my head and looked from one to the other down the line.

"It's all over the school." Jan spoke for them. "Bleaker made someone talk and now Daria's going to be expelled."

"Really?" I sat down on Daria's battered desk chair. We were all given one at the beginning of the year. Along with a desk, bed, and one lamp. Any other amenities you had to supply from home so our rooms were a collection of odds and ends donated by our parents or bought for the school year and then discarded. The castoffs of every year showed up in other people's rooms the next year, adding to the general thrift-shop look of the less wealthy kids' rooms, signaling to everyone just who was on scholarship and, in many cases, who was from a Quaker family. Quaker kids were given admission preference, even if they couldn't afford to pay the tuition. The school didn't tell us this. But it became part of the general knowledge that circulated like pollen settling on the student body. Like where you'd gone to school before you got to Foxhall and if you were one of the five or so percent of Jewish kids. Besides entering as a sophomore, I straddled the religion line and didn't quite fit in any category. My father had been raised Jewish and my mother was an Episcopalian. When anyone asked me what I was, that was my answer because I really didn't know what I was or where I should place my allegiance. I think that was why my parents sent me to a Quaker school. They thought in that environment I would be accepted for myself and not stuffed into a category that didn't fit me. Part of that was true. Even as I was rebelling against the school system, I realized I was absorbing something meaningful from Quaker teachings and practice. But then there was the pettiness, the arbitrary rules, the puritanical attitude.

"Well it wasn't me," I said emphatically. A general sigh filled the room and the atmosphere cleared as if a storm had blown itself out. "Anyway why would Daria be expelled and not anyone else?"

"Bleaker's been gunning for her since last year," Brady whispered, but the others could hear her I was sure.

"But why?"

"Because of Tim Payton," Brady put a finger to her lips.

"You can tell her," Daria interrupted. She sounded impatient. "For God's sake Brady, everyone else knows, or if they don't then they're just so out of the loop they don't matter."

"Well," Brady leaned into her story. "Last year, at the Junior-Senior Dance, Daria went to the dance with Tim . . ."

I'd seen him around already and heard about him, too. Now a senior, one year ahead of Daria.

". . . and they disappeared for about a half hour and Bleaker went berserk looking for them. When she couldn't find them, she went to Coach Sharply and told him to look for them in the boys' dorm because she suspected they were— she called it 'flaunting the rules'—and anyway, once you're at a dance, it's against the rules to leave until it's over. Well Coach told her to let it go, that school was almost over and, with graduation the next week, there was no sense making a big deal of it. That made her so mad she shut down the dance and sent everyone back to their dorms."

I looked over at Daria. She was grinning.

"What happened?"

"We weren't in the boys' dorm. We were in the mattress room. Tim had a key. I don't know who got it originally but it was passed around all year."

"What's the mattress room?" I must have sounded like a total idiot to them but I couldn't help myself. How else could I learn all the ins and outs of this new system?

"Brady, you tell her. You've spent the most time there of any of us." From her position on the bed, Daria leaned her back against the wall and pulled her knees up to her chest.

"Oh, so now I'm the group slut?"

Daria let out a little laugh. "Well it's true. You were the first one to tell me about the room."

Brady turned to me. "It's this room in the basement of Fox where they store all the extra mattresses. There must be about thirty of them down there. So if you want some privacy—you know like with a boy—that's the most comfortable place to do it."

"You guys are kidding, right?"

"Oh, man, like you are really out of it aren't you?" Daria sat up straight again. "Why would we be kidding? And anyway where were you the past two hours then?"

"Yeah," Jan spoke up for the first time since I'd entered the room. "We looked everywhere for you."

"I was in Bleaker's office."

"Then it was you," Daria's eyes narrowed and she moved to the edge of the bed as if she was ready to run.

"What did she say?" Faith asked in a clear voice. She was fair-minded, and supportive, always ready to forgive an offense. The younger girls adored her and often turned to her for advice.

"Oh, you know, she threatened me and then tried to make a deal with me."

"But you didn't squeal?" Jan asked. "I mean you kept us out of it, right?"

Looking back now, at everything that happened after that, I wonder what I was thinking at the time. I thought I was being noble, sacrificing myself to the greater good. At the same time, I think I knew what was really going on. I wanted them to accept me, to like me, to make me a permanent part of their circle, because high school girls' friendships can be as ephemeral as moonlight subject to a passing cloud. I was a new kid. I was lucky they'd taken me in and taught me the ropes. I didn't want to lose what I'd gained. And by taking the hit, I would have something over them and they could never reject me. At least not for that year. And by then I'd be in the upper class, and it would be up to me who to accept and who to reject. My time at Foxhall would be secure. They would owe me. It wasn't a bad thing to want to fit in. And there was no reason why I shouldn't.

"I didn't squeal," I told them. A collective sigh rose from the bed and they giggled nervously. Daria leaned back again and stroked her hair.

"Well, thank God for that," Brady said. "Sorry, Faith."

Faith never swore or used any words that might offend another Quaker. She was an odd combination of saint and sinner, hard to figure out so the other girls paid her a certain deference. And how she practiced the Quaker way of speaking to family and close friends, by using the pronouns thee and thy and thou rather than you and yours, was funny for me at first. Quaker faith could be quiet and yet visible in small ways. Faith was kind, pretty, gracious, and smart, a natural test-taker who always got perfect scores on every standardized test. Next to her, I felt every bit of my B average grades. Yet she always treated me with respect.

"What did you get?" Brady asked. "Study hall for a month?"

"The whole first semester," I said.

"Wow. She really was pissed, old Bleaker," Jan snickered. "God I wish I had a cigarette."

"One of the senior boys gave me half a pack yesterday," Daria whispered, as if she thought there might be a spy outside the door, ear pressed against the old wood, just waiting to get the goods on all of us together.

I reached behind me and turned the bent key in the old lock, thinking it would be easy to pick any of these locks, as old as this building was. It clicked and the girls seemed to relax some.

"Where is it?" Jan wanted to know. "Hand some over. We all need a smoke."

"Not in here, for God's sake," I told them. "That's all I need is detention for the entire school year."

"Yes," Brady muttered. "We don't need to get caught for smoking on top of everything else. But I know a place that's safe. We can go there one at a time and meet up. Out in the woods. There's a path where no one would see us sneaking out. It's an old shed out there. One of the boys showed it to me last year. He said they call it the pigpen."

"Which one?" Daria asked. She stroked her hair with elegant, tapered fingers. I noticed her nails were perfectly manicured and she had polished them a lovely pale pink. "Was it Boyd? He told me about that shed at a dance. He wanted to sneak out to it but I wouldn't go. He's got a reputation, you know."

"It wasn't him," Brady said. "I don't even remember who it was. But definitely not Boyd."

"What do you mean you don't remember?" Daria gave her a fishy stare. "You went out there with him didn't you?"

"Yes, but we were pretty drunk and I don't remember much about it." Brady giggled nervously.

"Are you sure it was one of the Foxhall boys? I mean could it have been . . ." Daria's voice trailed off.

LB GSCHWANDTNER

"No," Brady pronounced it with force. "It couldn't have been."

I looked from Brady to Daria as it dawned on me what was going on. Apparently the expelled girl wasn't the only one who had a thing for the cute townie with the initials WT.

"Why do they call it the pigpen?" I asked.

They all turned to look at me and Jan sneered, "Don't be stupid. Why do you think they call it that?"

I had no idea but I nodded as if it had just occurred to me and then Daria, her angelically gorgeous face masking any emotion, told me, "Because we can all behave like pigs out there and no one will ever find us."

My stomach felt like I'd been sucker-punched but I kept quiet and hoped my own face was as much of a mask as hers. That was, I was learning, the essence of cool here at Foxhall. Not to feel. And if you did feel, not to show it.

"Anyway I have the cigarettes for anyone who's not too chicken to come out," Daria offered.

"I'll meet you," I spoke up and the others agreed. All except Faith. She wouldn't smoke or drink. And no sex. But she also wouldn't tell. She was fair that way. We set a schedule for starting out one at a time so none of the faculty or hall teachers would get suspicious seeing a group of girls wandering into the woods. We each took something to make it look like we were just going outside to study. We'd pick a spot near the edge of the woods, sit down and then in a little while wander farther away until we found the path through the woods that led to the pigpen.

I took an American history book. It was a required course. I was also taking third-year French, algebra, second-year Latin, American history, English, and for a half credit, drawing. We had to do some sport so I tried out, and made, the girls diving team. I was a graceful and competent diver but nervous about boys coming to watch the meets. I'd been told at the tryouts that they came to ogle any girl who had a good figure and that made it hard to concentrate on the board and the pool. I was determined to ignore them but it was impossible and with every meet I developed a fluttery stomach that led to such serious jitters that for the rest of the season before and after every meet I considered quitting.

Once a week everyone also had to take one extra class— Quaker Life—where we learned the history, tenets, beliefs, and practice of the Friends way. The other new girl, Moll, and I sat next to each other around an oval table. It was the only class where we didn't sit in rows facing the teacher. I was surprised when it became my favorite class and maybe that was why I felt kindly toward Moll Grimes and encouraged her to think of me as her friend.

And so it progressed. One rebellious act led to another. Brady drew us a map to where she said we should meet and we split up after deciding on a time. It was Saturday and there were no games scheduled yet so we had free time. We were supposed to use that time to study. But only a week into school, we were pretty confident so far. I didn't realize how easy it was going to be to slip behind. Take one afternoon off, and pretty soon you were pushing the homework from one class aside and then another. It built until panic set in before a test or a paper was due. But that afternoon in early September, the sun was shining and I was still free. There was no study hall on Saturday and wouldn't be until Sunday after lunch.

It was hard to imagine it now, with rampant drugs and teen sex the norm, but back then, on the cusp of a young generation that would soon be at war with its elders, smoking cigarettes was the gateway to rebellion. I passed through that gate without a thought and, history book in hand, wandered off into the woods to find the pigpen.

Daria was already there, lit cigarette in hand. She motioned me to enter, which was funny because this really was not much more than a shed with three sides and a sloping, low roof. The floor was dirt, rutted and uneven, and there were what looked like old stalls along one side.

"Was this really a pig pen at one time?" I asked.

Jan came up behind me and slid past. "Who cares?"

I shrugged and sort of squatted next to her. "I don't know. I just wondered."

"Give," she said and held up two fingers for a smoke. When she'd lit it, she breathed in deeply, as if she'd been starved. "Ahhh," she said as she let out a misty, gray stream. "Finally. God I hate Saturdays here. Almost as much as I hate weekdays. There's not one damn thing to do."

I was about to ask why she came to Foxhall but at that moment Brady showed up and the ritual of lighting up repeated until we were all puffing away. So there we were, smoking like little locomotives, encased in the cocoon of our parents' protection, glorying in our rebellion and thirsting for ever more dangerous chasms where we could plunge headlong toward anarchy.

FIVE

Whatever Happened to Daria?

IN STARBUCKS, WITH *SKETCHES OF SPAIN* PLAYING IN THE background and a few laggards sipping on their Ventis and tapping away at their notebooks or checking their iPhones, I got around to asking Daria about herself. I guess I assumed she would be leading some glamorous life with yachts and trips overseas, maybe an apartment in Paris or London and a big house in Beverly Hills or possibly in East Hampton with a penthouse on Fifth Avenue. What other direction could Daria's life have taken? Over the years I had lost touch with almost all the girls from Foxhall and had only heard about a couple of the boys. Based on what she'd been like back at Foxhall, I thought she and Tim Payton would have gotten married, that they'd be incredibly successful, probably in the thick of a Hollywood or Tribeca lifestyle, that she would still be beautiful, that life would not have dared blemish her.

"So how are you?" I asked her. "Do you live out here? You were from Connecticut."

"Yes, Southport. On the Sound. A big old house with a huge lawn and a tennis court. We had a sailboat at the Pequot Club. My father used to take me out sailing every weekend. We raced in all the Atlantic regattas. Atlantics. They were a class of boat."

She's explaining it to me as if I came from some other world, I thought. Not like I came from the next town down the Sound where we also raced sailboats in regattas and went to the club for dinner dances. But that was before. Then the sixties happened and the world changed forever. Sex, drugs, rock and roll. Bobby Dylan, civil rights, the Kennedys, the assassinations. And The Pill.

"I wonder if anyone still sails them," her musing brought me back to Starbucks.

She had the remnants of the bearing she'd had then, a nonchalance, as if she knew nothing could ever really touch her because she was beautiful and privileged. Yet she had lost the certainty of position, at least as far as I could sense from our brief encounter, and seemed more tentative than I remembered. There was a furtiveness at the edges of her eyes, a tiny squint and a downward glance, that I didn't remember. She'd always been someone who would look you straight in the eyes, almost challenging you to stand up to her, which no one ever did.

She didn't answer my question directly so I asked again if she lived in San Francisco and, while she talked, I studied her face. It was the way it had changed that fascinated me. There was still beauty but where before it had been perfect in its symmetry and grace, now it was pulled hard, with deep creases at the sides of the mouth. Her hair was now the color of pale rust with white roots at her temples and it had no shine to it, the curls forced now where once they had cascaded as if caressed by a gentle breeze.

"I've been out here a long time," she said and held her mug in two hands. "I got married down in Monterey and we lived there for a time until we split up. I never go down there anymore. Have you been?"

"To Monterey?"

"Yes. It's beautiful. Weather's completely different. Here it's all fog and wind and sun. Sometimes the wind and damp chills your bones. Changing all the time. Jacket and scarf weather. Down there you get micro climates every few miles."

"No, I've never gone that far down the coast. But when did you come up here? Was it for work?"

"Yes work. I was still modeling then. A photographer asked me to come up for a catalogue shoot he'd lined up so I arrived up here with one suitcase and . . ." her voice trailed away and I could see in her eyes she was reliving something painful, or trying not to.

I imagined her back then. Beautiful Daria with snow-like skin and light auburn hair that draped in casual curls below her shoulders. Piercing green eyes, tall, slender, elegant, she was the nemesis of every girl at Foxhall School, and the fantasy of every boy. But she was still talking now, and I snapped back to the present.

"After my divorce came through—you know in those days divorce was not so easy and it took forever. I had to go to court. It was horrible. I borrowed the money for a lawyer and even with him there, this old geezer of a judge tried to talk me into going back and 'working it out.' Those were his exact words. Like I had done something wrong and it was up to me to make things right. My husband just sat there smirking. Oh, he wanted me to come back, all right. So he could get plastered and knock me around some more. But I was one of the lucky ones because after the last episode—"she talked as if she was retelling a story she'd heard, using words like "episode" as if this had all happened on a soap opera—"I had the photographer take pictures for me and kept the prints to show that day in court. Even that antediluvian judge couldn't deny what he saw. But he still asked if I could have possibly fallen down or been in a car accident. I could have killed them both that day. The judge and the husband."

"Why did you marry him? Not the judge . . ."

She let out a little "hunh" sound. Not a laugh exactly. More like a way of saying, "If I only knew."

"Well, he was rich, the east coast heir to a canned ham fortune. His father had sold the business out to some huge food corporation and promptly dropped dead, leaving his fortune to his only son. He was handsome. And charming. And he said he adored me and would always protect me and that was important to me then. He lavished me with gifts before we got engaged. He took me on fabulous vacations all over the world. He never seemed stressed or upset. He was the perfect host and he threw catered parties where all the best people showed up. It was like some dream life. My father had died suddenly of a heart attack. My mother had remarried and moved to Buenos Aires. My brother was working for some big oil company and living in Saudi Arabia so we got married with a huge ceremony and, even though none of my family could make it, it was all just wonderful. On the honeymoon, he beat me so badly I couldn't come out of our hotel suite for five days. He told me I belonged to him now and he could do whatever he wanted. And he did. For three years. It was like living in hell."

She stopped. Drank her coffee. Again that compressed

look appeared on her face. I didn't know what to say. Daria was the one who'd had the perfect life. The life we all wanted. There was nothing we wouldn't have given up to be her. And then she added, "Except that in hell you expect to suffer, to be punished for your sins. What sins did I commit? Why did I deserve what I got?"

I didn't know what to say. If she was looking for an answer, I had none.

"He wasn't a Quaker then?" I asked, more to move away from her painful memories than to gather information.

"But he was," she said. "Brought up attending meeting, both parents Quakers. From an old Main Line, Philadelphia Quaker family. Pacifists. He went to lunch counter sit-ins with his mother. His father ran the old family business. I think his being a Quaker made me feel safe. Before anyway."

"Wasn't Tim a Quaker, too?" I wondered what had happened to him—to them.

"You have a good memory," she mused softly. "Better than mine."

"You don't remember Tim?"

This is not possible, I was thinking. *She and Tim were inseparable.* I certainly remembered.

"How is it you've hardly aged at all?"

I laughed at that. "Thanks but I remember how we were back then." I sighed and said, "I'm happy with my life now. I wouldn't want to go back but I'd sure like to feel young. I guess you can't have both."

"So you're happy?" she asked as if it had never occurred to her that was possible. "I don't remember you as happy at Foxhall. But who's happy at sixteen?"

Foxhall School, where they tried to create a microcosm of the greater world with a 1950's notion of diversity. There were exactly four black students: one was the son of the ambassador to Sierra Leone, another was an exchange student from Liberia, the third was a Quaker girl from Illinois on full scholarship, and the last was the son of a judge from New Jersey. It may have been an institution attempting to be way ahead of the curve, yet all the kitchen and laundry workers were black men and women from the Philly ghetto. They came to work each day, crowded into a few cars and toiled in the background while the students attended class and played on teams in the afternoon.

On Sundays, the few Catholic kids were driven to Mass two towns away because you couldn't spit without hitting a Quaker Meeting nearby but Catholic churches were spread pretty thin near Foxhall. There were Jewish kids and Lutherans and even a few Presbyterians—one even a minister's daughter. But in those years, the school was over 50 percent Quaker kids and much of the staff and faculty were Quakers, too.

And where did I fit in with my Jewish father and Episcopalian mother? My parents decided before they married that ours would be a non-religious house. They saw sending me off to a Friends school as a way to get both a good education and some sort of religion without inundating me with doctrine. It was a good theory. A fine theory. The doctrine wasn't the problem. It was the way some people practiced it and, at that time in my life, I was not overly concerned with nuance in my judgments so I came to the conclusion that even peace-loving Quakers could be harsh and cruel and ignorant.

SIX

Moll

CLASSES BEGAN ON OUR FIFTH DAY AT FOXHALL. BEFORE that we went through Orientation. Like everything at Foxhall the schedule of student arrivals followed a pecking order. First to arrive were the football team members, a full week before everyone else. Teachers and coaches were already there. Next to arrive were the senior proctors—senior girls or boys who lived on each hall floor and guided and watched out for the younger students in their charge. Cool proctors were a bonus. Uncool, or sticklers-for-rules proctors were a drag. Finally new students arrived, looking bewildered and a little scared, or full of bravado to hide that they were bewildered or scared. I must have been a mixture of both.

The football team was tasked with helping new girls and their parents carry trunks and furniture and whatever else they'd brought, up to their dorm rooms. Sometimes these rooms were on the fourth floor. You arrived in the beginning of September and it was usually hot. Carrying all that luggage and furniture up the stairs was not pleasant but the boys never complained. They were happy to show off their muscles and scope out the new girls. The prettier the girl, the happier the boy was to be her porter. Arrival day marked the beginning of the race to date the prettier girls.

Moll Grimes was not one of those girls. I think I befriended Moll on that first day because I saw her struggling with a rather large ratty armchair and told the boy who was carrying a small suitcase of mine to help her instead. He took one quick look at her and was about to argue but I frowned and told him not to be a jerk, which, later on, got me a reputation as a smart mouth, and also placed a kind of bounty on my head. I later learned the boys in Hanniford Dorm had a pool going on who could get me to the mattress room first. But that wasn't all.

When I went out for, and made, the varsity dive team, Daria said, "You know the boys grade nipples, right?" She smiled that little snide smile of hers when she said it, and later it occurred to me that she was implying not only should I have known this, but that I probably was some kind of exhibitionist and wanted my nipples graded by a bunch of leering boys. Later a lot of stuff occurred to me but in that moment, I felt blindsided.

So I blurted out, "What? Are you kidding?"

"No, I'm not," Daria was still smiling in that cunning way of hers. "Every year they have a list of girls on the swim team and the dive team and they wait until you get out of the pool and you're cold. Then they write down in a log of the girls on the teams, who has the tautest, most pronounced, biggest, tightest, and maybe a few other categories. I'm not really sure. I only saw the list my freshman year and every year they refine it slightly. They appoint some boy captain of the nipple committee."

"That's horrible," I wailed.

"Not really. If you have great nipples, you'll always have a date for the dances."

sandwiched between Moll to my right and the light-skinned, black boy whose father was the ambassador to Sierra Leone, on my left. He was a quiet, studious kid, handsome in a rather effete way, and hardly ever spoke to me or anyone else in class. What he did beyond our classroom I couldn't have said. I never saw him at a dance or on the sports fields or in the library, except once in a while at meals, if he happened to be assigned a table near mine. Yes, we had assigned tables, seven students to each square table and one faculty member or senior proctor. To watch over us and make sure we behaved properly, although I never saw anyone do anything even remotely subversive out in the open in the dining hall. But also Foxhall school wanted to create a family atmosphere so the teachers acted as surrogate parents, albeit ones who encouraged us to talk about meaningful topics at the table. We couldn't have known it then but that ambassador's son would, in less than ten years, become the leader of a Black Radical group that would refuse to serve in Vietnam and threaten to blow up no fewer than three federal buildings. The FBI would consider him one of the Ten Most Wanted and a three-year nationwide search would come up empty-handed as he simply melted away into the ether. It took another ten years for them to find him, having forsaken his radical calling, living a simple life in a small apartment in Los Angeles from where he ran a dog-walking and telephone-answering service. He didn't even own a car, have a credit card, or keep his money in a bank. By the time they put him on trial, the country had moved on and he was acquitted because while they did prove he made a lot of speeches, his ACLU lawyer argued that free speech was protected, no matter what that speech was about, and he was simply exercising his right to practice what the Constitution allows.

Quaker Life class turned out to be more interesting than I imagined. On the first day, Mr. Brownell asked us one question. Before any of us could answer he also asked us to meditate on it in silence for fifteen minutes—a mini Quaker Meeting right there in class. So we all sat there, wondering what the hell he expected us to be thinking about for an answer.

"Is faith in your heart or in your head?" he'd asked.

We had not yet been instructed in the workings of "the inner light" that The Society of Friends considered within each of us and the force that, given a chance, could move all people to a life of purpose and principle. We were to learn about this, along with the history of the Quakers, over the next five months once a week, in a class that had no tests, term papers, grades, or, in fact, any possible way to fail. What was not to like in such a class?

While I silently doodled on a scrap of paper, awaiting the end of the fifteen minutes, Moll Grimes, with head bowed, appeared to be taking a classic class nap. At the end of the fifteen minutes, when Mr. Brownell looked up, Moll was the first to speak. She hadn't been napping at all. She'd been thinking about the question. It was the first time I'd heard her voice, and, for all I knew, it was the first time she'd spoken to anyone since she'd arrived. I know that is hard to imagine, so I guess I should explain about Moll.

Being a new kid arriving at boarding school was sort of like a whole bunch of individual dogs all running into a park at the same time. The dogs that had been coming to that park for a couple of years had all sniffed each other out and had come to an agreement on which ones were the alphas and which ones would roll over the fastest. The new dogs had to run the gauntlet, get sniffed, get growled at, maybe get nipped, until they learned just where they would fit in so the park could settle down again. But there were always a couple of dogs that hung around the fringes and didn't really understand—or couldn't fit neatly into—the system.

Moll skirted the edges of two groups in that she always looked submissive but at the same time, she hung back, as if trying to remain invisible so she didn't have to deal with any of the alphas or the groups that might pick on her or cast her out completely. Being homely in a way that teenage girls found easy pickings didn't help so she appeared to accept the designation of outcast. Except for one thing. She was brilliant.

I'd heard that she'd come to Foxhall because of Mrs. Doyle, who taught third, fourth, and even fifth year Latin. She also offered classical Greek to anyone who wanted to take it—there were none until Moll showed up. And Mrs. Pickery, who taught French, was a White Russian whose family had escaped the Revolution and migrated to Paris. So she also taught Russian. Again, no takers until Moll. That was on the language side. We also had Mr. Grazier, who had developed his own algebra text that was being introduced to the school curriculum in five states. He offered advanced students everything from limits to derivatives to integrals to vector calculus, none of which would be listed on my selected courses over the next three years so to this day I had no idea what those were or what they were good for but Moll did. And I found myself admiring her from that very first day in Quaker Life class, when she looked up from what I thought was a nap and told Mr. Brownell that faith borders on fantasy in that it dealt with hope when much information about the world around us defied hopefulness.

"I think to ascribe either heart or head, or even both, is to minimize what faith can do and to leave to fanatics the ability to define faith in their own limited, and often self-serving, terms."

So that was when I first took a liking to Moll and after class I walked with her to the door and we just sort of fell in together as we went to our next class. Me to third-year French (we were reading *Les Fleurs du Mal*) she to classical Greek (they were reading *Oedipus Rex* . . . in Greek).

I expected some sort of intellectual discussion of modernism or classicism or at least a description of her course work but instead she asked: "How do you get your hair to curl under like that?"

Her voice was very low and she almost looked as if she was going to pass out. I realized later that what I had witnessed was terror but, at the time, I was surprised so I blurted out, "Oh I just blow dry it with a round-bristled brush, you know. It's easy."

And that was when she really seemed to come apart because she started to tremble and her fingers got white around the knuckles where she was holding her books really hard and she just backed up against the wall. I had to get to my next class but I stood there kind of fascinated by her, the way you would be transfixed watching a speeding car you knew was going to crash just before the moment of impact.

And then she spoke again, very softly, looking at her scuffed, brown, decidedly-uncool leather shoes all the time.

"Easy?" she asked. "How can it be easy?"

"Well it's nothing special," I told her. "Anyone can do it."

"Anyone?"

"Sure. All you need is a blow dryer and a round brush."

She looked up at me then as if I was the one speaking Greek. And I felt as if maybe, without meaning to, I had said something awfully cruel because she looked as if she'd been stabbed and the blood was draining from her body.

"I have Greek class," she whispered and pushed herself away from the wall.

"Is that why you came to Foxhall?" I think I only wanted to know if any of the school grapevine rumors about Moll were true—that she'd been in a loony bin and that she was brought up in an orphanage were two of the ones I'd heard floating around.

"Not really."

She whispered as if we might be under surveillance. Then she looked around and I thought maybe she might be some sort of delusional and I wondered if I should be talking to her at all.

"It was because of the other place."

Other place? I thought. *Maybe I should drop this.* But I didn't know how and she went on.

"They were really mean to me there. I almost . . ."

Her voice trailed away and at that point I really had to know.

"What other place?"

"Benjamin Franklin High," she said and glanced down the hall. "Public school."

"Oh," I nodded. I had gone to public school when I was very young until my mother determined I was not being "challenged" enough and sent me to the girls' school.

"They locked me in the boys' gym one time and stripped me and stole my clothes."

"Oh, Moll, that's terrible."

"It was late on a Friday. They told me the girls cheerleading team was meeting there and wanted me to try out to replace a girl who was sick. It was pouring rain so that's why they were meeting in the boys' gym. That's what they told me. And when I got in there, they said I had to change in the bathroom and they all followed me in and took my clothes and left me there. No one found me until Sunday when the janitor came in to clean. I couldn't even find a towel. I covered myself with toilet paper."

There were tears in her eyes by the end of her story.

"Didn't anyone look for you?"

"Everyone at my house was away until Sunday night. No one missed me. I never went back to school. I told my mother it was the stupidest place anyway and I could learn everything on my own. But she said I had to go to school so here I am."

As she turned to go to her next class she asked, in a haunted whisper, "Where did you find a round-bristled brush?"

It didn't occur to me until much later what her unfinished statement "I almost . . ." might have meant.

SEVEN

French Braids

WHAT YOU ABSORB FROM CHILDHOOD COULD BE DIFFICULT to trace. There was what your parents told you and the ways they behaved and the things you picked up from them when they didn't realize you were paying attention. Then there were the things you learned and how you reacted to the things you learned. So, while you were learning facts and picking up information and cues, you were also learning how to feel. Sometimes those feelings got in the way later on in life when it could be hard to unlearn them so you didn't get stuck in an emotional rut.

Growing up, I had a Lutheran friend, Debra, a Baptist friend, Helen, Episcopalian relatives on my mother's side, Jewish ones on my father's, a Catholic friend whose name was Kandy, spelled with a "K" because her real name was Katherine, and assorted Protestants, including Jeannie whose father was an Episcopal priest, but until I went off to Foxhall, I never knew a Quaker.

I remembered each one of those girls for a different reason. Kandy had French braids that I adored. My mother never did my hair for me. When it got too long, she chopped at it and in old photos my bangs are crooked and look like they had been chewed instead of trimmed. While she was chopping away, she always told me to "just stand still" like it was me moving around that made my bangs crooked. Her hair, on the other hand, was always professionally cut and styled by some man named Mister Seymour. I never knew if that was his last or first name. In a way, I was glad she didn't drag me to Mr. Seymour to get my hair done because whenever she did take me anywhere it always ended in some sort of shaming incident.

Once she took me shopping for some clothes, she had the saleslady bring them into the dressing room. When I took off my sneakers so I could get into whatever I was trying on, my mother pushed me down onto the tufted stool and said, "Susannah, your feet stink. Don't you ever wash your sneakers? You should be ashamed of yourself."

Now, as an adult who has raised four daughters, I think back to that scene and wonder what in hell she was trying to accomplish. The fact that she had taken me shopping meant I was way too young to be washing my own clothes, let alone my sneakers. I'm sure nobody I knew washed their sneakers. As a mother myself, I'm well aware that all kids' sneakers stink. Actually I think they should change the name from sneakers to stinkers. But on that day, in front of that saleslady, I was ashamed. And shame could be a powerful feeling that sticks in you like a splinter, digging deep inside for years. I had no idea what clothes we were shopping for. I only remembered that my mother went on and on about how disgusting I was, while apologizing to the saleslady for the awful stink in that small dressing room.

One day Kandy's mother did my hair up in French braids

and I went home feeling like I was suddenly beautiful. I was ten. It was maybe my worst year of all the bad years from my childhood. And it was also the best year—or at least the most peaceful at home because my mother was in a hospital for thirteen straight months. During that year, I spent a lot of time with other girls' mothers. So I knew that some of them were sweet and kind and loving.

One Sunday, Kandy's mother invited me to go to Mass with them, so I went. I didn't understand taking communion or the catechism classes Kandy took every week, even though she tried to explain what she was learning.

Debra's family came from generations of Scandinavians and every summer at their small farm next door to our house they had a Lutheran church supper with hundreds of people. They balanced sheets of plywood on wooden horses and set out an endless line of covered dishes made by the ladies from their church. There were lots of kids running around and everyone ate delicious, homemade food. Once upstairs in Debra's house, she led me to the coveted bedroom where her elderly grandmother lived. Facing east, it looked out over the cow pasture and had a glassed-in porch. Debra pointed to a phonograph and told me when her grandmother died, she was going to get it. I remember there was a large, round, hooked rug in the middle of the floor. Debra's mother made them out of strips of old clothing. I couldn't imagine my mother doing anything like that.

Jeannie and I went to the girls' school where we wore those drab gray uniforms. It was called Griswold–King after some wealthy industrialists named Griswold and King who'd donated the money to start a private girls' school for their daughters. She had three older sisters and a younger brother whose name was Butler. She told me her parents kept trying until they got a boy. Every time I went over there, the wastebaskets in their house were overflowing. The kids all had chores. Butler's chore was emptying the wastebaskets. I never went to Jeannie's church because I never saw her on Sundays, maybe because her father was the priest and they were busy every Sunday. Her mother always seemed preoccupied, like she was looking for something and couldn't remember where she'd put it.

One Sunday after I'd stayed the night at Helen's house, I went with them to their Baptist church. My father had taught me how to play poker and after Helen's mother had said goodnight to us, Helen and I stayed up and I taught her the basics of the game. At church the next morning we sat way in the back row. Helen's mother sat with some friends a few rows in front of us. Helen's father had been killed in a car accident. There was a woman with him. She'd been killed, too. It was all kind of mysterious to me. Helen had brought the cards so while the preacher told us how sinful we were and how we would all burn in hell—his voice reached out to every corner of the big church on that one—if we did not repent and bring the Lord into our lives, Helen and I played stud poker on our laps and she beat me three games straight and then the sermon was over.

My father, I guess in an effort to give me some sense of where I came from, joined a temple—reformed of course— and signed me up for Sunday school. Except being Jewish, it was held on Saturday morning. I had a hard time explaining to all my Christian friends why I couldn't play on Saturday mornings anymore. And for that reason I hated Saturday school. I went for about six months and finally wheedled my father out of making me go anymore. He was not exactly a zealot himself so he let me off the hook. The only thing I retained from that brief inculcation was a book called *Behold My Messengers* that covered the highlights of old testament stories. I have to say, I didn't remember much from that book.

I remembered other things, though. My best friend throughout childhood was Melena. Her parents were Greek. Of course, they went to a Greek Orthodox church. I was never invited to go with them but when my friend turned thirteen she decided she was finished with church. Her mother was a sweet, gentle person who always welcomed me to their house after school. We would sit together and draw while we watched TV. Melena had a wonderful talent and all her drawings were lyrical and lovely while mine were tortured and harsh. Her mother would bring us a plate of cookies and two glasses of milk. And she would smile down at us and then silently disappear back into the kitchen, leaving us to giggle and whisper and make our drawings. I loved Melena as the sister I never had. She felt the same way about me. She was a girl who loved to sit and listen to the frogs croak in the pond her father had made, a girl with no guile or duplicity.

One day, she was at my house and my mother stormed into where we were playing. She took Melena to the kitchen alone, sat her at the table and accused her of stealing our live-in maid's money. I never knew how much money or when it went missing. Melena just sat there, dumbfounded. I listened at the door while my mother cajoled her, tried to get her to admit stealing the money, tried bribing her and, when that didn't work, threatened her. My mother called the police. Afterward Melena rode her bike home without saying anything to me about the interrogation before she left. I stood watching her pedal out our long driveway. I couldn't make any sense of it. Melena would never steal anything. She just didn't have it in her. I knew that then and I know it to this day. Her parents never said a word to me. Never shunned me or told me I wasn't welcome in their house. But Melena was very careful after that about coming to my house and would always leave when my mother came home. The money was never found. It was probably all of twenty dollars.

My scorn of authority dated way back and I think religion just got lumped in with all the other types of authority. If you considered my religious education on a proportional basis, I had probably been instructed in more New Testament beliefs than Old, given the years of flitting from one church to another versus the one season of Saturday school. All of it left me with a sense of spiritual hovering. I certainly saw no compelling reason to commit.

Then, at Foxhall, I went to my first Quaker Meeting. After being preached to, read to, hymnal-ed, and generally admonished in a variety of ways by all the other denominations that had galloped through my life to date, the quiet of Quaker Meeting was a relief. But it took some getting used to. It wasn't what I expected. Actually I didn't know exactly what to expect. Up to that point what I'd come to understand about religion was something like opening a cookbook and finding a recipe you thought you might like and trying it out. I hadn't given any one religion much attention but I had done a bit of tasting. I think I hoped Quaker Meeting would make me feel less suspicious of people in general, maybe more accepting, more tolerant of human frailty.

I had been at Foxhall for one week when the first Meeting was announced for Sunday at ten in the morning. By that time the whole student body had arrived and settled in. Classes were to begin on Monday. In the pamphlet on daily life at Foxhall, which was an addendum to the book of rules, we learned that Quaker Meeting was held for twenty minutes after Assembly on Wednesday mornings and a full hour on Sundays, same venue. Attendance by the entire school—faculty that resided on campus included—was required at both gatherings.

Even a cursory glance at our weekly schedule made it clear that the school routine was designed to keep us hyperbusy. That we also found time to lead our below-the-radar lives shows just how creative we could be when what we couldn't do was explicitly stated. Daily life at Foxhall was regulated by bells. Not chapel bells nor Santa's sleigh bells, but the kind that rang on every hall in every dorm, outside every classroom in every academic building, in the library, at the art center, even outside the greenhouse where we worked on botanical projects. The only places where we did not hear those bells were in the boys' gym, the girls' gym, and the pool that was connected to the girls' gym.

The first bell of the day rang at six fifteen in the morning. My room was in the middle of the hall so the bell was some distance away. Pity the poor girls whose room at the end of the hall was closest to it. Ten minutes later, another bell let everyone know it was *really* time to get up. The dining room doors opened at seven and closed at ten past. There was a mad rush to get in and out of the bathroom before everyone on the hall was up. There were eighteen girls on my hall and only six sinks, four toilet stalls, three shower stalls and one bathtub with a plastic curtain. We all had a small bathroom shelf where we could store a few personal toiletries and a hook below it for a washcloth but anything else you had to carry from your room.

At the sinks, which had a hot and a cold faucet, you had to push a square thing down to get water and it only stayed on for about twenty seconds and then you had to push it again for more water. You couldn't mix them so you had to fill the sink if you didn't want to scald yourself and wanted warm water. I took to getting up before everyone else just to get a clean sink and shower stall—at least, as clean as possible. At seven, a bell told everyone they had to be in the dining room seated at their assigned tables. The doors were shut, and all but one locked. Anyone coming in late was marked on a sheet by one roll taker stationed by that door. Too many lates for a student meant study hall or extra chores. Breakfast was over at seven forty-five with a lot of scraping of chairs against the old wood floor. What had begun with a minute of silent prayer before the food grab, ended with another bell and a rush for the closest doors.

On weekdays you had to get back to your room, clean it and make your bed for inspection by the hall proctors or your hall teacher, gather your books, and head to the Assembly Room. If you had a morning assigned chore, you also had to get that done by the next bell, which rang at eight fifteen, when the whole school trooped into the huge, two-story room with the wraparound balcony seats and the audiovisual booth at the very top of the balcony facing the stage below, to listen to announcements of various interest levels, sing some uplifting song like "You'll Never Walk Alone," and maybe watch a skit performed by students, or hear a speaker or some other short program, which sometimes included responsive singing or yelling from the audience, usually by boys.

Except on Wednesdays when we had the announcements and then a twenty minute Meeting For Worship. Meeting began with a general shuffling into the Assembly room, taking seats—thankfully these were not assigned so you could sit with your friends—and getting settled in. You were not allowed to bring books, except that a few kids brought Bibles, which were allowed, King James version in all the cases I ever saw, opened to some personally meaningful passage which a student could read silently, or stand and read aloud for a minute or two (they had chosen their passages carefully ahead of time so as to have something spiritual to convey to the rest of us) and then sit down. I guess we could have brought the Koran or a compilation of Buddhist prayers or The Bhagavad-Gita but I never saw anybody with those.

On the stage was a single row of about eight or ten chairs, known simply as the facing bench. In many Quaker Meeting houses, it is simply a wooden bench, sometimes with a pad, sometimes not. People who attended Meeting either volunteered to sit on the facing bench, or sometimes there was a predetermined lineup—or some combination. At Foxhall usually the headmaster, a few teachers and a few invited students—always high-performing ones like Faith—would occupy the facing bench.

Meeting always began with a general quieting of the

group. No one actually started Meeting. It was done by silence falling and the spirit entering into the space. This was a lovely concept to me. The existence of a spirit that resided inside each person, that when quiet descended, evidenced itself from inside to the outer world. Anyone moved by the spirit could stand and speak. Sometimes a person would simply sit and say something, usually short, spiritual in nature, or a comment on a particular state of the world or of their personal world. That was the only way the silence was broken. When the person finished speaking, there was only silence. Sometimes someone else would stand and expand on what the speaker had said, or go off on a related tangent. Or sometimes no one spoke at all and the twenty minutes moved slowly. Sometimes people fell asleep. Or passed notes. Not everyone had a spirit that was easily moved.

I had high hopes for Quaker Meeting, probably because it was going to be so different from any of the other forms of religion I'd dabbled in. At that first meeting, some girl I didn't know spoke about her missionary parents serving in Ghana. I didn't know it then but this girl would be a frequent speaker at Meeting. Not that anybody had the slightest interest in what she had to say. She was very short, had a face that looked as if perhaps it had been squashed in at birth, she wore thick glasses with decidedly uncool, powder-blue frames, and her clothes looked like fourth-gen hand-me-downs. I didn't think any boy ever spoke to her and I never heard she was particularly smart. It occurred to me later that maybe Meeting was the only chance she had to talk to anybody.

Just about eighteen minutes into that first Meeting, Mr.

Brownell got up and said, "We often question our purpose in life, especially those of us who are early in their life's journey. Purpose is something found in the service to others and in that quiet service, purpose becomes less important than serving." He sat down and in less than two minutes the headmaster, Mr. Williamson, sitting on the facing bench, turned to Mrs. Roberson and shook her hand. The rest of the people on the facing bench turned to their neighbors and in a few seconds everyone was shaking hands with their neighbors and Meeting For Worship was over. No hymns, no responsive reading, no preaching, no talk of sin or hell or damnation or heaven or interpretation of what Jesus said or did or meant. It was rather anticlimactic but also comforting in a way that made me feel we were all in this together.

Jan leaned over as I was about to stand and whispered to me and Daria, "Blah, blah, blah, just one of these times why can't she talk about the missionary position instead of her sainted missionary parents?"

When Daria giggled, I realized this particular moving of the spirit, sincere as it had appeared, had been something less than a spontaneous spiritual moment. Was I disappointed? I didn't think so. No matter what I had expected, the spirit had not moved me even one inch. I would wait for it, though. Maybe given enough time, whatever spirit was inside me would find a way to express itself.

EIGHT

___

Another Chore

I MADE THE DIVE TEAM WITHOUT MUCH TROUBLE. FOXHALL wasn't like some big competitive high school with a huge budget for sports. We competed in the Quaker league with signs in the gyms that said things like: "Root for your own team but never say disparaging things about your competitors."

There were a dozen girls trying out for five spots. Daria made it with me, or maybe I made the team with her because she was the best diver of us all, of course. Her swan was like an angel taking flight. There was a moment after she took off from the board and tilted up into the air, her arms spread wide, her neck arched and her face gazing toward the sky, that she seemed to suspend; it made the audience gasp with glee and awe, and even the boys stop ogling her body as it collapsed into one slender line and entered the water with the grace and power of a diving gannet.

We didn't have a platform, only a springboard. I had grown up swimming and diving at an Olympic-sized pool that had a springboard and two levels of platforms, so I was used to climbing up the board ladder and teetering on the edge of the platform before hurtling out and down. I liked those boards better. From a springboard, there was always the chance of cutting your approach too short or taking your bounce too high or cutting the bounce too soon and hitting the edge of the board on your way down. I'd had a few of those and it was the one thing that made me anxious during a dive. But the whole point of a springboard was to get as high a bounce as you could to make your arc clean and then come as close to the board as possible for your entry into the water straight down, leaving almost no disturbance so you'd just glide in as if a path had magically opened to let your body slip through unnoticed.

We tried out over one week in the early fall so we'd have plenty of time to practice leading up to the meets. During tryouts, I didn't have to worry about any spectators. No boys ogling my nipples or whispering who knew what up in the metal stands. Later I'd have to face the betting pool and hissed catcalls—at least until one of the coaches glared over at the boys to hush them up. But there was one spectator for the first two days of tryouts. Moll Grimes slipped into the pool area and sat over on the bleachers in the farthest corner. She watched for the first two days and, after I was assured a place on the team, I decided to ask her why she'd been hanging around the pool, which was hardly a pleasant environment unless you were in a bathing suit in the water. The building had that chlorine mixed with humidity smell, even though the pool water was not actually warm to the touch, moisture hung in the air with a cloying weight. We got used to it. Used to our fingers feeling wrinkly and our hair frizzy and that slight sting of chlorine in our noses.

"Hey, what's up with her?" Daria whispered between dives.

"She's okay. I don't know what she's doing here, though."

"She's been watching you."

"We sit next to each other in Quaker Life class is all. She's very smart."

"Of course she's smart. God doesn't give out looks like hers for nothing."

"What do you mean?"

"Just that there's always a counter balance. Like in nature. If an animal is not fast enough to outrun a lion, then it has some other really powerful defense like a strong kick. So of course she has something else going for her. She'd have to."

"Why are you so down on her? She can't help how she looks."

"She could try. I mean look at her."

We both glanced over at Moll hunched in the corner, her hair, from the greenhouse atmosphere in the gym, stringier than usual.

"She can't help the way she was born. Not everyone can be beautiful. You were just lucky."

I was taking a chance. Looking back now, it didn't seem like much of a chance. So what if I got drummed out of the cool girls set? But back then, even at a school that preached respect for individuality and independent thinking, even there, the cult of adolescence was powerful. We may have studied *Lord of the Flies* in English class but that didn't prevent us from casting about for powerful leaders and powerless victims outside class.

"Hey, Other New Girl," Daria called above the sounds of splashing and thrashing as girls swam their laps. "Hey, why don't you try out? I'll get you a suit if you don't have one."

She grinned over at me and nodded toward Moll. "Look at her. She doesn't know what to do."

"Daria, leave her alone. She's not hurting anyone."

"It hurts me just to look at her. If she's not going to try out with the rest of us then she shouldn't be here. Put up or shut up, I say."

"Your turn, Susannah," Miss Alderton called out.

I jumped up and tossed my jacket onto the bench. Before I hit the water, I looked over for Moll but she was gone. There was a ghostly quality about that girl, the way she faded out of sight.

Miss Alderton was our coach and one of the freshman hall teachers. She was also an assistant dean. One of three. Everyone liked Miss Alderton. She was young, sweet natured, and she never gave out demerits. Rumor was she was dating Mr. Hempstead, who taught American history. He was a hall teacher in one of the boys' dorms. He was also young and known for his Friday night pizza parties. Among the students there was an unofficial list of cool teachers, uncool teachers, and downright to-be-avoided-at-all-costs teachers.

Bleaker was at the top of the to-be-avoided list. Still I'd had to get special dispensation from her so I could try out for the dive team. It was pretty humiliating to have to grovel to Bleaker but it was the only way. Even Miss Alderton said I had to do it. So off I went because it was either that or be stuck with nothing but study hall in my life until Christmas break.

It's funny, the second time you see a person, what you notice about them that you didn't see before. Sitting in that spare office again, with Bleaker standing to the side of her desk—this time it had only a couple of pieces of paper on it and one pencil—I noticed her hands. Maybe because her hands were clasped in front of her as if she'd been caught praying. In that position, I couldn't avoid looking at them. No rings of course. And certainly no nail polish. Or was there some? Her nails looked shiny to me. I tried to sneak a look every now and then, tried to see if the light was playing tricks on my eyes. And yes, her nails were actually shiny. No color though. As she lectured me about being influenced by the wrong values, I imagined her in her little school apartment, long after lights out for everyone else, washing her dainty underwear and hanging it carefully from plastic hooks, imagined that she, underneath all the puritanical trappings of her dean-of-girls outerwear, like the rest of us, longed to be a cool girl, pretty, admired, courted, and desired. Maybe she even read steamy romance novels late into the night. Maybe that was why she always looked so rigid. She was holding herself in like a corset.

"Are you listening to me, Miss Greenwood?" She stepped forward. I flinched slightly, my reverie abruptly interrupted and wondered, for the briefest instant, if maybe she could somehow divine my thoughts. It was a pure moment of paranoia that passed as fast as a shooting star.

"Yes, Ma'am," I answered, sounding as dutiful as I could, knowing that I was only following proper form to get what I wanted. I was not going to learn any lessons from her nor would I bend to the rules any more than Daria and the other girls had shown me they would.

"In truth, I should extend your study hall demerit by the number of hours you'll be at practices."

She waited for me to react. Maybe beg or cry. I'd heard of girls breaking down in her office, pleading, promising just about anything to get her to relent. But then, inside my head, there were all those years with my mother screaming at me, blaming me for all sorts of behavior I'd never committed. Well, at least here at Foxhall I had participated in this infraction. So I felt justified, in some weird, crisscrossed way in my refusal to bend to Bleaker's will.

Instead of baring my soul to her I simply said, "You could do that. That would be a fair and even trade."

To my surprise, and perhaps to my slight disappointment, she said, "It might be, but instead I'll give you an extra chore. You'll sweep the Assembly Room aisles every Friday morning after breakfast, before Assembly begins. That's all. You can go to practices."

With that, she turned away from me as if I was nothing more than a piece of dust on her floor. The door to her office was situated just opposite the telephone operator's room, a small, square, affair where Mrs. W. sat at her console of wires and metal plug gadgets. It was Mrs. W. who transferred calls that came from parents wanting to speak to their kids in the hour and forty-five minutes between study hall and lights out during the week, or on weekends almost any time of the day until ten at night when she went off duty. And Mrs. W.'s telephone room was where everyone who entered Fox Building passed on their way to the deans' offices, the dining room for all daily meals, or up one flight to the second floor assembly room.

The Quaker way was alive and functioning at Foxhall—our daily life was informed by it in ways large and small. What I had just experienced in Bleaker's office was not called discipline. In the Quaker lexicon, it was known as "Getting Guidance" which had an accumulated effect of both discipline and learning lessons on the value of further self-discovery in the light. Students shortened this to simply "guidance" and, if you had just come out of a dean's office or, of even more significance, the headmaster's office and another student gave you a look that meant *what happened in there?* you would simply mouth *guidance* and that would explain it.

Lining the main hall of Fox were bulletin boards plastered with messages about work camps, sit-ins, service projects, overseas American Friends Service Committee offerings, soup kitchens, donation sites, service opportunities in schools and at elder care facilities. It was endless the ways you could serve others in a Friendly capacity. You could spend every weekend serving others, every break, every summer, even half a year for juniors. Many of these opportunities were also touted at morning assemblies during announcements, sandwiched between the daily hymn or uplifting song, and silent worship, allowing you time to consider your own place in the scheme of service to others.

Sunday meeting for worship was a different matter. No announcements. No hymns or songs. We simply walked in, took a seat, and quieted down while the facing bench on stage filled up. When the two people seated in the middle chairs on the facing bench lowered their heads, it was understood by everyone that Meeting had begun. A hush would fall over the room. A few coughs. Some shuffling of feet. One or two latecomers would hurriedly take seats in the back, and, until someone was moved by the spirit to rise and speak,

NINE

Secrets

FOX WAS AN OLD BRICK BUILDING IN THE GEORGIAN STYLE
with dormer windows on the top floor and a bell tower at
one end of the roof. In addition to the wake up, chore, class,
and study hall bells, that tower bell counted the hours
twenty-four seven, gonging us all through the days and
nights until we hardly noticed the interruptions. Fox Building had been constructed in the late eighteen hundreds to
house the entire school, classes, dorm rooms, eating hall,
everything, including a Meeting For Worship space which,
over the years was expanded to house the assembly room and
stage behind which was a back staircase that led up to the
makeup room.

The mattress room was located at the east end of a
sprawling basement, with staircases that led to it from both
the west and east wings of the building. At the west end was
the school laundry, known to students as the button crusher.
They had some kind of massive ironing machine down there
that they fed with clothes and sheets all day long. Everything
that went in one end came out the other board-flat, buttons
and all.

The basement housed all sorts of creepy rooms and alcoves off of its main hallway, a low-ceilinged affair of rough concrete painted white. I remember a buzzing sound at certain points, probably emanating from a gigantic electric room where all the switches and fuses were located. Besides the mattress room, there were various storage rooms filled with old desks, chairs, lamps, bed frames, and assorted other extra furniture.

Up above, on the first floor, you could enter Fox Building from one of three sides. On the east side a wide porch, which happened to be almost directly beneath my window next to the offending dogwood trees, led to an old fashioned double wood doorway with glass panes. Inside there was a generous foyer type area with a decorative and rather large round wooden table with those curved legs and a bowl of something—fruit or flowers—in the middle, especially when alumni or benefactors were in town. Off to the sides were ample rooms with comfortable couches and armchairs and more tables and lamps.

These were the "for show" rooms of the school, the places where important people were greeted, passed cups of tea, and generally fawned over in a quiet, Quakerly way. It was also where—sometimes—prospective students and their parents met with an admissions officer for a "conversation" which was really an interview. It was rare that an actual student ever saw the insides of these rooms except to glance at them in passing on the way to the door. But even that was rare as few students used the east door, it being the farthest from anywhere we normally would be heading, like the gym or a classroom. And anyway, all the action was on the south porch, which was the main entrance to Fox Building with an even wider porch and a semi-circular set of six steps that spanned the entire width of the high-ceilinged porch.

This was the entrance that led to the telephone operator, Mrs. W., and across from her cubicle, Bleaker's office and next to that, the assistant deans' office and farther down the hall, the mail room where we each had been assigned one of hundreds of little, metal mail doors with small windows that allowed you to see if you had received mail. In those days now long gone, before iPhones, email and texts, the mail-room was a boarder's link to the outside world.

Beyond the mailroom, the hallway opened up to a large space surrounded by built in benches along the walls where students sat to read newspapers or just hang out before and after meals. They were called the social benches. Flirting happened here. Also gossip and general teasing. At certain times of the day, this rather wide hallway was as quiet and empty as a museum after closing hours, but at others it was like a train station at rush hour. These times were all predict-able. Meals three times a day and Assembly each morning prior to the start of classes.

In one corner where the benches met, the phone booth stood with its little seat inside and its door that pulled closed from a hinge that ran up and down the middle between two glass panels. If you wanted privacy, you banged the door shut. If you didn't and you wanted air, you left it open. This was before calling cards, so you had to come armed with coins and time your call to the minute or bring a boatload of coins if you didn't know how long you'd be on the phone.

In her sophomore year, Jan, in concert with a boy called

Stocky for reasons that were never clear since he was tall and rather gangly, came up with an ingenious contraption that billed the phone company out of hundreds, if not thousands, of dollars in calling charges over the years that we attended Foxhall. They managed to divine the exact shape of the inside mechanism that dropped the coins into the coin box when you placed them in their individual slots at the top. They then constructed, from a coat hanger, a wire line that replicated the precise path the coins took until they hit a latch that opened up like a trap door. But they went one step further by including in this wire mechanism an extra bend that corresponded to the coin return pull. And that was the genius of it. With the coat hanger carefully shoved up into the phone from the bottom following the inside path precisely, you'd plunk your money in one end, and when you heard it descend, you'd flip the wire sideways diverting the money from the coin box and pull the coin return open and like some Vegas slot machine, your coins, and anyone else's stored inside, would tumble out into your lap from the other end. They called it, simply, the wire.

Stocky had a crush on me, I was told, so one evening after dinner on a Tuesday night when we had a whole extra half hour before study hall just to hang around, a bunch of us were sitting on the benches just yakking. Stocky motioned me aside and kind of cornered me by the phone booth.

"Want to call someone?" he asked.

"Right now?"

"No. Later, after study hall. I could meet you here and let you use the wire."

Of course, by then I was an officially designated cool girl

so I'd heard about the wire but had never actually used it. Still I must have looked guarded so he said, "Just meet me here at eight forty-five and I'll bring enough coins to call whoever you want. I'll show you how it works."

By then I was going to study hall while everyone else could stay in their rooms for the two hours we were required to study weeknights. Study hall for anyone on demerit was held in one of the larger classrooms in the quad where all the academic buildings were located in the middle of campus between the boys and girls dorms.

Not everyone knew about this coin contraption, but those who did used it widely. Of course they had to use it at odd times since it wouldn't have done anyone any good to be discovered robbing the phone company. But, at least consciously, nobody thought of it that way. We all just thought of it as exerting a measure of frugality. Someone always stood guard when one of us used it. The wire was transported in a brown paper bag so no one could see what it was. Better to keep it quiet, we all agreed. Such was our moral compass that while we knew it was wrong to rip the coins from the pay phone, we also thought of the telephone booth as just a thing at our school, completely disconnected from the real world. Just something inside our make believe school bubble that was there more for our amusement than for any other use. It was the clandestine nature of this tripwire contraption—not unlike the mattress room or the pigpen or even the makeup room—that attracted us because all the kids who used it could readily have reversed the charges when calling home or certainly afforded the few dollars it would take in quarters to call our friends back home. And, after a year or two at Foxhall, most kids didn't have many friends they kept in touch with outside school anyway.

"I can't make it back from study hall at exactly eight forty-five," I told him.

"I'll wait for you by Mrs. W.'s then."

"What if we get caught?" I was already in so much trouble, my parents had even called to reprimand me and tell me to watch my "behavior."

"If anyone's around we'll just wait."

"Wouldn't it be better on the weekend when fewer people are outside the dining hall?"

"Maybe, but I don't think there'll be anyone around tonight. Just meet me at Mrs. W.'s and I'll take care of everything."

I didn't know it then but Stocky had put money into a mattress room bidding war on me and this was his first move to gain my trust. Boys were only allowed in the public areas of Fox Building until nine thirty on weeknights so that didn't give us much time and, if anyone happened to walk by the telephone booth while we were extracting coins, I could really be in big trouble. But part of fitting in meant taking ever-bigger risks so I told him okay and, after two hours reading *Tess of The D'Urbervilles* for English class, I met Stocky outside Mrs. W.'s. He held the brown bag and my mind was filled with the awful things that happened to poor Tess at the hands of men.

"Here." Stocky gave me a handful of coins while I hit "0" for the operator and gave her the number. I'd decided to call my friend, Melena, back home. No sense alarming my parents any more than I'd already done.

When the operator said: "That'll be one dollar and sixty-five cents for three minutes," I plunked the coins in one at a time while Stocky adjusted the wire. After a few seconds the phone rang and my friend's mother answered. When Melena got on, we started to chat as if I'd never left home, and I forgot all about Stocky and the wire and the demerit and everything. We giggled and whispered until the operator came on and said it would be fifty cents for another minute, so I plunked in two of Stocky's quarters and we kept on talking. Well, by this time, Stocky had positioned himself directly against the phone booth door, which was half open, in a way that anyone walking by couldn't see inside. And as Melena and I chatted like birds in a tree, he pushed himself closer and closer so that finally his thighs were right up against me and he was practically straddling me seated in the booth with my knees facing out. And then the operator came on and demanded more coins so I reached for the slot and Stocky placed some in my hand. Now he was rubbing against me, and all I could think was how could I get out of this situation?

"Hey, Melena," I breathed, "I should probably go. Write me okay? And I'll write you."

"One more thing," she said, "remember Bill Poole? Well he asked me out for this Saturday. To a dance at the high school. Should I go? You remember what a reputation he has?"

"Of course you should go. Just make sure he doesn't drive you home alone on any back roads. Hey, I really have to go. Love ya."

I could feel something going on with Stocky that did not seem to be his leg muscle and I also thought I saw someone coming down the hall toward the phone. I looked up and he had this far-away look on his face and all I could think was, *Good God, what have you gotten yourself into, Tess?* So I kind of smacked Stocky on the arm and he snapped out of it. I hung up and he yanked the wire and all his coins came back out at us in a rush like a dam had burst. I giggled and kind of pushed him back so I could collect the ones that fell on the floor.

When I looked up to hand them back, he was grinning and said, "Oh, keep them for next time."

He slid the wire back into its paper bag and stepped back away from me.

"Maybe Saturday, after the dance, we could meet up—you know—downstairs?" He pointed down toward the basement. "I think I could get us some wine or maybe something stronger."

Oh, God, I thought, *how do I get out of this now?* At that moment another girl, a junior from one of the east side halls, walked over and told us she needed to make a call so we stepped away, which gave me a few seconds to think of an answer. I didn't want to turn him down and it get around that I was a bitch or something. But what to say?

"I don't know, Stocky. I mean you're really sweet and I like you and everything. It's going kind of fast, you know, and I really don't want to tie myself up with one person yet. I mean so many girls are after you, it would be unfair to you at this point." I hoped it sounded convincing.

He didn't look wounded or anything and I thought he was really out to lunch, and then he said something that really stung, for some reason.

"Oh, I get it. You're a virgin. An ice queen." He started to walk away and then turned back. "Well, you had your chance. Maybe someone else will have more patience but not me. Take care." And he sauntered away down the hall as if he'd made some big score.

TEN

The Nipple Pool

DARIA AND TIM PAYTON WERE EXCLUSIVE AND THE WHOLE school knew it. At the Saturday dances they clung to each other. All the girls were jealous of her and all the boys were jealous of him. They were the perfect high school couple and talk was they would end up married with the perfect life, perfect family, loads of money and possibly even fame because of Tim's Hollywood connections.

Tim was one of five students who'd made the trek east to Foxhall from the west coast. One even came from Hawaii, a boy named Rennie, who took me to my first Foxhall dance. He was so blond, he almost glowed. Tim's father was some big muckety-muck movie studio exec. Tim was tall, broad shouldered but with a mop of curly, black hair that made him look like a boy in a man's frame, with cow eyes and long, thick lashes that all the girls coveted like crazy. He had a shy and deferential manner and he adored Daria. He'd wait for her outside class, walk her to the dorm, and sit with her to study in the library. The most attractive thing about him was the way he moved. It was kind of a slow amble but his shoulders seemed to shrug a little with each step so he almost appeared to be slow dancing. Anyway, it was pretty sexy to watch him.

This was their second year dating and you could tell he felt lucky to have her. The way he clung to their relationship made all the other girls even more envious of Daria. At the school dances, he'd hold her as close as he possibly could without some teacher or Bleaker coming over to separate them. The only time he'd let go of her was when they'd play a fast dance. He couldn't fast dance and the other boys would take the opportunity to ask Daria for a dance and, when they did, she'd dance rings around them and the other kids would snicker at the boys who couldn't keep up with her. Tim didn't seem to mind because she'd always come back to him.

Most relationships at Foxhall followed one of two patterns: fast and furious with a quick breakup or tethered for the duration. That was actual coupledom. Then there were all the kids who just couldn't seem to manage to date anyone in particular at all and hung around at the edges. Moll, for instance, never even came to the dances, probably because she was so shy and had no social skills. Or the social skills you needed to make it at Foxhall, which was not the real world, after all.

But there were all kinds of couples. I once passed what was known as the Social Room, situated across the wide-open hall from the Assembly Room on the second floor of Fox Building. This room was located above one of the fancy rooms where donors were entertained. It had a bunch of old couches and chairs, a couple of desks, even a rocking chair. It was right next to my room so I often passed through that hall. On this particular day, as I passed, I heard soft talking so I glanced in because I thought maybe some friends were in there and I glimpsed one of the steady couples, seniors both of them, and hall proctors, too. They were seated next to each other on one of the couches, very close together. His arms were wrapped around her like a python and she was taking out her retainer and putting it in his mouth while he did the same to her. I thought I was going to gag and maybe hurl lunch so I got out of there as fast as I could, but not before I heard her giggle and say, "Ooooh, tastes like your tongue."

When I told Daria about it she said, "Those two are totally disgusting. If they got married they'd probably produce a bunch of brats with no teeth at all."

We were at the indoor pool waiting to practice our dives for a meet the next day. My stomach had already started to flip-flop just thinking about that meet.

"You know they're all going to be here," Daria said as we watched another girl execute a half gainer. "Oh, that was ugly. We'll never win tomorrow, belly flopping off the board like that. Come on, Greenwood. It's up to us to pull it out."

I stood slowly and made my way down the bleachers to the board. It was easy at practice, with only the team there. I could concentrate on my approach, the three long steps to the end, the bounce—once, twice—and up as high as I could go and as close to the end of the board as possible to get the maximum arc. Then, tuck, twist, come out, enter the water clean, and down like a bird going after a fish. That was the best part. Down there in the water, everything blue and quiet with only the beating of your heart to break the stillness of that perfect moment of freedom. You'd think it would be up there at the crest of your jump, when you flipped or twisted and you were, for a few seconds only, defying gravity, but that wasn't it. Not for me. It was those seconds in the water, after the dive, before you came up to see your score, when anything was possible and no one but you had any control of what happened to your life.

And then I was up and my face broke through the water and I gulped in air and looked over to see what Miss Alderton had marked on her big card. It was okay. I'd done what I had to do. She waved and smiled and nodded at me to let me know I was good to go.

"Nice diving," Daria said in the locker room. We were drying our hair.

"You too."

"Yeah, but can you do the same tomorrow at the meet? You've got to ignore the guys. They don't mean any harm. It's just a game."

"How do you ignore them?"

"I just think of their dicks cold and wet and shrunken like little beans."

"I'll have to keep that image in my mind."

She didn't say anything else and when I looked over she nodded toward the door. Moll was standing there, just sort of looking lost so I walked over. My hair was dry by then and I had gotten dressed before. All I had left to do was put on my shoes.

"Hi," I said to Moll.

"Hi."

She looked down at her feet and didn't say anything else. I waited. Finally she looked up at me and said, "Good luck tomorrow."

"Are you coming to the meet?"

She shook her head.

"You should come out. It'll be fun. And anyway, if I can face the crowd, you should be able to."

"What do you mean?" She looked confused.

I didn't want to tell her about the nipple pool so I just shrugged and said, "Oh, you know, all the people and everything. Come out, though. I'll look for you."

"You will? Really?"

"Sure. Hey I've got to go. Dinner's in half an hour and then I have study hall."

"You're still on study hall. I know."

"Yeah, well, what are you gonna do?"

"It was very moral of you."

I smiled at her and she beamed. It was the only time I ever saw Moll smile.

It was worse than I expected. Twelve boys showed up for the meet together and sat in a group in the bleachers. At meets the team sat on a bench to the side of the pool. I kept my swim jacket on until it was time to get up to dive. You got two chances. If you thought you could improve on the first dive, you got a second chance and the judges took your average score. My stomach was in such a knot I thought I was going to keel over. The problem was that the ladder to get out of the pool faced the bleacher side so you had to climb up and when you got to the top you'd be facing all those boys straight on.

When my turn came to dive, I stood up and shucked my

jacket, walked fast to the board, and then something just kicked in and I forgot all about the boys and the gym and Bleaker and study hall and everything. Before I took my three steps, I looked out and there was Moll, sitting at the very end of the bleachers all alone, watching me. I took my three steps and jumped as high as I could and hurled myself off into the air. My dive was perfect and deep down at the bottom of the pool, all alone in the stillness, with the buoyancy of the water tumbling me slowly, slowly to the surface, I came up with an idea.

When I broke the water surface, knowing I'd nailed the dive, I turned to face the boys. They had their little pads out and their pencils and were all glued to my face, just waiting to see me emerge all wet and cold from the water. I bobbed up a little, and then turned to face the other way. With quick strokes I swam to the edge of the pool and hoisted myself up onto the coping and out of the water. All they got to see was my back. I slipped into my jacket and heard them yowling and muttering. Daria grinned and gave me a thumbs up.

"Now why didn't I ever think of that?" she whispered as the judges flashed my score. I didn't take another dive that day. Moll left before the end of the meet. The boys drifted away. My stomach settled down. And that was that. Or so I thought at the time. I had no idea they dubbed me "Watery Ice Queen" that day. It would stick for the semester.

ELEVEN

Daria's Life

I'VE NEVER BEEN MUCH OF A STARBUCK'S DEVOTEE SO I nursed my one chai latte while Daria got up and ordered a second skinny mocha. She was very thin, I noted, the way some women are in their sixties. It's funny, although I think I have the average level of female vanity, I'm not nearly as concerned with how I look as I used to be. Age does have certain advantages and that's certainly one of them.

Daria seemed in no hurry to leave. When she came back and sat down with that second coffee, I did want to hear the rest of her story, although it's always chancy to delve too deeply into people's pasts, especially when you haven't seen them in a very long time. They tend to give you all the wrongs that have happened in their lives in a form that makes it seem as if a tsunami of grief just washed over them all at once with no warning. I think they're so relieved to be able to off load all that pain that they just can't stop. Still, I assumed the terrible marriage must have been a long time ago by now so she must have remarried and pulled her life back together, which is what I would have expected of Daria. Still there was the haunted look. The darting eyes. The lines at the corners of her mouth. The nervous laugh.

"So what about you?" Daria asked as she slid the chair closer to the little table. "I just went on and on about my sorry self. And anyway what happened so long ago, well . . ." She made a little gesture with her hand as if waving away a gnat.

Her question caught me off guard. Ever since Foxhall I had made a vow to live in the present and prepare for the future because, no matter how many times you go over what might have been and what different decisions you could have made, you couldn't reverse the clock; you couldn't redo what had been done and only in science fiction stories could you time travel. No. We swim in the soup we've made.

"You said you've been happy," Daria stated rather than asked. "Isn't that what you said? Or did I imagine that?"

I told her that's what I'd said.

"I don't think I know anyone who's happy." She shook her head and sipped her mocha.

"Happiness is all about how you define it," I told her. "If I defined being happy as depending on great wealth or staying young forever or being queen of the universe, then I'd be unhappy because none of those things would have happened for me."

"What did happen that made you happy?"

So she wasn't going to talk about herself anymore. I wondered if she felt she'd revealed too much or if maybe she felt like I was challenging her.

"Well, this, for one thing." I held up my phone with the picture I'd taken at the hospital of tiny JJ all swaddled with his little hospital cap, saucer eyes wide open, lying next to my exhausted daughter, her husband leaning over the two of them, smiling as if he'd just been beatified.

"Oh," she said. "Grandchild?"

"You know, I'd been told what a wonderful thing it is to become a grandparent but no one could possibly have prepared me for the actual feeling. I've been literally floating all morning."

She looked at me then, a look that told of losses unimaginable. And her story poured out. About the plans she and Tim had when he went off to college. They were going to be the storied high school sweethearts who stayed together for life. And then Vietnam happened and Tim, who felt obligated, with all the turmoil swirling around his generation, to support his country by serving in the ambulance corps, especially since he'd decided to apply to medical school later on after he came back.

"But he never came back." She said it in a flat voice, as if she'd said it so many times before, she'd become inured to any weight it had once carried. "That's why I married the ham hock heir. I thought he would protect me from ever again having a broken heart." She shrugged a pathetic little shrug of one shoulder, her head tilted to the right, a rueful expression on her face with one side of her mouth curled up slightly. "I think that's one of the reasons he beat me so badly. He knew I would never give him my heart. And, it so enraged him that he wanted to break it permanently. But, that had happened long before I met him. He just didn't know it."

She sighed and sat back holding her coffee mug in both hands and I noticed that her nails were bitten down to where I thought it must have hurt. She was a walking reminder of those girls who become anorexic. We'd had none of that back at Foxhall. It seemed to me we all looked healthy. But I probably didn't know half of what was going on back then.

"There was so little left of Tim, they couldn't even send home a body. Just his dog tags and a small box of bone fragments."

"That's awful, Daria. I'm so sorry."

I really was sorry. I'd had no idea they were that committed to each other beyond Foxhall.

"I was nothing without Tim," she said.

"But you were the girl who had everything. I mean we all envied you."

"I know. I think that fed me, kept me going. I needed to be envied. Tim was the only person on this earth who really saw who I was. He knew my soul. And he was willing to look beyond it."

At that moment, I finally realized what had bothered me about Daria all those years ago, what had stuck with me, why I had remembered certain things she'd said long after they had any meaning or import. She was like one of those cutouts of a famous person you could stand next to and have your picture taken. It looked real. But it had no substance. I saw Daria now, sitting in front of me, still with a kind of beauty, but now she seemed somehow transparent.

"So how about you?" she asked. "About being happy. I'd like to know someone who's happy."

When she looked at me, I could see such longing in her eyes, so I told her about my marriage, about the event of that morning before I ran into her, about my other three daughters, my work, my husband, who would be arriving that night to meet his new grandson.

We didn't talk much after that and I started to fade, the enormity of the previous night having finally caught up to me. Outside the Starbucks, she hugged me and held me for a long time like someone who felt she was falling with nothing to grab onto for support. We exchanged emails and phone numbers, said our good-byes and keep-in-touches but I knew we would never see each other again. Whatever had united us all those decades before was long gone and all that was left was the memory of what each of us had experienced in our own ways.

TWELVE

_____

Falling in Love
(or something like it)

AFTER THE SWIM AND DIVE MEET AND DINNER, THERE WAS
a Saturday night dance scheduled. But at dinner something
else happened that completely surprised me. I was sitting at
my assigned table as usual. Here's how seating in the dining
room worked. When you first arrived at Foxhall during orientation, you could sit anywhere because not even a quarter
of the school had arrived yet. The football team generally sat
by themselves and the senior proctors for the halls mixed in
with the new arrivals, almost all freshmen, except for Moll
and me, of course. Then there were the other fall teams—
girls' field hockey, cheerleaders who weren't necessarily the
cool girls the way they were at big high schools, and the
teachers and coaches and hall teachers and all the boys and
girls deans were there. So, until the rest of the students arrived it was pretty much a free-for-all at the dining room.

Once school started and everyone was there, you had assigned tables. It was supposed to be a time to meet and mingle
with kids you might not ordinarily talk to and to get to know
teachers outside the classroom. There were a few meals each
week when you could sit where you wanted—Friday and Sat-

urday lunch and Sunday dinner, which was the only meal without required attendance. To police attendance at meals there were roll takers, always girls, who would eat early and then walk around the dining room marking people off on a long list. Two roll takers handled the entire dining hall, each taking one side. The roll takers worked shifts of eight weeks each, which was how long the table assignments lasted before you were rotated to a new table with different people. In this way, the school always knew just where you were three times a day.

If you had to leave school for any reason, or you were in the infirmary, or had an absence for some other legit reason, your name was on a list at the deans' office and the roll takers had access to it. After they finished accounting for everyone in the dining hall, the two roll takers retired to the deans' office to add up their numbers and check off names on another long list. If these didn't add up, the school knew someone was either missing or skipping, which was not allowed. If you were a roll taker, you got to know everyone at Foxhall and everyone got to know you. There were four sets of roll takers. Once you had put in your eight weeks, you didn't have any other chores for the rest of the year.

So everything was tidy and neat. Just like The Foxhall Handbook of Rules. Uh huh. Thing was, being a roll taker was the only plum chore at Foxhall. Everyone had some assigned chore. Most involved sweeping floors or stairs in the dorms, or, God help you, working the early morning kitchen chore which meant getting up in the dark so you could spread plates, glasses, cups, and silverware on tables for five hundred plus people who'd rush the doors the minute they opened. Or you could be even unluckier and get the weekend dinner kitchen chore, which meant while everyone was already at the dance or the weekend entertainment you'd be scraping half-chewed chicken wings and gummy macaroni off about a thousand plates and stacking them in the huge industrial dish washers that looked like they'd been recycled from Fort Dix.

Yeah, roll taker was way better than that. And here was why. Roll takers didn't have to sit at assigned tables. They got to eat before everyone else and they could fudge the numbers. If their friends wanted to sleep in or disappear for a day, the roll takers could make it happen. And then there were return favors. I wouldn't say roll takers ever exacted actual kickbacks, but there was an understood arrangement that roll takers took care of their own because at the end of each year, the roll takers assigned who would take over for the next year if any of that year's roll takers were graduating. See, that was what I meant by tidy and neat. If you were selected for your sophomore year, you could be a roll taker until you graduated. It was a position of responsibility, like a senior being chosen as a hall proctor. Because the school had to know where everyone was at all times. Classes were small, and missing a class didn't mean much because teachers didn't necessarily keep track or hand in reports about an absent student unless it became routine. But meals were the leveling field.

So that Saturday at dinner, I was at my assigned table and the roll taker, who just happened to be Brady, slipped a note onto the napkin on my lap and gave me a stare that said, "Open in private." I excused myself in the middle of dinner and nearly ran from the dining hall to the girls' bathroom.

Once I got inside, I checked under all the stalls to make sure I was alone before carefully unfolding the crumpled piece of paper, which looked like it had gone through the button crusher. All I could think was someone was in trouble and didn't want any of the deans knowing about it and Brady had marked them in. But who?

This wasn't like one of the bathrooms on the halls where we lived. Those were a big, open room. But in this bathroom on the main hall there were only three stalls and a sink so I had the place to myself. It had a cloying, closed-off feeling and the light was bad but I leaned against the wall and slowly uncrumpled the paper.

Scribbled in pencil, it said "Would you go to tonight's dance with me?" and was signed "Wes."

Wow, I thought. *Wes Ritter. Me?* Okay after I got over the initial shock, I started to wonder why, out of the blue, Wes Ritter was asking me to the dance. I mean he was cute. Very cute. And popular. Very popular. And kind of shy in a way that was still confident. He was one of those boys all the girls thought had a lot going on inside, like in his head, that he wasn't necessarily going to show everyone. Only someone special. Like James Dean or someone like that.

I hadn't noticed him at the meet that afternoon, so he was probably not in on the nipple pool so that couldn't be why he wanted to take me to the dance. So maybe he liked me. But usually when a guy liked you he showed it in some way. Not like with Daria and Tim. They were special. But other ways. You heard about it from someone. Some little hint dropped, maybe by a friend of his. Or of yours. Like a go between to feel you out. But this? I studied the paper in my hand as if it were a treasure map with hidden clues. The crumpled paper—well, that could mean he asked someone for a piece of paper because he was in the dining hall and just used whatever someone gave him. And that could mean it was a very last minute thing and he hadn't planned it at all. But maybe he'd been carrying this paper around in his pocket for days and finally got up the nerve to ask Brady to pass it to me. Okay then, maybe it was still last minute but should that matter?

It was kind of a big deal if someone actually asked you to go to the dance with him. Most of us—at least the ones who did go every week—went on our own in groups. We'd stand around until some boy asked one of us to dance. Usually you didn't dance with him the whole time. Maybe a couple of dances. Then a dance with someone else. Or you'd stand around and just talk and joke and stuff. Sometimes there were break-ups at the dance. Those were pretty rough because it was never mutual. So someone always left hurt and confused. Then all their friends would group together and tell them he or she wasn't worth getting all upset over. But if you went with someone who'd asked you, that was it for the whole night. You'd be at the dance together and then you'd sit in the Assembly Room together for the Saturday entertainment, which was usually a movie.

I personally saw *Friendly Persuasion* three times—once every year. The kids who started as freshmen saw it four times. Gary Cooper was pretty great and there was some actress who had two ugly daughters she was trying to marry off. She was funny. She traded her horse for Gary Cooper's because her horse liked to race and wouldn't let any other horses pass and she thought that was keeping suitors from being able to catch her daughters. But that was a sub plot. The real point of the movie was that the Civil War was coming and Gary Cooper's family were Quakers and that presented a moral dilemma for their community. Also, a black man worked for them on their farm and, although he was free, it presented a different dilemma for him. So there was the issue of slavery—albeit oblique—and the issue of war, and there were a couple of other sub plots about love and sex and horse racing and betting. And of course, Quaker Meeting, which was heavily covered in the movie. The only other movie we saw that had a Quaker in it was *High Noon*. Also Gary Cooper. But Grace Kelly played his new bride, a Quaker who would not stand by him in his hour of need when he chose to stand and fight. Later, after Foxhall, I saw another movie with a Quaker in it—*Angel and The Badman*. John Wayne was the badman. He got shot and a Quaker girl nursed him back to health while convincing him that shooting people would kill his soul—or at least damage it beyond repair. In the movie she actually used Quaker terms like thee and thy. Same with Gary Cooper in *Friendly Persuasion*. Because so many Quaker kids went to Foxhall, and many of them used the familiar thee and thou and thy to their friends, we were used to hearing that so it didn't seem odd in the movie.

I didn't know what the movie was going to be that night. So there I was, hiding out in the girls' bathroom, trying to decide what to do. If I said yes and we had nothing to talk about, it could be a disaster. If I said no, I would be blowing a chance to date one of the popular boys. And if I was honest with myself, I did have a little crush on him, which I'd been trying to hide.

THIRTEEN

The Dance

I WORE A POWDER BLUE CASHMERE SWEATER AND A NAVY pencil skirt with little heels. Not the best dancing skirt, I admit, but I looked good in it.

"Are you sure it's okay?" Brady and Jan were helping me dress. It was like I was getting married and they were the maids of honor. Except it was only a stupid dance.

"You look sexy," Jan said. "Sexy's good. I wish I could look sexy. When I wear a pencil skirt my ass looks enormous."

"How does my ass look?"

"It looks good," Brady stepped from behind me. "You look great. You need a necklace."

"Really?"

"Yes. Something silver against the powder blue sweater."

"I have this." I held up a linked chain necklace.

"That's good," Jan reached out and helped me fasten it in back.

"Aren't you guys going?" I asked them.

"Of course. We wouldn't miss this for anything," Jan said and stepped away to look at my outfit with the necklace. "Perfect," she patted my shoulder. "You're—like—ready for anything he throws at you."

I glanced from Brady to Jan. I must have looked worried because Brady laughed.

"Relax," she said. "When he gave me the note he smiled."

"What does that mean?" I asked.

"How should I know?" Brady laughed again. "I'm not a mind reader. But if I was one, I'd say he has a major crush on you."

"Where's Daria?" I asked. She would be able to tell me how to interpret all this.

"She's already downstairs with Tim. You know how he waits for her like a puppy dog. I wonder if they're off having sex," Brady said to no one in particular.

"What?" Jan almost shouted. She flopped down on my bed. "You think they are? Now, before a dance?"

Jan was an information pack rat who always wanted to know every little detail of everything anyone had heard. Come to think of it, she was pretty much a pack rat about everything. I was once in her room before inspection. When she saw the hall proctor coming down the hall, Jan would grab all the stuff all over her room—and there was always a lot of it—gather it up in a big wad and stuff it into her closet, shove the closet door as hard as she could, stand against it with her backside and push it closed with all her strength, then reach around while her weight was still against the door and turn the key to lock it and hold everything in. When she unlocked it later in the day, everything would fall out on the floor and she'd just leave it there and pick through it for whatever she needed.

Jan came from Atlantic City and her father managed the hotel where the yearly Miss America pageant was held. Her family always hosted two of the girls competing in the pageant, which meant the girls lived in their house for Miss America week. That year, they were hosting Miss Montana and Miss Alabama. Jan adored Miss Alabama and her room was full of all kinds of autographed items from her, including the sash she wore when she got her state crown, autographed—*To Jan, Miss Bama Loves You.* Of course this was before pageants were under attack for being shallow and demeaning to women or before the girls who entered them had to be biophysics majors who could also belt out an aria from *La Bohème.*

"She's certainly passed around the key to the mattress room," Brady offered.

"That's right," said Jan. "I forgot about that. So they must be doing it down there. The little sneak. I'm going to get her to spill at the dance."

"So do I look okay?" I asked. My stomach had started flip-flopping again. "Because I have to meet him in ten minutes at Mrs. W.'s."

They surveyed me one more time and both agreed I looked perfect, which meant not too sexy, not too eager, but just enough to make him glad he was taking me to the dance. It was a precarious balancing act. I didn't want to be like Juniper Barksdale who wore her skirts so tight you could see when she wasn't wearing panties and turned her cardigans backwards so they stretched tight across her chest and you could see her nipples through her bra. But she got asked to dance a lot.

Brady said maybe I should have worn a fuller skirt for dancing but I didn't know what kind of a dancer Wes was yet, so it might be too risky to wear something that said I really wanted to dance. All I'd noticed was when Wes came to the dances, which wasn't every week, he usually didn't dance at all, unless some girl really pressured him. There were only a few boys who were great dancers and all the girls took turns with them. The other boys only wanted to slow dance anyway and anyone could do that.

As I put on a little makeup, I started to get stomach flutters and tried to calm myself down by saying nothing important was going to happen. *Just relax.* It was just a Saturday dance. It wasn't working and by the time I got my hair finished I was in a definite state. After we'd meet at Mrs. W.'s I'd have to walk over to the gym with him. What was I going to talk about? My French exam? American history? Then I remembered something my mother had told me once. She was sometimes completely on point, especially when it came to attracting men.

"Just ask him a question and let him talk."

So that was what I would do. But what question? At least now I had something to concentrate on so my stomach settled down. Brady and Jan went off to get themselves ready and I locked my closet and was heading out the door when, out of nowhere, Moll appeared, looking even more nervous than usual.

"You look really pretty." Her voice trembled a bit and I wondered what was going on with her, but on the other hand, I didn't have time to really get into it right then.

"You're so lucky." She twisted her fingers in a funny way. "I mean to be going to the dance."

"Why don't you go?"

"Oh, I couldn't. I'd be too embarrassed."

"About what?" I shouldn't have asked that because I really had to go. But I couldn't just walk away from her.

"You know," she began and faltered and shrugged one shoulder. "I don't know how to dress or wear makeup or anything. I mean I just wouldn't fit in."

"Well, do you want to?" I didn't know why I asked that because of course everyone wanted to fit in.

"I never could so what does it matter?"

"Look, Moll," I said. "Just throw on anything and come over. Nothing will happen. It's not like public school here. You know, Quakers are all about being inclusive of everyone, about accepting everyone. And maybe you'll get used to the dances and next time you'll feel more confident about going. But, look, I have to run."

"You have a date, don't you?"

"Yes." I started to leave but then . . . "How did you know?"

"I heard some girls talking. They said Wes Ritter asked you. Anyone would want to go with him."

"Yeah, well, it's only one dance," I said, more trying to reassure myself not to expect too much than to make Moll feel better by letting her know it was nothing special. So people were already talking about me, as if Wes and I were a couple. "If you want, you can walk over with us."

The minute the offer was out of my mouth I regretted it. What would Wes think if I showed up with Moll trailing along like a bumbling baby sister? He'd probably think I didn't want to be alone with him. Not exactly the best way to start whatever might happen between us.

"Oh, no," she said and blushed so red I thought she might explode all over my door.

"Anyway I have to translate the second act of *Oedipus Rex.* It's not the same as modern Greek. It's much more complex and there are odd idioms and lots of footnotes. Well," her voice drifted off, "I guess that doesn't much matter. I don't know what really matters anymore."

———

When I got down the hall from Mrs. W.'s, I couldn't see Wes waiting for me and my heart took this little flop like a dying fish. What if he forgot or changed his mind? Then, through the glass panes of the double doors that led to the front porch, I saw him standing outside with some of the other boys. So then my heart took another flop only this time it was a flip up and a couple of pounding beats. I thought, *Get hold of yourself or this is going to be a horrible night.*

He caught sight of me at about the same time and raised his hand in a little wave. One of the other boys fake punched him on the arm and they all started hooting at him, although I couldn't hear it and could only just see them razzing him. He pushed one of them away and opened the door. When he was inside, he had this cute little smile on his face and I thought then that everything was going to be fine.

"Are they giving you a hard time?" I asked, nodding toward the boys outside.

"Nah," he said. "They're just being goofs is all."

"Well," I said and stopped.

"Yeah. Want to go over to the gym?"

"Sure." And then I added, "Want to go out the other way?"

"You mean the north door, out the back?"

"Yes. We wouldn't have to walk right past them."

"Good idea. Fake them out."

So instead of going through the front doors, we turned and headed down the long hall of Fox Building, past all the offices, all of them locked up, giving the hall a deserted feel. Finally we got to the north door. This door was different from the other two. There was no porch here, only a small landing at the bottom of a fire stairwell that had been installed because of new fire regulations, which was a joke because if this old wooden building ever caught fire there would be nothing left.

It was a massive metal fire door with a push bar and heavy metal hinges. It was locked every night at nine but I had heard about kids going out there at night and propping it open so other kids who wanted to sneak out could get back in. There was a night watchman who made rounds all night but it was easy to figure out his schedule and time your escape and return in between his rounds. It took him four hours to make the complete circle so he only checked this door twice a night.

Wes didn't say anything until we got to the fire door. Then he spoke.

"You look really pretty."

I didn't know what to say so I just said, "Thank you."

"You always look really pretty."

"You've hardly ever even seen me," I said. I didn't know why I said that and the minute it was out of my mouth it sounded stupid.

"I've seen you," he said quietly.

We just stood there by the door. No one else was around. It could have felt awkward but it didn't.

"I've seen you since the first day you got here. When Joey Eisenstadt helped carry your stuff upstairs. I was jealous he'd gotten you."

"Really? Why didn't you ever talk to me? I mean if you were jealous."

He shrugged and turned his head away and I realized he was blushing.

"I guess I was afraid you might turn me down."

"I wouldn't have turned you down."

"Really?"

"Sure. I mean why would I turn you down?"

He let out a big sigh then and took my arm and put his other hand on the push bar.

"You never know. Maybe you liked someone else?" He pushed the door and it swung open and cool air came in at us. It was almost dark, a clear night. Stars had begun to appear and I could see Venus bright and steady above the horizon.

"Look," I said and pointed to it. "It's Venus. Planets don't twinkle like stars because they're not on fire."

"I'm glad you said 'yes,'" he said.

"Me too."

FOURTEEN

Advice About Boys

AFTER THAT SATURDAY, I KNEW IT WAS GOING TO BE REALLY hard to concentrate on my classes. At the dance, we were glued to each other. I kept peering around Wes to scope out Bleaker but she was like a hound sniffing at Juniper Barksdale and Curt Brosius, a mattress room regular. Juniper had on her tightest white sweater and black skirt combo. Skirts were mandated to come at least down to the crack at the back of your knees. Juniper's was really pushing it. Bleaker had been known to stand outside the dining hall with a yardstick to measure skirt length and push at the hem to see if the knee crack at the back of a girl's leg was fully covered.

I didn't want to dance with any of the boys I usually danced with just because they were good dancers. Wes was pretty good. But it was not the dancing that kept me by his side. It was the way I felt. And there was also the acceptance factor. Instead of standing around with the girls who were there alone, we were surrounded by other couples. Daria and Tim of course, but also the other senior and junior couples. And I was the only sophomore. It was like I'd been inducted into the most exclusive club on campus without having to apply at all. To be with Wes was simply to be accepted. I didn't question it or doubt myself. I didn't want to know why or how. I wanted to be next to him forever.

At some point during one of the slow dances, I came out of my trancelike state and happened to glance toward the gym door. Standing to the side, neither inside nor outside, Moll stared at me from the shadows. She was still wearing the same clothes she'd had on when I saw her on my hall. She hadn't taken off her glasses or even fixed her hair. She looked as if she'd just traveled from a long distance on foot, weary and dusty, needing both cleaning up and rest.

I pulled away from Wes.

"What's wrong," he asked and looked down into my eyes.

"Nothing," I said but not convincingly.

"Yes there is."

If it's possible to fall in love at fifteen—and I think it is—and all in one instant, that's when it happened to me. Because no one had ever sensed when something was bothering me or even had the determination to push past my assurance that everything was all right. And here was Wes, without really knowing me at all, understanding that I was upset. He understood it even before I did.

"It's just Moll over there." I nodded toward her.

"What about her?"

"I saw her before I left to meet you. She wanted to go to the dance so much and I told her she should come over."

"She looks kind of out of place," he said.

"She always looks that way. I feel sorry for her."

"Why?"

"Because she's so lost, I guess." But it was more than that. It was about my mother, really, about having this built-in need to rescue someone because not being able to rescue my mother had created so much misery in my life. There are so many ways of being lost. On the outside, Moll appeared to be fixable while my mother, as far as I'd seen, was irretrievably broken.

It wouldn't be until much later in my life that I could sort out the conflicting feelings my mother engendered in me. I hated her at times, pitied her at times, raged at her at times, feared her at times, wistfully longed for her love at times, avoided her at times, circled back to seek comfort from her at times, listened to her at times, and tried not to hear her at times. Any desire I had to rescue my mother was subsumed into attempts to improve the lot of certain people I perceived as potentially redeemable. Moll fit into that mold and she must have, in some imperceptible way, sensed my need was as strong as her need to be fixed. And I fit right into the Quaker ethos. The world could be saved from itself through peace and love.

"We could go talk to her," Wes offered.

At that moment the night's deejay, actually one of the AV boys, the one with bad acne and a scrawny frame that seemed out of proportion to his height, put the needle down on *A Teenager In Love*. I pulled Wes onto the dance floor so we could take advantage, and I had a feeling it would be designated as "our" song. We danced as close as we dared until it was over, both of us singing the words softly to each other.

"Okay," we held hands going off to the edge of the gym. "We can go talk to her now."

But when we looked around for her, she was gone. I forgot about it for the rest of the night. After the dance and the movie, we hung around the front porch of Fox with a bunch of other kids until the bell rang and it was time to go to our dorm rooms. The night had gotten chilly and we all huddled together, drawing out the few moments we had left to feel unencumbered by homework or tests or term papers detailing the rift between the Papal See and Henry the Eighth over his serial divorces and remarriages. In those last few minutes on the porch, we all felt nostalgia for that moment in time. Maybe it was the approaching winter, or our own sense that our youth would not last long. Whatever it was, I felt intensely happy and intensely sad at the same time.

Wes gave me a soft brush of a kiss on the cheek and our hands separated.

"See you tomorrow."

He squeezed my hand one last time before taking the steps down from the porch two at a time. He looked so happy and I felt it to be such a bittersweet moment although, if asked, I couldn't have said why.

A bit later, in my room, splayed out on my bed, surrounded by assigned history books, my mind was far away from dances and holding hands and fitting into my new school. I was comfortable by now, accepted, on the inside looking out. So I could afford to think about studying, which had begun to actually interest me in a way that it never had before. On Saturday night, we could stay up late. There was no lights out bell and no proctor telling us to quiet down and get to bed. Of course, even that privilege had limitations. Midnight was the absolute deadline unless you were a senior. It was eleven forty-five and my mind was somewhere in the

Reformation around mid-eighteen hundred when there was a soft knock at my half-open door.

I looked up and there was Moll, who looked like she couldn't decide if she would come into my room or turn and run down the hall to get as far away as possible.

"Oh," she said, "I'm sorry. You're studying."

"That's okay. Come on in."

"No, I don't want to bother you."

"Hey, I'm ready to quit anyway. There are only so many wives of Henry I can get through in one sitting. What's up?"

She edged a little closer into the room, keeping her back against the doorframe as if she needed support to remain standing. There were dark circles under her eyes and I wondered if she had trouble sleeping. I'd seen eyes like that before. When my mother had migraines, the skin under her eyes would darken and she'd get this haunted look about her. She'd lie on a chaise lounge in her bedroom all day with her arm slung over her forehead, an ice pack behind her neck, her cocker spaniel, Ginger, curled on her thighs like a small lap rug, the dog's head down, eyes darting here and there at every little sound, silky ears flapped to the sides of her head.

"We saw you at the gym tonight. We were going to come over and talk to you but you disappeared."

"I know. I . . ." She stopped and rubbed her palm against her cheek. "I, uh, didn't feel like talking to anyone."

"Moll," I said it in a soft voice, trying to make her feel comfortable, "is there some boy you like?" It was a shot in the dark but I thought maybe it would hit a target.

She turned red like she had before and I thought she

might spontaneously combust and then how would I explain that to Bleaker?

"So there is someone." I stood up and walked over and closed the door quietly. "Who is it?"

"I can't say."

She shrank even farther back against the doorjamb and looked at the floor as if there was some hidden message down there.

Then she whispered so softly I could barely hear her. "Donald Wingart."

I knew who he was because Daria was the photography editor for the yearbook and one day she asked me to come help her in the darkroom when she was developing some black and white prints she'd taken. She'd done a bunch of shots of the school orchestra. That term was a bit inflated because the string section was two girls on violins and the horn section was one trumpet and a tuba. On a chair, strad-dling the tuba, his head completely hidden behind its bell, was Donald Wingart, his little legs sticking out underneath and his fingers pressing on the valves.

"You mean the tuba player?"

She looked up at me and I thought I could just make out tears glistening in her eyes.

"Moll, there's nothing wrong with having a crush on a boy. It's normal."

"But it feels so odd," she said. "It makes me nervous."

I wondered what nervous felt like to Moll since she seemed nervous all the time anyway.

"Well that's normal, too," I said and sat down on the end of my bed facing her. I folded my hands and waited but when she didn't say anything else, just to keep the conversation going I asked, "Hey, Moll, tell me about your family. Do you have any brothers or sisters?"

She nodded. "An older brother. He has a doctorate. He teaches at MIT. He's very brilliant. He's really my half-brother."

"You're smart, too. I guess you know that already. So he's much older than you, huh? What about your parents?"

"There's only my mother. My father died when I was two. He was in his sixties already when I was born. He was hit by a train. He was a doctor and a lawyer. He was married before he met my mother but his wife died. She had cancer. He worked for a big pharmaceutical company in New Jersey. My mother's a microbiologist. She still works there. That's how they met. At work. My mother was at the station to meet him and he walked across the tracks to her and a train came. She was forty-two when I was born. I was a mistake."

"Oh, Moll, nobody's a mistake. You were a gift." It sounded like a pat answer and I was uncomfortable that I'd said it. But I did feel sorry that she felt that way. No one should feel they were born by mistake. I lived with my own sack of weighty mother messages so the empathy I felt was really for myself as much as it was for her.

She sighed and moved one step away from the door into my room.

"Do you think he would ever ask me to a dance?"

"Donald Wingart? I don't know. Have you talked to him?"

"No."

"Well, are you in any classes together?"

"No."

"Do you see him at the library?"

"I did one time."

"Well that would be a good way to talk to him. Just sit down at the same table and sort of drop a book or something."

"Why would I do that?"

"So he'd notice you and help you pick it up."

"Oh."

"Try it and let me know what happens. Maybe he's been watching you, too. You know boys can be very shy."

"Really?"

"Sure."

She said she'd better go, thanked me for talking to her, and left my room slowly as if she was thinking about how to solve some gigantic problem. I got into bed, and by then all the room lights, except for the seniors' rooms on another floor, had been automatically turned off from some main switch that controlled the electricity to the rooms in Fox. I saw a crack of light from the hall under my door as Daria opened it and slipped into my room.

She shut the door quietly and whispered, "Shhh," before she climbed onto my bed and sat with her back against the wall.

"I just got out of the mattress room and didn't want to go up to my room yet. Jan's in there now."

"In your room?"

"No, in the mattress room.

"Really? Alone?"

"Don't be stupid. Of course not."

"Who's in there with her then?"

"Jan's with Stocky. He can be a real ass."

"I know. He tried to get me to go in there with him. He let me use the wire as a bribe."

"I don't know why Jan bothers with him. Maybe she thinks she can't do any better but I think she can. I saw Moll coming out of your room. What did she want?"

"Oh, some advice, I guess."

"About what?"

"Boys."

Daria started to laugh and then clapped her hand over her mouth.

"Oh shit, I forgot it's after lights out. If they catch me in here we're both cooked," she whispered. "What did she want to know about boys? How they're different from girls?"

"No. She was, you know . . ."

"What?"

"Oh just asking about the dances and stuff like that."

"Come on, give. It must have been more than that."

"Well, yeah, she said she has a crush on someone." I immediately realized I shouldn't have said anything. It was a confidence and I had blabbed it, probably because it was Daria.

"No!" she hissed. "The other new girl likes someone. Who?"

"I can't tell you. She'd be upset."

"Come on. You have to tell me. We're a group and whatever any one of us does or hears, she has to tell the others. That's the way it works."

"Really, Daria, it's not right. She trusts me."

"And so do I. But if you're going to keep things from me, well, then I can't trust you and the others won't either. Anyway, who cares if she trusts you or not? If you tell me, she'll never know."

I thought about that for a minute and it seemed to make sense.

"It's Donald Wingart."

"Who's he?"

I let out a breath I hadn't realized I'd been holding. She didn't even know who he was so it couldn't possibly matter that I'd told her.

"Nobody really."

"I don't know why you bother with her. She's so strange."

I wondered the same thing about myself but had no answer so I let it go.

FIFTEEN

The Trestle

IT WAS ONE OF THOSE BEAUTIFUL DAYS WHEN THE SKY IS SO blue it hurts your heart and the air feels clean and cool on your skin. Wafting scents of newly mown grass and baled hay came to us as the river gurgled lazily by down below. We huddled high up under the train trestle, strictly forbidden to students, where nonetheless generations of them had come in ones and twos to have a private and quiet moment. Even climbing up to the trestle was forbidden, as was venturing through the woods as far as the river. Generally, the Nonnahanny wasn't deep at this point but there were fish in some pools in the middle and occasionally someone would appear, rod in hand, to fly cast out while wading near the banks on the pebbles that made up its bed.

On this day, with the sun shining brightly, the river glittered and danced as if to its own music and I felt almost drunk on its beauty. We'd had a few chilly nights but winter seemed a far off cloud on this day. We scrambled up the riverbank to the trestle as fast as we safely could. I'd waited for Wes behind a clump of honeysuckle that spread itself into a kind of nest grown wild over a group of saplings. I looked around but figured if anyone had walked this far and taken the chance we were taking, they would want to be seen even less than we would. Our only companions seemed to be twittering wrens and the occasional drifting cloud high up in that blue sky.

The turning leaves were at their hot peak. It was like looking out through a kaleidoscope with every gust of wind.

"You go ahead of me," Wes said. "In case you slip, I'll catch you."

It made me feel good when he said that—to know he was looking out for me.

"Okay." I went as fast as I could. The bank was dry. Leaves and twigs were not easy footholds but every once in a while there was a patch of rock outcropping to hold onto with one hand, while balancing with the other. I had to make my way half on hands and knees where it got really steep and I dared not look down or back. Once I did slip and felt Wes grab my ankle and hold it firm. I stayed like that longer than I had to.

"Go ahead," he said quietly. "It's okay."

"I can't look down or I'll get dizzy."

"Right. Never look back on a climb. But you're doing fine. Once we get up there it's all flat."

We continued like that and soon we'd made it to the top of the bank, which was really more of a ridge where they'd built the trestle for the railway bridge.

"Phew," I said and sat down to look at the trestle spanning the river. "I've never seen a trestle from below before."

"Yeah, it's kind of cool." Wes sat down next to me and put his arm across my shoulders, which was fine and felt totally normal, as if we'd just accomplished something together. From far off we heard a train whistle.

"Here comes one," he said and hunched closer. "It's going to be loud, you know. Just warning you."

"So you've been up here before?"

"Sometimes. Last year."

I nodded. He was a senior, so this was his fourth year at Foxhall. Of course he'd done more things there than I had. Probably with other girls. What was I thinking? Of course with other girls. Other girls here at the trestle? We could hear the train slowly clacking far off in the distance.

"Here she comes," he said.

"Wes," I started to ask, but then stopped.

"Yeah?"

I wanted to ask but I also felt stupid asking about other girls when he was sitting here, taking this chance with me. If we'd been caught, we'd be suspended, maybe even kicked out. I was so deeply in trouble already, I was taking an even bigger risk by sitting here under the trestle with him. He must have known that. The whole school seemed to know I was on demerit until Christmas break. And Bleaker giving me an extra chore sweeping the Assembly Room on top of that was humiliating, which was probably what she was trying to do. But if he were kicked out, his college plans would be a shambles. We were both risking a lot so I backed off.

"You're taking a big risk coming out here with me," I said instead of asking what I really wanted to know.

"You're worth it," was all he said.

Then we could hear the train just rounding the bend before the river.

"Watch under it when it comes across. It's really cool. You can see the wheels turn and all the gears. It's the coolest thing. Last year I used to come down here when I was all stressed out and just lie back and watch as many trains as I could."

So he didn't bring girls here. He came for the trains. I smiled and stretched out on the sweatshirt he'd spread on the ground under me so I could see the bottom of the trestle better. He slid down next to me and turned sideways so he could put his arm across my waist. He put his head against my shoulder and I could feel his chest rising and falling with each breath. His shirt smelled a little like oats and it made me think of a barn where I worked one summer feeding horses.

The train got louder. It was almost to the bridge now and we watched as it started over. The clacking turned to a kind of humming and a thrum-thrum-thrum sound with the train rolling along. It was a freight train and as the engine reached the middle of the trestle, the whistle sounded again. A long blast that was a chord like music and then two short blasts and then a very long one that lasted until the engine was directly above us, and Wes was right. You could see every detail of the train's underbelly as it rumbled along.

It was so loud, I could barely think. The noise from it echoed off the water and came back up as if it was hitting us like echoing thunder. I could see Wes saying something to me but I couldn't hear him. I smiled and pointed at my ears and shook my head. I turned to face him to try to read his lips and he kind of shrugged at me and lifted himself up on one elbow and leaned down and that was when it happened.

I felt his lips touch mine and felt his soft breath on my face. The train rumbled on and on, each car passing overhead with a kind of drumming and sometimes the whine of metal against metal. He didn't pull away and neither did I so he moved over closer and slipped his leg across my thighs so his body was over me and I was flat on my back. He leaned in so I could feel him against my thigh. What I felt at that moment confused and also excited me. I felt like I had some kind of power I'd never felt before and when his tongue touched mine, my brain went kind of wild with thoughts and feelings all jumbled together.

Neither one of us pulled away so he kissed me a little harder, and then I opened my mouth and that seemed to make him go a little crazy because he rolled over on top of me and placed his hands on either side of my face, holding it in place and kissed me and kissed me until I had to gasp for breath, and then he pulled back and looked at my eyes as if searching for the answer to some hidden question, and the train finally clattered off into the distance.

But the silence that followed was full of another kind of sound because my ears were ringing and I could feel blood pounding in my temples.

Wes didn't say anything but he reached down and started to unbutton my sweater.

"Don't worry," he whispered. "I just want to touch you. You're so wonderful and pretty. I'm crazy about you. I want you to know that. I want us to be a couple. For the rest of the year. Will you?"

I didn't know what to say. I hadn't expected this. Not any of it. Well maybe I thought he might try to kiss me. But not this much. Not this fast. Not this . . .

His hand had found my right breast. With the other he fumbled with the rest of the buttons of my sweater. He had to use both hands to finish and when the sweater was completely unbuttoned, he peeled it back and then reached behind me to unhook my bra. It was then I started to feel panicky.

"Wes," I said. My voice sounded shaky.

He got my bra unhooked and pulled it down off my shoulders. How did he know how to do all this, I would think later, but at that moment I had no ability to think. I felt as if I'd been swallowed by the river and it was pulling me along at its will.

Now he was touching my breasts and when he leaned down and put his lips around one of my nipples, I thought I would evaporate like a drop of rain in the sun. And all I could think was that I had to know. I just had to.

"Wes," I whispered because now there was only the sound of a soft breeze rustling the leaves and the gurgling river way down below us.

He stopped and raised his head. His lids looked heavy and I'd never seen anyone with that particular expression before, like someone who was groggy with sleep but heavy with . . . what? Wanting.

"Yes," he said and moved up to kiss me again, which he did, slowly and softly but with a kind of urgency that made me squirm under his weight.

"Have you been up here with other girls? Last year maybe?"

"No," he said. "Never. Why?"

"Why do you think?"

He smiled and kissed me again. "I love kissing you," he said. "I've never been up here with any girls before."

"Then how do you know so much about . . ." I stopped

because it suddenly sounded silly, what I was asking. I felt like a baby. But it wasn't like I had any experience with boys. Oh, I'd been kissed before. Even done other stuff. But not like this. It never felt like this before. And those boys all seemed to fumble around a lot, like they were looking for something and didn't know where or how to find it.

He let out a little laugh, which I hadn't expected. Then he reached out and stroked my face with his fingertips, which made me want him to kiss me again.

"You're a cutie, you know that?"

"No, I'm not," I said. "I'm just curious. And nervous. And . . ."

"And what?"

"I don't know what. I've never felt like this with anyone before. You make me nervous."

"That wasn't my intention."

"What was your intention?"

He smiled at me in such a disarming way I smiled back and before I knew what was happening he had pulled my bra and sweater off and pulled me to a sitting position and was holding me against his chest with his arms around me and his hands on my bare back. There was no more talking after that as he kissed my neck and shoulders and moved his hands down to my jeans and unzipped them and pushed them down as far as he could. I could have stopped it. I could have pulled away but I didn't want to and I let him feel wherever he wanted and where he wanted to feel no one had ever touched before. Soon he had my jeans and panties down around my thighs and his fingers were moving around like a musician playing an instrument, now fast, now slow, and I was unable to think at all and heard myself moan a couple of times and heard Wes call my name and then I think I must have lost consciousness altogether because all I remember was waves and waves of feelings cascading like a waterfall over and through me and Wes was doing something against me and I could feel him against me until all at once I heard him gasp and then it was over and he pulled his hand away and rolled away from my body.

After a few moments he sat up and looked at me, still lying there with my bra and sweater off and my pants and panties down around my thighs.

"Don't worry," he said. "I didn't even take off my pants. You're okay."

"I'm not worried," I said it but at the same time felt I should have been worried.

"Let me help you get dressed." He picked up my bra and handed it to me. When I held it up to my breasts, he slid the straps up my arms and hooked it in the back.

"If you haven't come up here with other girls," I began.

"If what?"

"Well if you haven't, then how do you know so much about . . ."

"About sex?"

"Yes," I said. "And about girls' underwear and stuff."

He laughed. It sounded reassuring. At least he wasn't angry with me for asking.

"I met this college girl this past summer," he said. "I had a job at a country club in the pro shop. She had just been dumped by her boyfriend and she was really sad and lonely and we started talking and got to know each other and one thing led to another. So I learned a lot. But I didn't have real feelings for her, you know. I mean I liked her and she was nice to be around but not for more than a summer. And she had a lot of needs."

"You mean sexual needs?"

"That and other needs. Anyway, she went back to college and that was that."

He stood up and helped me with my sweater. I wondered what other needs she could have had. While I was buttoning it up, he pulled my panties and jeans up and pulled me to him by the belt loops and zipped them up for me. But he didn't let go.

"I could do it all over again right now, you know," he whispered close to my ear. "Just say the word."

I should have been embarrassed and mortified and shy and everything but instead I felt triumphant.

"So what about it?" he asked.

"About what?"

"Are we a couple now?"

I leaned forward and he took the cue and kissed me again and that was the answer. Whatever else might happen that year, I assumed it would be okay.

SIXTEEN

Talking Past Each Other

I HAD NO IDEA MOLL WOULD SHOW UP AT A DANCE ONE night. How could I have known? In all the years that have passed, I still think about how different things might have been if only I had seen her first. Maybe run into her in the dorm or seen her at dinner where she could have mentioned her plan for that particular Saturday night. After sitting next to her in Quaker Life class for seven weeks, I thought we'd developed, if not a close friendship, at least some kind of trusting relationship. We'd all talked about some pretty deep stuff in that class and it felt like we'd developed a kind of respect for each other separate from whatever other friends we had—or didn't have—at school. It was like in Quaker Life class we were on an island of equivalence that elevated our sense of ourselves and gave us a notion of what our places in the world might be.

Since that first dance, Wes and I had become inseparable. I was still on demerit and he couldn't go to study hall with me. So he made a point to go to the library while I sat in a classroom down the hall.

"I hate to make you do this," I told him the first time.

"It's okay," he said. "It gives me a quiet place to study.

Even during study hours, the dorm is a hard place to knuckle down. Guys are always coming into my room and stuff."

It was true that some people went to the library voluntarily just to have a quiet place to study. See, the way it worked was, dinner was from five-thirty to six fifteen every evening. Then we had what was known as social hour, which really lasted forty minutes. Then a bell rang everywhere in the school as a five minute warning before you had to be either in your room, in the library, or in study hall for the two hours between seven and nine at night. Then another bell rang at seven telling you it was quiet time and you had to stay put wherever you were for study hours.

I must have looked skeptical because he fake punched me in the arm and said, "Really. It's okay."

Wes was that way. Never seemed stressed by anything, as if he was on a cloud slightly above everything going on around him. Other guys asked him for advice and hung around him as if there was something important happening. In general, boys were a mystery to me. What they talked about and what was important to them—it seemed like sports was the only thing they cared enough about to get really intense. The smarter guys—the ones who would end up at places like Yale and Cornell and Harvard—studied hard but didn't seem to make a lot of noise about it. The girls who had competitive college dreams were always saying things like: "Oh God, I really messed up on that test," or "The exam was so hard and I studied all the wrong stuff." Then, when they'd get an A, they'd say they were just lucky.

Knowing Wes was nearby made my demerit easier to bear and the weeks rolled by. Wes didn't ask me to the dances after that first one. It was just understood. He'd say, "Meet you at Mrs. W.'s?" and I'd say, "Yes," and that would be that. I knew Bleaker was still watching me, but I began to ignore it and just enjoy being away from home and sort of on my own. At least as on your own as you could be at boarding school. That was the funny thing about it. You didn't have your TV and your refrigerator or your own bathroom. You had to check in all the time and prove you were where you were supposed to be, like at meals. You couldn't just meet your friends somewhere. Being at boarding school was a lot more restricted than being at home. But that all depends on what home was like. And how happy you were at home—or at least how much home was a place of refuge and safety.

That Saturday night was kind of different from the others because of what had happened at the trestle the Sunday before. The weather was starting to turn. The air felt snappy cold on your skin and the skies were that clear autumn blue with a hard edge to it. We had to wear heavy sweaters or jackets and the boys couldn't get away with T-shirts anymore. Leaves speckled with brown were falling fast now. Soon, Thanksgiving break would arrive and we'd all scatter like the blowing leaves. I didn't know what would happen with Wes and me when the break came. He was one of a few kids who came east from California for prep school. His mother was a Quaker and she wanted him to have a Quaker education. We hadn't talked about it much—about being apart—because I was confident that things would be fine. I assumed he felt the same way. But as the weeks went by, and the Thanksgiving break moved closer, I began to worry. It crept up on me in small ways.

And that Saturday night I was keyed up. When he met me at Mrs. W.'s he noticed something.

"What's wrong?" he asked right at first.

"Nothing, why?"

"There is something. Tell me."

"I don't know. I just feel kind of antsy."

"Like how?"

"Honestly I don't know."

"About me?"

"I don't think so."

"What then?"

"I told you; I don't know."

"You do. You just don't want to tell me."

He sounded kind of petulant. It was the first time I'd heard that tone in his voice.

"If I tell you, you might get mad."

"No I won't. But if you don't tell me I will get mad."

It was our first fight and it wasn't much of one at that because I capitulated pretty fast. We were standing right by Mrs. W.'s and it felt too public to talk so I suggested we go up to the Social Room on the second floor—the room where I'd seen that couple exchanging tooth retainers. It was un-likely anyone would be in there on a Saturday night. You never knew for sure, of course. Sometimes kids used that room to study or have hall meetings or hall parties. But not on a Saturday night so we walked down the main hall and headed up the stairs to the second floor.

The Social Room was empty. We chose a couch in the farthest corner over by a window as far away as possible from any of the standing lamps that dimly lit the room in spots. A half-moon was coming up in the east and its light slanted through the window and cast soft shadows on the floor.

It was the first time I'd felt uncomfortable with Wes and I guessed he could sense it. I crossed my legs under me and kind of backed myself into the corner of the old couch.

"So what's going on?" he asked as soon as we sat down.

Coming from the kind of turmoil at home that I'd grown up with, I'd gotten very good at hiding and keeping things to myself. I was not so good at expressing what was going on. I had a lot to fear at home and mine was not the kind of family where you got a fair hearing. So this was hard for me, and not what I had anticipated when we started going out. Actually it had never occurred to me that we might have to talk about anything serious. Or even about our feelings. Guys didn't seem to me to be interested in feelings anyway, so I thought I wouldn't have to deal with them either. Naturally I had feelings. All kinds of feelings. They sometimes leaked out like a dripping faucet. But I tried to get them under control. And this was one of those times. Except that I noticed I was wringing my hands and squirming on the couch cushion.

"Hey," Wes whispered close to my ear, "I'm over here right next to you."

He meant it as a joke but it only made me feel more under the gun and I almost jumped up and ran to my room, which was not far away outside the door and down the hall. And if I did run he couldn't follow because boys weren't allowed on the girls' halls except on one day a year known as Open Dorm. This was not that day.

Then he leaned over and kissed my neck. Well that did it. I turned to face him and tears pricked at my eyes. I didn't know when or how I'd gotten myself so upset but there it was and no denying it. The light was too dim for him to see, so I tried to hide the tears and just looked down. He put a finger under my chin and lifted my face and tried to kiss me but I turned away, fearing that if I let him kiss me he would feel the wetness on my cheeks and know I'd started to cry.

Well that just made things worse because he pulled back and moved away from me on the couch and kind of sat there with his hands hanging between his knees. He didn't say anything and I didn't know what to say to explain how I felt. I didn't even know how I felt, only that something was bothering me and getting worse, like something stuck in your throat that just annoyed you at first and then you started to cough and before you knew it you were afraid you couldn't breathe anymore. I felt like the room was closing in on me. I wanted to run but I was frozen to my spot on that couch.

"Well," he said finally, "I guess that's it then."

I could feel him looking over at me, waiting for me to say something. My mouth was so dry and my throat so constricted that I couldn't have uttered a word at that moment even if I had known what I wanted to say.

"I guess I was wrong about how you felt about me—about us," he said.

He sounded bitter and angry and it just made me feel awful. I didn't know what to say or do.

"Aren't you going to say anything?"

He stood up then and walked to the window.

"I guess the other guys have the right idea," he said.

Without thinking, my body suddenly relaxed and I asked, "What do you mean?"

He turned back to face me but stayed where he was by the window.

"You know, stuff like the nipple pool is a lot safer than getting involved. I guess I should have listened to them. But I thought you were different."

"Different from what?"

"From girls who just lead a guy on and then dump him. Girls who care more about how they look than about really connecting with a guy. Girls who are flighty and needy and all over the place."

"Is that what you think of me?"

"I didn't. Before. But now I don't know."

"Wes," I was almost whispering now because I was so scared of the answer. "If you're trying to break up with me, you can just say it straight out. I'd rather hear it all at once than in little bits and pieces."

And this is the thing about the teen years. What you imagine is as potent as what you actually experience. The two states are intertwined like a vine that's wound itself around a tree, depending on the tree not only for support but also, after the initial embrace, by embedding its roots right into the bark, for sustenance of a kind different from what its roots pull from the soil. I know this now but only because I can look back over the decades and see the confusion that fueled my behavior at that time. So I imagined Wes was breaking up with me. Even though, separately and logically, I knew that it was me creating our stalemate. Yet I felt powerless to stop myself.

Which is another irony of my state of mind at that age. In front of Bleaker I could use the blocking tactic that had protected me from my mother's rages and depressions, scoldings and accusations about things I never did. It was not serving me well with Wes.

"What are you talking about?" he asked.

That question snapped me back to the moment.

"I mean if you want to break up . . ."

He came back to the couch and sat down close to me again.

"I don't want to break up. I thought you did."

"No," I shook my head. "That's not what I want."

"Then what is it?"

I still didn't know what to say and I started to cry again because I was just stuck in neutral and couldn't move forward. Wes put one arm around me and hugged me to him.

"What's wrong? You can tell me. I won't get mad or anything."

"Thanksgiving's coming up," I started.

"So?"

"So I have to go home."

"So?"

"And so do you."

"Yeah?"

"What's going to happen to us?"

"What do you mean?"

And at that moment it occurred to me that guys just didn't get what was going on with girls.

"I mean are we still going out or what? If you're in California, and I'm in Connecticut, then what happens to us? I mean 'us' is based here, at school. This isn't the real world. It's the school world. And here we're fine. But we have to be together here. At home we don't. And then what happens?"

"First of all, we don't have to be together here. We choose to be together. And Thanksgiving is only like, what, less than a week? I don't think we'll forget about each other in that amount of time. Do you?"

"I guess not. But . . ."

"But what?"

"Oh, nothing. It's not worth talking about it."

We sat there in silence for a few moments. I didn't know what Wes was thinking. I was beginning to realize what was bothering me and it felt too huge to bring out into the open. I never talked to anyone about my home life. It was painful, sure. But I also didn't think anyone would understand about it. It was complicated enough for me to get my mind around the situation with my mother, much less to expect anyone else to get it.

"You could come out to Carmel with me for Thanksgiving."

Carmel. It sounded so exotic. I'd never been to California. So if ever there was a time to tell him about my mother, it was now.

"Wes," I began. He took my hand and laced his fingers between mine. "Look, when I said we're together here, what I meant was . . . well I meant that but I also was thinking about home. My home. See it's probably not like yours."

"You mean in Connecticut?"

"No, I mean my home life. Besides my parents also have an apartment in New York. But the thing is, I probably would be going to the house in Connecticut for Thanksgiving. That is I would if . . ." I stumbled again.

"If what?"

"Well, yesterday I got a letter from my father."

"Are you trying to tell me your parents are getting a divorce? Because if you are, that's not a big deal. I mean it is a big deal but it wouldn't matter to me."

"No. That's not what I'm saying."

"What was the letter, then?"

"It's hard to explain." I took a deep breath.

SEVENTEEN

My Mother's Not
Like Other Mothers

EVEN NOW, AT MY AGE, WITH GROWN-UP ADULT CHILDREN, and now a grandchild, it's hard for me to get my head around how I felt about my mother back then. I know how I feel now. I know what I've forgiven and what I've come to understand. I know what pain and hurt I've let go of, and what anger I've gotten past. I know that your past is always a part of you but it doesn't have to define you. I don't know about the philosophy that what doesn't kill you makes you stronger but I do know that survival depends on the way you heal your wounds. Broken bones that knit together well can be stronger than before the break. In the Japanese art form of Kintsukuroi, broken pottery is repaired with gold or silver lacquer to make an even more beautiful work of art from the shards. If I know one thing now, it is that my struggle to make sense of my mother, while a work that seemed too monumental ever to be realized when I was fifteen, at last devolved into acceptance and forgiveness, even love, although not the kind relegated to the cloying sentiments on a Mother's Day card.

So how to explain to Wes, in my fifteen-year-old world, this complex, shameful, hateful, desperate, lonely, and con-

fusing relationship with the one person who was always supposed to be on my side, standing up for me, supporting and
defending and nurturing me? For none of these was she doing, and none of these was she even attempting. Yet to the
outside world, she seemed to be your average, every day
mother. Well, not exactly average. In the world I know now,
the world of my grandmother years, the world that's gone
way past what I knew as a child, these things are talked
about, written about, discussed on TV and played by famous
actresses in movies. Everything is out in the open now. But
in those days, when I was a teen, what happened in people's
personal lives was considered private and even if you wanted
to talk about certain things, you couldn't. It was like some
unwritten law prevented everyone from bringing up certain
topics. So outside of a few politicians and reporters, no one
knew about John Kennedy's affairs or that certain famous
people were alcoholics or drug addicts or had sexual prefer-
ences for little boys or little girls or abused their children.
We were all protected from these images. The world was
cleansed for us. Except inside the home, inside the family,
inside the lives of people, yes, there, these things went on
and no one talked about them.

The moon had risen higher by then and was moving beyond
the windows to a position in the sky that put it over the roof.
Our eyes had become used to the dim light in the Social
Room and we sat huddled together on one corner of the
couch, Wes with his arm around me, my feet tucked in be-

tween two of the couch cushions. Wes had waited patiently for me to answer his question about the letter from my father but I didn't know how to begin.

"Just tell me," he said, and ran a finger down my cheek. "Whatever it is, it can't be all that bad."

"The letter I got just said my mom is in the hospital and I'll have to go to my aunt and uncle's for Thanksgiving. That's all."

"Well, that's not so bad, except about your mom being in the hospital. What's wrong with her? I mean is it serious?"

"You don't understand," I said and shook my head. "She's in the hospital again."

I knew he didn't understand, couldn't understand, wouldn't understand. How could he? How could anyone? I couldn't understand it and I'd been living with it ever since I could remember.

"So it is something serious then? I'm sorry. But she always got better before, right? So she'll be okay. I mean she got out of the hospital before, right?"

I shook my head again. "How can I explain it to you? It's not like she's sick the way you think. It's not that kind of hospital. She's not physically sick."

"Well, what is it then?"

"She gets funny."

"Funny how?"

"Not right. Not herself."

"I don't understand."

"No, you don't. You can't. No one can. So let's not talk about it anymore. Let's go to the dance." I slid my feet out from between the cushions and slipped them into my shoes.

"Wait a minute."

I turned to Wes, hoping this tension would go away and never creep between us again. And then I hated my mother. For making me feel this way. For all those times she made me feel wrong when I had no idea what I was wrong about . . . just that I was wrong. It was a terrible thing to be punished when the authority wouldn't or couldn't tell you what the crime was and makes you suffer as if you had done something simply because the authority, whoever that is, has the power and control over you. It might be easier to understand if there was a profit motive involved. Or if there was the threat of anarchy. We were heading into a time when that threat would be used as an excuse for all sorts of mischief and damage. But that was a government. Not a mother.

I remember being shut up in my room before breakfast until after dinner with nothing to eat or drink because I had done something. I don't remember ever doing anything that would warrant such treatment. I was neither a thief, nor a drug user, nor promiscuous; I did not talk back or wreak havoc on the house or burn things in my wastebasket. I lost a watch that my mother had given me in second grade. I was sure there was some retribution for that. On her birthday, I once gave my mother a beautiful, very fine cashmere scarf that was large enough to be a wrap. It had delicate crewel stitching of flowers and birds at the ends. I think it came from India. I was thirteen at the time. She opened the box, lifted out the scarf, looked at me with a kind of scowl on her face and said, "I don't need anything like this." With that she put it back in the box and handed it back to me. I think that hurt more than all the screaming and punishments.

So it wasn't going to be easy to explain to Wes why my mother was not like his.

"Explain it to me. I want to know. Where do your aunt and uncle live?"

"Oh what's the difference? I have to go there for Thanksgiving and that's all there is to it. My dad won't be home and my mom will be in the hospital. So I can't go home."

"How do they know how long she'll be in the hospital? I mean when my brother had his appendix out they told us when he would be able to come home. So how come they don't know with your mom?"

"Will you just let it go for now? I'd rather be at the dance than think about all this stuff."

I stood up and was about to walk away when Wes said, "I thought you trusted me. I mean at the trestle and all."

So I turned around, and in the fading moonlight I looked at him, but his face was in shadow and I couldn't tell if he was angry or what.

"I did trust you. I do trust you. I just don't want to talk about this anymore."

"Why not?"

"Oh, Wes, you can't possibly understand. You have this nice normal family with this nice normal mother. You have everything just right. And I . . ."

"You what?"

"I don't. Okay? I just don't. Let's leave it at that."

EIGHTEEN

The Last Dance

THAT NIGHT HUNG OVER US LIKE THE RISING HALF-MOON, half-bright and glowing, half-dark and unfathomable. We held hands walking to the gym, in sync and out of touch at the same time. I longed to be back at the trestle, in his arms, no need for words, only the clanging metal above as the train thundered along. The closer we came to the gym, as I heard music over the loudspeaker, a feeling of dread enveloped me. Wes squeezed my hand. I knew he was trying to reassure me and I also knew he had no idea what I was facing, nor could he possibly unless he moved into my house as a small child and grew up with all that I had experienced.

Just before we got to the gym steps and the dance monitors who would be watching our every move to be sure no signs of physical affection occurred between us, he put his arm around me and kissed my cheek.

"I do understand," he whispered but to me it seemed more a whisper of uncertainty, as if he was trying to convince me—or himself—of an intimacy that I had never acknowledged. A part of me had closed off years before I ever met Wes and no one could have opened that door in those years. Touching my body was allowed. Touching my hurt was off limits, even to myself. The safer course was a cynicism that I wore like armor, and a knowing sophistication that was only as deep as the milieu I had been born into rather than anything I felt I had accomplished on my own.

I guessed he was trying to see inside my world beyond Foxhall and maybe that was enough. At least for that evening, at that time, for where we were. Still the feeling of impending doom that had settled inside me didn't lift. At that moment, I thought it meant the inevitable would overtake us, that time away from each other—even a short break—would irrevocably untie the connection we had and I would be left floating. At fifteen, every little word, or touch, or glance carried such import that it could shatter the moment into tender fragments or imbue it with a kind of ecstasy.

The others were in the gym already. Daria and Tim huddled in a far corner in some replica of dancing, determined to make the most of the last dance before Thanksgiving break. Tim would go home to Beverly Hills and Daria to Southport, Connecticut, to what I considered her cushy life, where I believed she had at least a Beemer waiting for her in one corner of a five-car garage situated just to the side of the pool and barbecue pit. Over Christmas some of us would get together away from school, especially the ones who lived in or near New York or whose parents welcomed school friends to stay for a few nights. We'd all go to shows or just hang out in the city. But Thanksgiving was known as family time so when we scattered we'd stay apart four days. Four days away from prep school seemed like an eternity once you'd become acclimated to your friends and the school routine. I guess it was like any regimentation—army or jail—where you became part of the mill, each cog working in its own way inside the machine of life in an enclosed system, institutionalized, in our case within a privileged class of elites, although Quaker life was expected to be anything but elite. We weren't like the kids at Exeter or Choate, especially in the early sixties before those schools went coed and we wouldn't be together at all, girls and boys. That was one of the reasons we, or our parents, had opted for Foxhall. That, and what was deemed a "family" atmosphere, inclusive and supportive.

Wes and I joined the group, milling around at the edges of the floor. Stocky was working on Jan at the moment, a big push to get her alone one more time before the break. Brady and a senior named Michael Keating had just broken up. I wasn't sure why, but that left Brady open and Stocky was also making moves on her when Jan wasn't paying attention. He may have been crude but he was buddies with all the cool boys, so we let him dog us around and every once in a while he managed to get somewhere with one of the girls. He could be charming, if obvious.

Faith had come to the dance with a really sweet boy name Steve Lippincott. He was from a fourth-generation Foxhall family and came from Quaker bluebloods. Jan whirled and dipped out on the dance floor with Josh Lichtenstein, one of a small group of Jewish boys from New York, and a Foxhall dancing star. This was the only place she ever even talked to him. He looked completely absorbed in whatever combination of ballroom dances they were blending. I knew Jan didn't care about him particularly because she'd said, "He's a good Saturday night partner as long as we're in the gym." We'd laughed and moved seamlessly to some other thoughtless barb about someone else. Much later in life, Josh would run one of the biggest corporations in the world and be worth a few billion dollars. But in the gym that night, his gift was dancing and that was all we cared to know.

The gym was crowded for this last dance before we'd part. The music was sweet. Lots of kids came stag and stood around the edges of the floor in groups, just hanging around or talking as best they could above the music. After the dance was over at nine, there would be a movie in the Assembly Room, a serious movie about murder and racial prejudice. The title was *Sapphire*. At Foxhall we were rarely treated to entertainment that had no social message. We were supposed to think about the ills of the world and what we could do about them. A large part of being a Quaker means practicing faith in tangible ways. We were supposed to be activists for the greater good. Which was why, that morning, without telling anyone, I had surreptitiously taken a pen to the posting board outside Bleaker's office where notices were taped or pinned for everyone to see, and signed up to work in a Philadelphia soup kitchen over Thanksgiving break. It was easy. I pulled off one sign up sheet and wrote my name and placed it in a box in the dean's office. If accepted, anyone who volunteered would be bussed there and put up at a local Quaker family's house for the holiday. I didn't yet know who else would be going. Not any of my friends, I was sure of that. Probably only exchange students or kids who'd come from countries where Thanksgiving meant nothing or were too far to fly there and back for only four days. Definitely not Wes. I liked to think all the education about Quaker values was making me a better person. In truth, after my father's letter, I didn't want to face going to my aunt and uncle's house, to see the brave faces they'd put on for me, to think about my mother being sick yet again, away at a holiday, our home disrupted (for the umpteenth time) by her inexplicable illness, my needs shunted aside and everyone focused on her and her problems.

At the movie, Wes and I sat together way in the back of the balcony. As soon as the lights dimmed he put his arm around me and began to rub the back of my neck. It was nine-thirty on Saturday night. We would leave Foxhall on Wednesday morning. On Monday and Tuesday I had tests and papers due. This was the last time that Wes and I would be together until after Thanksgiving break. I still felt a distance between us. I wondered, there in the dark with the movie credits rolling by up on the old screen—apparently it was a British movie, which was kind of a novelty, and a recent release, another novelty for us—if I had put up this space between us or if it had happened on its own. Or, a much worse thought, if Wes was pulling away.

As the sensation of his fingers on my neck spread down through my body, it occurred to me that he had never mentioned the mattress room, never said he could get the key or asked me to meet him there. I turned to look at him but he was watching the movie. I reached up and twined my fingers through his but he seemed not to notice.

I leaned close to his ear. "Do you want to leave?"

He shook his head. And then . . .

"Do you?"

I didn't know what to say. I wanted to feel close to him. I wanted him to feel the same way I did. I wanted not to feel this crushing sense of something being over. I wanted not to feel.

"Yes." I said it with a nod and started to get up. There was no one sitting near us so no one noticed when we picked our way to the aisle and slipped out the door.

After the dark Assembly Room the light startled me like a camera flash. I blinked and leaned against the wall. This was a weird space outside the balcony. At either end of it was a door leading to one of the girls' halls. There was also a fire door to the stairs leading either up to the fourth floor, or down. On the level below us was the Social Room. But up here, there was nowhere to go in this no man's land so we stood there getting accustomed to the bright light.

"Well?" Wes finally said.

The air felt heavy, or maybe it was my limbs, or my heart. I cleared my throat and said, "Let's go to the Social Room." My voice sounded strange, like something was wrapped tightly around my neck. Either Wes didn't notice, or I was imagining it. Or maybe he did notice but chose not to say anything. These thoughts built a kind of panic of what ifs. But I had made a decision and I would follow through with it so we pushed the fire door and headed for the second floor.

The Social Room was empty.

"Everyone must be at the movie," I said.

Wes slumped down in a cushy old armchair. He stared at his hands, which he had placed on his knees. I turned off the overhead lights leaving only the standing lamps on, which gave me more the sense of a living room and less of an institutional feeling. Then I sat down in a chair near Wes and leaned forward.

"Wes," I began.

"Look, you don't have to say it. I'll make it easy on you. Anyway, I'm leaving early on Tuesday to catch a plane so we don't even have to see each other after tonight if you don't want."

"You're leaving Tuesday? Everyone else is leaving Wednesday morning."

"Yeah, well my mom made some arrangement for Thanksgiving up in Sonoma so I have to fly to San Francisco a day early."

I hated it when Wes seemed far away, when he got a certain look on his face. It was a combination of worry and isolation, a slight knitting of his eyebrows and a downward cast of his eyes, his shoulders set hard and it felt to me like he had some invisible barrier around him. I had noticed it the first time after he'd started walking me to study hall—we'd meet at the door to Bedford Hall which had the biggest classroom and thus was the designated study hall—we had developed a routine. He arrived first and stood to the side of the doorway off the concrete path beyond the arc of the outdoor light and I would come around from the side of the building because my dorm faced the side of Bedford. Concrete paths crisscrossed the campus connecting dorms, gyms, academic buildings and the paved road that led from the street outside campus. This road snaked around the buildings and off down the hill behind the dorms and skirted the edge of the woods then came back up on the far side of campus behind the outdoor graduation theatre and met up with another road in and out of the school. The whole thing formed a big circle, which also connected to parking lots, the infirmary, and the back of the kitchen where trucks backed up to a loading dock for deliveries.

As I came around to the front of Bedford—we had to meet in front because the side doors were locked at night—Wes would slip his arm around my waist and pull me to the tall bushes and we'd kiss and he'd sneak his hands under my sweater or jacket and feel my breasts. He called it getting his just desserts for coming out at night. We both found it hard to concentrate after this.

One night I said, "We shouldn't do this. What if we get caught?"

"Who's going to catch us? No one's going around poking in the shrubbery."

I giggled at the word shrubbery and he leaned down to kiss me again.

"But it makes it hard to concentrate on studying."

"For me, not for you I'll bet."

He was wrong about that. And he seemed able to turn it off when it came to actually getting the books open and homework done.

"You study just fine. I'm the one who's having trouble with algebra. You're the whizz kid who's going to Stanford."

He ran his hands down my hips.

"Hey," I said and he put his hand over my mouth.

"Shhh. Someone's coming. We'd better go in."

We waited until the shadow passed and then he looked around before motioning for me to come to the path. Inside, we tromped up the stairs to the room where study hall was about to start and then, just before we split up, he to the library, me to my jail term, I saw that faraway look on his face.

I didn't know what it meant but my imagination and insecurity told me it was about me, about Wes wanting to be free of me.

"So you're leaving early?" I asked because I wanted to open the subject again in some perverse way to pour vinegar in my own wound.

"We're going to Sonoma," he repeated. "It's up north, wine country. My mom rented a winery for my eighteenth birthday. It's the day after Thanksgiving. My whole family's coming. Aunts and uncles and everybody. Big deal." He raised his hands and placed them on the fat, worn chair arms.

"Your birthday? Why didn't you say anything? I had no idea."

"Yeah, well, you haven't been exactly present lately."

"I know. I'm sorry." I wasn't sure what else to say. "But we talked about this before. I mean earlier tonight. I thought you didn't want to break up."

He just stared at me then. "I don't."

"Well then we don't have a problem. Because I don't either."

"Then why did you want to leave the movie?"

"Because . . ." I didn't know how to say what I wanted to say. It all seemed so complicated. And on another level so simple.

"I hate my mother." That was the simple level.

"What?"

"Yeah."

Wes sat up in the chair. All of a sudden that sullen, faraway look was gone.

"Why?"

"Remember earlier, when you wanted to know why my mother was in the hospital?"

"Yeah. But you wouldn't tell me."

"I know. I never tell anyone. I mean I feel like what's the point. Nobody can understand unless they've been through it like I have."

"You said that before. So what's different now?"

"I want to try to explain it to you. Because how she is affects how I am."

"Okay. I think I get it."

"But you have to listen to the whole thing. Because it's not easy to talk about and even harder to explain."

"I'll listen. I want to know."

NINETEEN

Greenwood's Confession

"WHEN I SAY I HATE MY MOTHER, YOU HAVE TO UNDERSTAND that hating someone is not disliking them. I mean, hate and love, they're entwined. Like on a seesaw. All the weight is on the same end. On the other end is dispassion—just not caring one way or the other. And it's impossible for me not to care about her. Matter of fact, most times I think I care too much about her. Everyone else does, too. And that makes me angry and makes me hate her. Because there's no room for me in there. She takes up all the emotional room and leaves nothing for anybody else.

"But not always. That's the other thing I hate about her. She's not the same all the time. I can never rely on her—not for anything. Like now. She's in the hospital again. She's in and out of the hospital like a bouncing ball. I never know when I go home what I'll find. If she's there, she may be in one of her super aggressive moods, yelling and blaming me for things I didn't even think about doing, telling me all the things that are wrong with me and all the ways I'm wrong. Or she may not be there at all. She may be in the hospital again. Or she might be just lying in a lounge chair in her room in the dark with an ice bag on her head because she has such a bad headache. For hours and hours, just lying there not doing anything. Or maybe she'll be crying. Or just lying there in the dark. And you can't go in and you can't do anything about it."

"Shit, that's tough," Wes said when I stopped to get my breath.

I looked out the window and spoke, not directly to him but it was meant for him of course.

"I'm not looking for sympathy or empathy or for anything like that. I'm just explaining to you what my world is like. I mean my world away from here, away from Foxhall. I think my parents wanted me to go here so I would be in what they thought would be a nice family environment, because my family environment is so far from nice. Also my mother wanted to get me out of the house so she wouldn't have to take care of me. I was brought up by my nurse, until I was five, and then live-in maids until last year. It may sound glamorous to some people but to me it was lonely. I always felt there must be some reason why my mother didn't teach me how to cook or sew or keep my room clean or wash my hair or any of those things. I learned about Tampax away at camp. I figured out where to put them by myself one day in the bathroom."

"I could have helped with that."

I could hear the grin in his voice even though I was still looking out the window. I turned and expected to see him smiling but he wasn't. He looked so sad, I almost thought he might cry.

"I'm sorry," I said.

"For what?"

"For telling you all this stuff. It's sad and gloomy and frustrating and makes me angry every time I think about it. But here's the thing. The main thing about it all. After I came here and got a little distance on my mother, I realized that she's broken. She's a broken person and there's no fixing her. And all this time, all my childhood, I wanted to find a way to fix her so my life could be better. It was—it still is—painful to see her going off the rails all the time. But the real pain is knowing that she can't be fixed."

"What exactly is wrong with her? I mean what happens when she goes to the hospital?"

"That depends. She sometimes gets very—I don't know what to call it—agitated I guess is the best way to describe it. Like she has so much energy she can't stop. But she also gets angry and goes into rages during these times. And then other times she gets really depressed like when she's lying alone in a dark room or when she has a headache. And if that lasts too long then my father takes her to a doctor and she gets sent to a hospital. Sometimes she stays for months at a time. One year she was gone for thirteen months. My whole fourth grade year.

"I remember that as a good year because the house was at least peaceful. No yelling or blaming or hiding or running off to the woods to be alone. And no picking on my friends. That's another thing she does. Berates my friends, tears them down, tries to make them look bad to me."

"I hope I measure up if I ever meet her."

"Oh, she loves guys. She never picks on guys."

"What about your dad?"

"He never picks on anybody."

"What happens when your mom's away for so long?"

"He travels a lot. He has to go to companies and study them and it takes time and then he has to report back to his company about whether they should invest or not. So he's out of town a lot. And if she's in the hospital, sometimes she can't see anyone because of treatments she's getting or stuff. He'll be away over Thanksgiving staying near the hospital where they sent her this time. I don't know where it is but I'm not allowed to see her for a while. At least that's what my dad told me."

"Why don't you come out to California with me?"

"I can't now."

"How come?"

"Because I signed up for a work camp in Philadelphia over the weekend. It's a soup kitchen or something and I've already been accepted."

"Wow, you're doing one of those?"

"Yeah, well maybe I can help fix someone else's life. You never know. Anyway, since I've been here at Foxhall, I've started thinking that my life is pretty shallow and I should really try out some Quaker ideals."

"Yeah, I know what you mean."

"You do?"

That clouded looked came over his face again and I thought maybe I shouldn't have told him all this stuff.

"When I turn eighteen in January, I'll have to register for the draft."

"Oh, God, that's right."

TWENTY

The Car Ride

IT WAS SORT OF LIKE WHAT I EXPECTED AND THEN AGAIN IT wasn't. Mr. Brownell and his wife drove five of us to Philadelphia in a school van. We were an odd assortment.

There was Dieter, the German exchange student, who'd gotten into a shouting match with Benny Newman, a Jewish boy from Long Island. The shouting turned ugly and caught Wes in the middle.

It happened one day at the track right after Wes had finished his extra laps. I was walking out to meet him so we could talk a little before he had to go shower before supper. Most of the track team had already left and the coach was on his way to the gym. Wes was drinking some water when we both heard shouting coming from near the bleachers. The shouting got uglier, Dieter said that Benny was typical of his race. That sent Benny into a rage and he took a swing at Dieter, hitting him in the nose, which started to bleed. By then Wes dropped the water and ran over to where they were yelling at each other. Benny called Dieter a fucking Nazi bastard and Dieter punched Benny, his knuckles making contact with Benny's left cheekbone just below the eye. Before Wes could stop them, fists were flying and they fell to the ground pounding each other.

I had never seen a fistfight before and the thing that sickened me, besides seeing blood flying, was the sound the fists made when they hit bone. It was like a crack and a thud at the same time. It made my stomach turn over but Wes started to pull Benny off of Dieter, who was the smaller of the two. A couple of other boys from the track team piled on and finally got them apart. They were both bruised up but it didn't stop them from screaming at each other while they were restrained by the boys.

"Hey, you guys," Wes admonished them, "you're going to get into big trouble if you don't cool it." He led Benny away, talking to him in a soothing voice. I heard phrases like, "I know he's a little prick." And "Don't let him get to you, man." I don't know what the other boys were saying to Dieter but in the car driving to Philly I thought about that day.

Dieter could come across annoyingly arrogant at times and Benny was pretty hotheaded. It wasn't a surprise that they'd gotten into it. In those days there were still people, like some of my father's relatives who wouldn't buy a German car.

The girl who always talked about her missionary parents at Meeting for Worship sat in the middle row of the van with me. Her name was China Noice, named for her parents' first missionary posting. We all knew that because she'd slipped it into one of her Meeting soliloquies. In the car she talked about "the poor" as if they were personal friends of hers and she was going to spend the holiday with them. On my other side was Arlene Sanderson, whose family lived in Guam and therefore she hardly ever got to go home and was glad to get away from school for any reason as she told me in a whisper while China prattled on about the poor and needy.

Behind us was Donald Wingart, the tuba player. His father was in the State Department stationed somewhere overseas so Donald couldn't go home either. He was so small and frail looking that I wondered how he ever managed to hoist that tuba and carry it around. He looked like he was about ten years old. He wore brown leather shoes with non-matching laces, one black and one tan. I could just imagine the original brown laces breaking and Donald searching absent-mindedly for replacements, no matter what color they were. I thought about talking to him about Moll and tucked that thought away for later in the weekend when there might be a lull in soup ladling.

The one bright spot was Faith, also sitting in the back seat with some of the gear we'd brought. She had told her parents this was what she wanted to do to show her thanks for all her blessings and they were one hundred percent behind her, although they told her the whole family would miss seeing her smiling face and cheerful grace. Those were their exact words, Faith told me. I thought it must feel warm and hopeful to be in a family that told their children such things. No wonder Faith was such an easy person to befriend and why she was sought out by the younger girls. I didn't count myself among the younger girls since I wasn't a freshman and my main friends were juniors. The pecking order at Foxhall wasn't all that rigid. There were even instances of a senior girl dating a junior or sophomore boy—if he was hot and cool, which may seem like two qualities that should cancel each other out if you only understood literal definitions for words and weren't tuned into teen speak, which changes from year to year and generation to generation.

Since these were the days long before seat belts were mandatory, I could turn around freely and talk to Faith while Mrs. Brownell turned to talk with us and Mr. Brownell drove—maddeningly slowly—in the far right lane on the interstate.

"Have any of you children ever been to a work camp weekend before?" Mrs. Brownell smiled benignly at us, looking from one to the other while I was busy whispering to Faith, who leaned over to listen and so Donald couldn't hear.

"Do you think we'll have time for any fun?"

"Doubtful," Faith whispered back. "They keep a pretty close watch all the time."

"Are we going to be serving food the whole time?"

"Shhh," she whispered and motioned subtly to Mrs. Brownell.

I turned back to face front. Mrs. Brownell was explaining something to Dieter.

"You see, Dieter, by serving others we express our faith in a tangible way. The rewards of giving come back to the giver and the rewards of receiving multiply the faith."

"Ya," he pronounced with his thick accent. "Ya, I see but how then does the receiver express faith? Is he not simply taking what he has not worked to obtain?"

Hearing this I felt a little stab. Who in hell was he to be questioning the very thing he was embarked on doing? He could at least go into it with an open mind. No wonder Benny had punched him in the face. These were not Quakerly thoughts and I mentally admonished myself while at the same time thinking them.

Mrs. Brownell, still turned toward the back, smiled at Dieter.

"We have compassion for those less fortunate, Dieter. Our hearts are large enough to hold love for all humanity. Not everyone is as fortunate as those of us in this car."

"Ya, but how come then they are strong enough to come to soup kitchen to get handed out food? Can they not work for that? Work is good for them, for everyone. Why should I give hard earned fruits of labor to someone else?"

Mrs. Brownell looked at Mr. Brownell's profile.

"That is a question societies ask themselves the world over," Mr. Brownell said. He looked in the rear view mirror to see us in the back seat. I could see his eyes. He looked so calm. I was ready to smack Dieter. But he went on.

"There are always strong ones and weaker ones in any society. Societies that treat the weakest of their members with dignity and respect, with loving kindness and a helping hand, are stronger for it. It's said that a rising tide lifts all ships. Well the tide can be helped to rise."

That sounded completely sane to me. Of course, I thought of my father. Of his love for my mother, of helping her no matter how sick she became. Of waiting for her to come back to him. I often marveled at his patience. She was one of the weaker ones, although, when she was in one of her high moods she appeared strong, almost invincible, strong and angry and frightening. But certainly not weak. Her voice and manner had an imperious aspect to it that told you she would suffer no impertinence or defiance. Yet she had those crushing bouts of depression where she could not function. Weak did not begin to describe it. Should we have tossed her out? No matter how much I hated her at times, I also felt a deep sadness for her and, even as a small child, I realized she was fragile in some way that I didn't understand.

"Ya, but I still say if a man can work he should work. Work makes for dignity. Being fed by someone else's work is for women."

"*Arbeit macht frei*, huh, Dieter?" I said, not loud, but not under my breath either. Mrs. Brownell turned to look at me, eyebrows raised, which I took to mean I should cut it out.

The car became silent and I wished I'd sat in the back with Faith. I felt like Dieter's last remark was directed at me and the other girls in the car. So annoying that he could get away with that just because he was an exchange student. At least I'd shut him up. But then China found her Meeting For Worship voice.

"In Ghana, all the people my parents serve have little. But they're all generous with each other, no matter how little they have. My parents say that's what makes a strong community. This summer, after school is over, I'm going back there to help with the school. My parents have gotten the whole village together to build it and now they need teachers. I'm going to teach English and geography."

All I could think was *Run, Spot, Run.* It kept repeating in a singsong in my brain. At the same time I was having trouble controlling an excruciating urge to giggle. I reached back and motioned for Faith to take my hand. She squeezed it so hard, I knew she understood.

"That's very nice, China," said Mrs. Brownell. "I'm sure you'll be a big help out there."

I watched the suburbs skim by as we drove. Houses and streets and gas stations with signs screaming low, low prices, old shade trees and parking lots, industrial buildings that looked like warehouses of some sort, traffic lights and railroad tracks. And then we could see the city. Traffic got heavier, buildings packed tightly together and up ahead, in the distance, spires atop a few stone structures taller than the rest, buildings that spoke of an elegant time long ago with multiple layers of windows in elaborately detailed structures. Compared with driving up to New York, this looked small, almost compact, easy to navigate. Mr. Brownell turned off at an exit and headed past buildings that had an air of squalor. Streets with trash blowing around, people sitting on stoops. We passed by and nobody seemed interested in us or any of the other cars. A bus roared by from the other direction, leaving a plume of dirt-gray smoke.

Soon we came to a different neighborhood of small, compact houses, clapboard with wooden shutters painted in colonial colors, with front yards and little gardens. I looked out the window past China—I didn't want to look out Dieter's side—and then we were winding our way from traffic light to traffic light until we came to a sign that said Rittenhouse Square. Lovely, large mansions surrounding a park with stately old trees. People were walking dogs, sitting on benches reading, a police station at one corner, and a fancy hotel at another. We drove around the park until we turned off at a side street, turned again, drove for a few blocks then stopped. I think it was Pine Street where we pulled up in front of a brick house that looked old but had obviously been restored, like the others on down the street. It was the kind of block that, except for the cars, could have looked the same a hundred years in the past. Preserved like a dried flower, picked at its peak and locked away like a bug in amber. The front garden was incredibly tidy with not a leaf on the ground or a stem out of place. This would be our home for the next four nights. It looked crisp, inviting, if unadorned.

We unloaded the car while Mrs. Brownell rapped the doorknocker up and down. After a few minutes an old lady opened the door and put one foot outside on the stoop, peering at Mrs. Brownell. It took a few seconds for recognition to flood her face.

"Oh, Elizabeth," she flung her arms around Mrs. Brownell. "Thee have arrived. I've been waiting and waiting. Just ask Virgy. And where's that boy of mine?"

"Right here, mother," Mr. Brownell took the steps up to her two at a time. They embraced as if they hadn't seen each other in years.

"But it's chilly out here. November has arrived, I can tell thee. Virgy set the fire going in the living room so it would be toasty warm for all of thee." She looked beyond Mr. Brownell to the rest of us standing on the sidewalk by the suitcases.

"Come in, children," she motioned with a wave of her hand for us to come up the stairs. "Thee are all welcome."

"Mother," Mr. Brownell stopped at the door, "Elizabeth is not staying. Remember I told thee she's visiting her Aunt Martha for the weekend? Her aunt took sick and she's so wanted to see Elizabeth."

"Oh yes, dear, I do remember that. Virgy," she called out. "Bring my daughter-in-law those car keys I left on the hook, please."

I could have sworn I was watching an episode of *Leave it*

To Beaver, the way they talked to each other. But then Virgy arrived with the keys while we were all standing there on the steps waiting to get into the house. Virgy must have been about a hundred, stooped over, with wiry gray hair and gnarled finger joints. She walked bent to one side and her dress hung loosely as if she had at one time been a much larger woman. Her skin was medium beige and one eye was cloudy gray.

TWENTY-ONE

Ladling at the Soup Kitchen

WE GOT UP BEFORE DAWN, STUMBLED AROUND IN THE DARK in unfamiliar rooms, me and Faith in one room, China and Arlene in another with a shared bathroom between, Donald Wingart and Dieter up under the roof eaves in bunk beds. Our floor had a toilet, sink, and small shower in one corner. We were told to wear jeans and sneakers, shirts and sweaters because it would be cold most of the time, not to carry any money and not to wear any jewelry. We were not to wear any gloves or hats or anything that we would have to take off during the day because there would be nowhere to store it safely and the mission would not be responsible for anything lost or stolen.

Until that morning, fumbling around in the dark, I hadn't really thought about what to expect. I'd been so focused on avoiding going to my uncle's that the reality of here and now had escaped me. But pulling up a pair of old jeans and grabbing a sweatshirt, that I mistakenly put on backwards and then had to slide my arms back out of to turn it around right, it occurred to me that the situation at a shelter on Thanksgiving week might not be a whole lot of fun.

That was when I began to worry about the people who

would be there for free food. Icky people. Dirty people. Sick people. Thugs, thieves, or worse.

"Faith?" I called into the dark. She had pulled open a shade so I sensed where she was over by the one window. I didn't remember where the light switch was in our room or that there was a small lamp between the twin beds.

"What?"

"You've done these mission things before, right?"

"Not really. All I've done is work camps and sit-ins."

"You mean like lunch counter sit-ins?"

"Right."

"Where?"

"In Philadelphia. Last year."

This was news. It would be three more months before the term sit-in became a common part of our language, a full three years before the images of fire hoses and German shepherds turned on demonstrators in Birmingham erupted on the one black-and-white TV in the rec room of Foxhall school.

"What happened?"

"A group of Quakers from Philadelphia Yearly Meeting organized an interracial group and we went to the Woolworth's counter downtown. It was very orderly."

"But I don't understand. There's no segregation here."

"No but there's something called de facto segregation and that's an integral part of racism in this country."

Although this was my first introduction to the term, de facto segregation was an accepted part of life. It was like the kitchen staff at Foxhall or the series of black women who'd lived, one after the other, in the room behind our kitchen in the house where I grew up. From them I learned how to cook and sew, how to take care of my personal needs, what it was like to feel safe with another person. All things I should have learned from my mother.

A soft vapor of daylight, the slightest whisper as if filtered through cheesecloth, now outlined vague shapes as it crept into our room, defining that momentary patch between night and day. We finished dressing, brushed our teeth, and headed downstairs. The others joined us and Mr. Brownell's mother met us at the front door.

"I wanted to give thee a good breakfast before thee leave but my son insists that everyone eat at the mission. Thee will be fine." She smiled at us, a cheerful and patient smile. Wisps of white hair surrounded her face, giving her the look of one of those medieval angels. She reminded me a little of my grandmom, Bess, who'd read me *Heidi* in weekly installments when I was nine, the year my mother was in the hospital for thirteen months. The one time I saw my mother that year, she had a blank expression on her face as if someone had conked her on the head and left her in a daze. I think I felt like Heidi, stuck up on that mountain with the old man, secluded from everything but goats and cows and wildflowers and snowcapped peaks. But my isolation was not of the physical sort.

"I'll be here when thee get back."

She waved us out the door and we stepped into the cold morning and the waiting van with Mr. Brownell at the wheel. It didn't take long to get there. None of us said a word on the way. I wanted to ask if anyone else was nervous, but I didn't dare and told myself to stop sniveling and just get through it.

As we parked, we could already see the line that had formed outside the old stone building. I imagined greasy sausages and stale bread, powdered eggs like the kind I'd once had at a summer camp and retched up before swim practice. My stomach was already in revolt at the thought of sharing what these people were about to gobble down for free and I imagined taking a cab over to the fancy hotel my parents had booked us into the weekend they'd brought me to Foxhall for my interview. I tried to remember the name of it in case I could make a break for it but then remembered we had not taken any money along. So I was trapped here. I decided to keep my head down, do what I was told, and not really look at anybody.

———

They came in shifts. The first would be the breakfast shift. Lydia was the organizer of this Thanksgiving soup kitchen, a small, thick-waisted woman wearing overalls and big, brown, tie-up shoes that looked like they'd seen more time in a garden than a soup kitchen—which, as it turned out, was a misnomer since no soup was served the whole time. The doors for breakfast opened at seven and closed at ten. Then would be the cleanup and cooking for the afternoon shift, which began at three and ended at nine.

The hall, as Lydia called it, was the hulled out remains of a rather broken down old stone church—Baptist we were told—that had moved to classier quarters and taken the gift of the old church as a charitable tax deduction, which I didn't understand since churches were already tax exempt.

Lydia gave each of us a task. She spoke abruptly, not with

any ill will, but as one who has a lot to do and not much time to do it in.

"You," she pointed to Dieter with a stubby index finger, "carry plates and bowls and stack them here." Again she pointed, this time to the nearest end of a long serving table.

"And you," she pointed to China, "stack the cups over there and you," she pointed to Arlene, "lay out the silverware and napkins."

She motioned for little Donald Wingart to follow her. The next time we saw him he was struggling to control a huge steaming vat of something that I could smell but not place as anything I had previously eaten. I almost laughed to see him behind this metal tub; almost as large as the tuba he sported back at school. I thought we must all be destined for something and poor old Donald was to be always half hidden by some huge metal object. I could have no idea that one day, not too long after we had all left Foxhall behind, he would be hidden from view behind an eight-inch self-propelled howitzer somewhere in Vietnam. But on this morning, it looked like he was about to give in to the weight of his burden. I saw his legs buckle a little at the knees so I grabbed a couple of dishtowels and rushed over.

"Donald," I breathed, "here, let me help you."

I clamped my hands, bound in the towels to avoid burning my fingers from the hot vat, under the handles to support Donald's grip and together we kind of waddled the huge thing over to one of the long serving tables. After we set it down, Donald seemed unable to extricate himself from the handles sticking out at the sides of the vat.

"Hey," I said. "You can let go now."

"I . . . can't."

Poor guy had gripped the handles so hard he couldn't let go. So I gingerly took each finger and loosened it from the big potholders. Some of the stew—I finally got a look inside the vat and determined it was some kind of meat, potatoes, vegetable thing in a thick broth—had slopped over and stuck his pot holders to the handles.

"Are your hands burned?" I continued peeling his fingers away one by one.

"I don't think so. Maybe a little. Maybe just my thumb."

He held it up. It looked red but there was no break in the skin and no blistering.

"Maybe you should ask for some first aid," I suggested.

"No. I don't want to be a bother. I'll put it in cold water for a minute."

He turned to go to the kitchen, I assumed to run his hand under a faucet, but then he turned back to me.

"Thank you," he said, looking at the ground like he was embarrassed.

"That's okay," I said. I thought about Moll. They would be a perfect pair, it seemed to me. They'd never look at each other. Maybe they'd be able to hold hands in the dark. Or maybe they'd both love music. The thought made me bold.

"Hey, Donald," I said.

"Huh?"

"Hey you know you should come to a dance at school sometime."

He looked up then and his gaze met mine. He looked stunned as if I'd seriously suggested he fly to the moon on a broomstick.

"Why?" was all he said.

"Well, you might meet someone, you know, a girl, and get to talking and find out you have a lot in common. And maybe you'd get to like each other." I shrugged. "It's just a thought."

He did turn then and disappeared into the kitchen.

"When the doors open," Lydia told us by way of warning, "you'll have to move fast to keep up the line. We don't want any traffic jams here."

She and Mr. Brownell brought in more vats of food and Donald went back again and again carrying trays of bread, jams, honey, sugar, large pitchers of milk and juice. Mr. Brownell brought in and placed on the serving table what I figured to be the world's largest coffee urn and ran a cord back somewhere to a plug.

There was no bacon or sausage as I had expected. One vat was filled with chipped beef, which I had never seen before. Another with slabs of ham. There was French toast, piles and piles of it. Grapefruits cut up, and a huge griddle with dozens of eggs frying and getting flipped by Mr. Brownell himself.

Once it was all in place, a bell rang. Not like the bells at Foxhall, more like an alarm clock, which is what it turned out to be, stuck back in what passed for a kitchen behind us, where huge industrial ovens had been installed along with a gigantic gas range with twelve burners. I had never seen anything like it nor have I since. It must have been army surplus from World War II because where else would such a contraption ever be needed? When the bell sounded, Lydia slid a long bar through two iron rings on the front doors, pulled them back, and placed a large stone against each one. The people who'd been waiting outside the door crowded into the church in a long line that funneled through the big hall set up with row after row of long tables and benches.

"Take your time," Lydia called out. "No need to push or rush. Plenty for everyone. All are welcome." She repeated this song over and over.

The people surged forward in an orderly way although it occurred to me, seeing how many there were, that if anything set them off we could all be trampled like the running of the bulls in Pamplona.

Then there was the sound of it all. Shuffling feet, scraping chairs, the bumping of plates onto tables, clinking of silverware, slurping, chewing, raising forks and spoons to mouths and then dipping down for more and repeat, repeat, repeat. Even the pulling apart of bread, with so many hands attending to this task, had a sound, like a muffled pillow fight through the other side of a wall.

Faith and I were assigned to dishing out food onto plates held out to us by shaky hands, dirty hands, hands in gloves with tattered fingers, men's hands, women's hands and then, what I had never expected and finally what made me look into the eyes of these diners, children's hands, small, neat, needing both hands to hold a heaping plate.

The first gaze I met, reluctantly, but I could not stop myself from looking up from the big spoon in my hand. Those first eyes, full of pain and longing and fear, and yes, friendship and trust; those eyes gazing into mine, no barrier between us; those eyes, dark circles floating in white, surrounded by silken chocolate skin, wide cheeks and below the eyes a little mouth almost curled in a shy smile, which, when I spooned on a slab of ham beside the fried egg—over easy—murmured the words, almost so low I could not hear them, "Thank you, ma'am," so disturbed the mistrust I had brought with me that I answered, without thinking, "You're welcome, honey. Enjoy it."

Of all the things I could have said that day, why I said that remains a mystery but it must have been simply the conditioned response of someone who's been taught manners. As was hers.

TWENTY-TWO

Talk of Politics

BY THE TIME WE FINISHED DOLING OUT THE LAST THANKS-giving meal of turkey, stuffing, sweet potatoes, cranberries, green beans, and pumpkin pie to the last of the thousands of people who had marched in what seemed like an endless line of hands holding out plates, and we had piled into the school van for the trip back to Mrs. Brownell's upstairs bedrooms, we were all depleted and at the same time, in a way that I never expected, uplifted. On that last morning, old Mrs. Brownell was allowed to make us all breakfast. Elizabeth Brownell had returned and she helped in the kitchen. We ate like we'd been starved although we'd done nothing but look at, dish out, cook up, and clean up food for three days. It was one thing to be doing the serving and another to be served.

"Well," Mr. Brownell said as he pulled his chair up to the table, "a moment of silence is in order."

We held hands around the table and lowered our heads. It lasted less than ten seconds, I would say, this moment of silence, until we let go of each other's hands. I was seated between Faith and Elizabeth Brownell. I didn't mind them touching me and was glad I didn't have to hold hands with Dieter at all. It was in these moments of silence, when according to the tenets of Quakerism, I was supposed to be allowing the spirit to move from within and give me—what? —guidance, hope, charity, peace, fulfillment, a sense of my place in the world? Or all of these together perhaps. And in those moments, I invariably found myself thinking about what was wrong in my world, what was wrong with me, who had insulted or injured me, who I would like nothing better than to get back at, who was annoying me at the moment. Or a song would get stuck in my head and repeat itself until I just wanted to scream.

Yet on this day, after serving food to so many strangers whose needs were absolutely basic, that little girl's eyes came to me and I thought: *I will try to do better, to be better, to think of others more than myself.* This thought glanced by me so quickly I barely recognized it and then with not a space between it and the next, I thought: *Wes, what are you doing right now?*

With the kind of smile that crinkles the eyes, Mr. Brownell raised his round head and we let go of each other's hands. There was a general shuffling, not nearly so pronounced as in that big hall with all the tables, but like a miniature version, as we took up our forks and spoons and reached for hot rolls and passed each other plates of waffles and eggs and cut-up fruit.

"I read some rather disturbing projections in the paper last week," old Mrs. Brownell said out of nowhere.

"What were those, Mother?" Mr. Brownell spooned some mixed fruit into a small bowl for himself.

"About what they think might happen over there in, Laos or Cambodia or one of those countries over in—where is it?"

"Southeast Asia?" Elizabeth Brownell helped her. "I read

the same thing, Mother. A prediction of what we might do if those little countries fell into communist hands. The crux seems to be Vietnam, according to what this article said."

"Is that so?" Mr. Brownell looked at his wife and then his mother. "Don't we already have what they call advisors there? Didn't Ike send them in?"

"What does this mean, advisors?" Dieter asked between bites.

Even the way he chewed made me angry. I decided not to engage in this conversation.

"It's hard to know for sure but from what I've read it means military people who are there to train and help facilitate the existing indigenous military but not engage in active fighting. It's all sad. Very sad. And I'm afraid our country will not be able to stay out of whatever happens there."

Mr. Brownell's happy expression had shifted to a furrowed brow and downcast eyes.

"Ya, this country seems always looking for a fight."

Okay so now Dieter was getting on my nerves.

"We didn't go looking for either of the world wars. They sorta came looking for us. Begging for us in fact," I said.

"Now, now, let's not get ahead of ourselves. What do you young people think of the presidential campaigns?"

"I hope Kennedy wins," Arlene hadn't said much the whole weekend so it was a surprise when she had any opinion at all, much less a political one.

"And what do you like about Mr. Kennedy?" Mr. Brownell asked her.

"Nixon is creepy," she said softly. "He always looks like he's hiding something. Sort of shifty."

"So you would vote for someone against someone else?"

"No. I like Kennedy."

It seemed like she wasn't going to give any specifics.

"He's quite charming," Mrs. Brownell smiled at her son. "I'm sure the ladies will vote for him."

"Who, Mother?"

"Well not that Nixon character. The other one. The young, handsome one."

I can't say, at the time, I was particularly interested in politics or elections or talk of military advisors. The one brief thought about Wes had kindled a longing to see him and I was ready to be on our way. But the meal dragged on and then we helped clean up, climbed the wooden stairs to the rooms we'd slept in, stripped our beds and, in the middle of our chores, in walked Virgy, wearing the same print dress she'd worn the first day we'd arrived. She was carrying a large white wicker basket, the paint chipped in places and the handle held together with some tape, partly covered by a pale blue ribbon.

"Miz Browen-elle axed me to give you chillrens these baygs."

She set the basket on a chair and handed Faith and me a paper bag each. There were four more in the basket. I could tell from the scent that rose in front of us that they were muffins, warm from the oven.

"Thank you, Virgy," I said.

Faith gave her a tender hug. "You didn't have to climb all the way up here. You could have given them to us at the door," she said.

"I gots to come up here anyways, once you all is gone.

No differn to me. You had a fun time, feedin' them peoples?"

Faith looked at me and then at Virgy. Neither of us knew how to answer that question but it turned out we didn't have to.

"Peoples gots a hard time nowadays. Thass right. I know that mission. I goes there ever Friday evening and doles out supper to 'bout a hundred or more souls. Old peoples, young peoples, Negroes and white, some bring chillren in there and them's the ones tear at my heart the most. Innocent little chillren never done nothing to nobody and they hain't got nuff to eat. Well, you enjoy them muffins. I baked up fresh this mornin'. Give you somethin' sustains you back at the school. And then, when you gets ready, you can go on and change this ole world for a better place."

TWENTY-THREE

The Kindness of Bearer

EVERY ONCE IN A WHILE AT RANDOM TIMES DURING THE week, the deans called for unscheduled dances that lasted only forty-five minutes. The Monday after everyone returned from Thanksgiving break, a dance was called with a sign on the deans' bulletin board in the main hall of Fox Building. It was posted there because everyone had to pass by it on their way to the dining hall. Usually these dances were not well attended. No one really paid much attention to choice of music so that was one reason. And the time was so short that the weekday dances felt rushed. A lot of kids just went off to the library or stayed in their rooms to study. I was still tied to study halls every night but the dance happened before study hall began so I could go and Wes wanted to so I agreed.

As I walked past the dean's office, Donald Wingart was standing in front of the sign for the dance, just staring at it as if it was written in Sanskrit. As I walked by, I slowed down just as he turned and saw me.

"Is this what you meant?" he pointed to the sign.

"Sure," I said, and smiled at him. I was trying to be reassuring but the look on his face had a tinge of terror.

"You mean just show up?"

"Sure. Like anyone else."

"Alone?"

"Do you want to go with someone?"

He shrugged and backed up so he was flat against the wall. "I don't know."

"Do you want me to ask someone to meet you there?" This opening was more than I had hoped for.

"Who?" Now he looked really petrified.

"Well, not someone like Daria."

He suddenly relaxed and slumped forward.

"How about Moll Grimes?"

"Why would she want to go with me?"

"Why wouldn't she?"

"What if she says no?"

"She won't say no, Donald. Trust me. Just be at the door and she'll show up. I promise."

He walked off, kind of weaving back and forth as he moved toward the front door.

———

I'd expected an emotional reunion with Wes Sunday when I got back from the soup kitchen mission, but his plane was delayed and he returned so late that all we had time for was a few stolen moments outside the back door of Fox Building before the doors were shut and locked. We didn't say much, standing to the side of the steps in as hidden a corner as we could find out there. Hardly an ideal spot for rekindling our passion but that didn't hold him back and I remember being swept up in the moment. There were the usual exchanges.

"I missed you so much."

"I missed you, too."

"I dreamt about you every night, about what we would do when we saw each other again."

"Me too." Although in reality I was so tired after every day at the mission that I'd fallen into bed like a boulder and sunk into an unfathomably deep sleep.

"I couldn't wait to hold you again. Your hair smells like sunshine. I missed that."

As these exchanges were going on, it seemed to me that something a little desperate had crept into his tone. Or maybe it was the way he clung to me. Or that his breathing seemed different. There was a slight gasp at times, as if he'd been running hard and his lungs were empty.

"Are you okay?" I asked.

He didn't answer but leaned down and found my lips. At that moment we heard the push bar at the back door and we broke apart hurriedly. He backed away and gave me a little wave and disappeared around the building so it would seem to whoever was at the door that I was just getting some fresh air.

"Anyone out here?"

It was Miss Alderton, the dean everyone liked. Some faculty members—Bleaker for one—would have questioned me being out there in the dark, would have wanted to add to my demerit if at all possible.

"Only me." I came up the steps slowly. "I just wanted some fresh air."

She held the door open and, for a few seconds, I thought she might call me on this lie, but she turned aside and let the door clamp shut behind me. Maybe it was her own youth—after all she wasn't much older than the students—that allowed her to ignore certain infractions. Whatever it was, my luck held out and I wandered down the hall and up the back stairs to my room, where I would sit down to study my Latin text and ponder that feeling about Wes.

Once there, I read, "By diplomacy and arms, Caesar had at last brought all Gaul under the power of Rome and there was now peace in the land. But it was not the peace of contented and free men; it was a peace imposed by force and maintained by fear."

And then there was text in Latin, which I started to translate beginning with: *Gallia est omnis divisa in partes tres.* All Gaul is divided into three parts.

I had signed up for Latin because I was also taking French, which I hoped to use one day, and I thought Latin would help with that. The irony of studying the workings of the mind of a military general and dictator along with Caesar's own record of his military conquest of Western Europe at a Quaker school did not escape me. I also knew that to get to third year Latin and more poetic readings like *The Iliad* or *The Odyssey*, I'd have to slog through Caesar's military campaigns, something a fifteen-year-old girl had little interest in pursuing. Not that either of the more advanced texts weren't replete with battles and gore. And then there was the violence and warfare in much of Shakespeare, yet my Latin and English teachers never seemed to address the dichotomy of immersing our minds in the bloody history of man while at the same time exhorting us to non-violence and peaceful problem resolution based on silent consensus. From where I sat, that didn't seem to be an option that had taken much root upon the land.

At Foxhall there was a sweet tradition of sending notes, folded in a complex origami-type pattern into a small, thick square that made it impossible for anyone to read unless carefully unfolded by the recipient. These folded paper squares began as a normal sheet of three ring binder paper, creased lengthwise twice, then folded over and over from one end on a diagonal until you had one end that could be tucked into the first crease, creating a fat little square with a hole in the middle. The KOB, as they were called, short for Kindness Of Bearer, ended up being about two inches on all four sides. On the outside the sender wrote the name of the recipient and any coded message he or she wanted to add. After study hall was over, in the forty-five minutes we had to wrap up our personal needs and get to bed, a designated person from each hall in each dorm hurried down to Mrs. W.'s to leave a batch of KOBs at the ledge outside her telephone operator cubicle. The messengers then waited for all the dorms to report and the KOBs were sorted and then delivered to their respective halls and dorms. Most KOBs were between boys and girls although every once in a while a girl would send one to another girl, usually if she was upset or having some kind of trouble, usually with a boy, as a sort of cheer up things will get better message.

That Sunday night, after the four-day hiatus, Mrs. W.'s little ledge could barely contain the overflow of torturously folded love papers. My hall designated me as collector for the week so down I ran, not expecting anything since Wes had never sent me a KOB. I had thought of sending him one a few times but didn't want to seem desperate, even though it was a struggle to hold myself back.

Yet, when I collected the ones for my hall, my name and hall number was scrawled on one of the outside triangles so I pocketed it and was about to run back up the stairs to deliver the mail when Daria appeared from nowhere.

"You get one?" she hissed near my ear.

"Um, yeah. How did you know?"

"Tim told me Wes was mooning around in their dorm."

"When did he tell you?"

"A few minutes ago when he brought over the KOBs."

"You mean . . ."

"Yes," again she hissed in my ear. "Listen tonight we're meeting in the mattress room after lights out. He's getting the key from someone. I have to jam something in the back fire door lock so he can get in the building then we're meeting in the basement by the laundry."

She meant the back door where Miss Alderton had found me earlier that evening.

"Have you ever done it?" she asked.

"Gone to the mattress room?"

"No, stupid, propped the door open enough so the lock doesn't catch?"

"No, I never had to. What are you going to use?"

"I don't know. I thought maybe a knife from the dining room but that's too big."

"How about a wad of chewed gum?"

"Oh, God, that's perfect. That's why I'm friends with you. You can figure all the odds for getting around the crap here."

"What about Wes, though?"

"What about him?"

"You said Tim said—"

She cut me off. "Oh, that. Never mind. Just some guy stuff I expect. Anyway Tim and I haven't seen each other for five whole days, so I gotta run."

"Be careful."

"Right."

She said it with irony, like it was dumb of me even to suggest caution, but I had a bad feeling about something. At the time, I thought it might have been about her risking the mattress room right after returning from the break. But she was gone before I could say anything else. Gone with all the KOBs for her hall, and when I turned to go, I almost bumped smack into Moll lurking behind me like a shadow. She looked furtive, like she had some secret and was struggling with herself about spilling it. Then I thought maybe she'd heard Daria.

"Hi," I said and backed up a little.

"Did you get one tonight?" she asked.

"One what?"

"A KOB."

"Oh. Yeah I did." It was in my jeans pocket and I wanted to get upstairs to my room to read it. Also, I had others to hand out and I knew the girls were waiting for them.

"You're lucky."

"What do you mean?"

"That a boy likes you enough to send you one. I'll never get one."

"You know, Moll, I just spent the break at a soup kitchen in downtown Philly and Donald was there too. He's really sweet. Why don't you at least talk to him?"

"Oh I couldn't. I wouldn't know what to say."

"You could ask him about music. He plays that tuba so he must like music. Isn't there any music you like?"

"I do like opera."

"Well there. Ask him if he ever listens to any opera. And if he says yes ask him which ones."

"But when could I ask him anything?"

"Well you could come to the dance tomorrow and if he's there, you could talk to him. The music at those weekday dances is always kind of haphazard so that might be a good time to talk about music."

Before she could object I patted her on the shoulder.

"I have to get these back to the hall. See ya' later."

TWENTY-FOUR

A Small Packet of Kindness

THE PROBLEM WITH GETTING A KOB WAS YOU COULDN'T answer it right away. So if a boy made a declaration, wrote something intimate, poured out his heart, or just told you he'd been watching you, you had to sit on it until breakfast the next morning when you'd be certain of seeing him. If he broke up with you by KOB at night, you had to confront him in the morning when presumably all his friends knew you were not a couple anymore. It would be all over the school in a matter of minutes and you could be humiliated right there over the half-boiled eggs the kitchen cooks churned out by the vat. I dropped off the KOBs for my hall and shut my door. I sat down on my bed, for some reason reluctant to unfold my KOB.

I didn't know it then, but opening that KOB initiated a tumble of events like a rockslide that would crash down not only on me but on the entire school in ways no one without a clairvoyant streak could have predicted. It was a week that stayed with me and that always defined for me how the choices we have made have consequences that can last over a lifetime.

On the outside, along one of the folds, Wes had written

my name in his small, left-handed scrawl. On another fold, on the same side of the little square packet, he had drawn two tiny hearts, one overlapping the other. I thought this was so sweet that it was a shame to open the note and find anything else. But I did. Unfolding it carefully, butterfly-like it transformed into a creased piece of notebook paper folded twice lengthwise. I further unfolded this and there, in his precise slanted handwriting, was the following note:

"I don't know how to begin this. I've been thinking about it since that day at the trestle. Which by the way was the best day of this whole year so far. And I don't mean just the school year. I mean the WHOLE year. Which will be over soon and when it is, I will face a decision..."

So far so good, I thought. It didn't sound like he was breaking up with me. I exhaled hard and slid my butt back until my back hit the propped up pillows. I pulled my knees up and spread the crumply notebook paper on my thighs. With my eyes closed, I pictured Wes the way he looked running the track behind Bedford Hall. Long cheetah strides like he was after some prey, each foot barely grazing the ground before it lifted and the other touched down, a clockwork of precision and constant forward motion. It was like watching a ballet of one, thigh muscles flexing, calves pounding, his head pitched slightly forward, neck taut, his face blankly determined. I opened my eyes and looked down at the paper lying against my thighs.

"...I've known this decision was looming. I've wanted to talk to you about it but it never seemed the right time. Also I think I feel a bit ashamed to talk about it. When I was home for Thanksgiving my mom tried to discuss it but I put her off because I know what

she thinks and my dad didn't even try to talk to me practically the whole time I was home. Just how did you sleep and want some more stuffing and how's your running time; are you staying in shape for spring track and stuff like that. So I guess what I'm saying is I don't know how to say what I want to say..."

Oh, God, he was going to break up with me. I felt this something-stuck-in-my-throat constriction like a cat choking on a hairball, and my chest felt like a foot had stomped on it. I took a deep breath and tried to shake the panic-room feeling.

"...On January tenth I'll turn eighteen. And then I have to register for the draft..."

The DRAFT, I thought. That was what this was about? Of course. Guys had to think about that. But he would be in college after graduation. He would get a deferment. Everyone like us got a deferment. As long as a guy was in school, he was safe. And anyway, they hadn't started calling guys up for the draft in forever.

I looked down at the paper again.

"So maybe I'll just say I'm not sure what to do. And I want to know what you think. I could register as a CO (he meant Conscientious Objector . . . we'd learned about that in Quaker Life class*) but that's what the problem is. See, part of me feels like that's a cop out, like I'm not really a man if I do that. I mean, who lets somebody else go do their fighting for them? Not that I've ever advocated fighting. But when do you draw the line? It's okay to say in Meeting for Worship that pacifism is the only moral choice. But what would have happened if the Allies didn't fight the Nazis? What if someone with a gun breaks into your house and threatens to kill your family? Is pacifism going to stop that person? I don't know. I can't imagine every situation that could happen. But I think that every person must have some fight threshold, some point*

at which they would do violence to another person. Maybe as a species we are programmed to fight under certain circumstances. This may all be academic. But from what I've read, we don't seem to have a strategy for getting out of Vietnam. And we seem to be getting, step-by-step, more, rather than less, involved. We've talked about it in history class with Mr. Gerstle. Most people are more concerned with the Berlin Wall, but Mr. Gerstle says we're sending advisors to Vietnam and Laos and we'll probably take over in Vietnam after the French give up completely...

I'm probably boring you with all this. I was happy to see you tonight. Even if it was only for a couple of minutes. I kept your image in my mind the whole time I was home in California. So far away. But it was like I was waiting to come back to a piece of candy I'd hidden away—a tasty treat that I could look forward to rediscovering.

Good night, my treat."

TWENTY-FIVE

Eyeliner and Lipstick

I TOLD MYSELF AT LEAST A THOUSAND TIMES, *I COULDN'T have known.* But that was later. After. Before, I couldn't have told myself anything because before something happens, you are unaware of the swirling currents that could rock your boat. I was just happy to be back with Wes, back at Foxhall, back in our little world.

What I did tell myself throughout that first day back was that after my "experience"—and I put it that way because that was how I thought of it, as a *big* experience—at the soup kitchen, now I could see other people's circumstances with a clearer eye, with a softer heart, with a deeper understanding. I should be a better person after all that, I told myself. But really, behind all those thoughts, I knew I was no different. I was the same me, the way other people are the same them, doing what we had always done and thinking about ourselves first because that was what nature intended. Nature. The nature we referred to when we want to think that every act, every instinct was predetermined. We were, after all, mostly animal instinct. Like nature. We followed our natural urges. We ate and slept and had sex. Because we were programmed to do what would keep us—the collective us—going as a species. Nature. We relied on it as the backdrop for all existence. And it always treated us so well. Didn't it? Nature . . . always dependable and reliable.

It was a chilly night. Winter was just over the hill. A crisp, clear, moonless night. Stars were just beginning to show themselves in a shy display. Wes and I walked hand in hand to the gym. No deans around to point and tell us that was a no-no. I felt as if I were floating rather than walking.

"I want to talk," Wes said.

"Yes?"

"About the KOB I sent you."

"Okay. At the dance? It might be hard there."

"We can't go anywhere else with the dance on. You know the rule. Either at the dance or in your room or at the library."

"Right. Well, we can find a quiet corner maybe."

The future was sealed right there. And I was oblivious. Or maybe the future was never simply a matter of one decision in one split second. Maybe it was not only one event. Maybe it was a series, like a cascade, starting with a trickle and then building, building, to a rush that couldn't be contained. And afterward you ask, what if I had done this or said that or not gone there or been more alert or a million things, what if they had been different. Well, of course, if a million things had been different, everything would have been different. The Greeks offered a tidy explanation of how our lives unfold. Three fates spinning, measuring, and cutting our lives. A fantasy view of the universe. A poet's view. A fatalist's view. A quaint, but untenable, locked-in view that utterly denied a human free will. I didn't know how the ancients wrapped their collective mind around that view but we had evolved. We had choices. We made choices. They may have seemed obvious or expedient, even forward-looking at the time we made them, but they didn't always yield the expected results.

One of the AV boys had brought his entire collection of forty-fives to the gym. He stacked a batch on a record player—the kind with a fat tube that fit the large holes in forty-fives—and set it to run on its own, oblivious to the gym half-full of students, more of them than usual at an unscheduled dance, milling around in tight groups against the walls or out in the middle dancing to Elvis ("Don't Be Cruel"), The Fleetwoods ("Come Softly To Me"), The Drifters ("There Goes My Baby"), The Everly Brothers ("All I Have To Do"), with most of us lip syncing the lyrics—*You ain't nothing but a hound dog / Cryin' all the time / You ain't nothing but a hound dog / Cryin' all the time / Weeeell, You ain't never caught a rabbit / And you ain't no friend o' mine.*

And then they played the latest hit—*Georgia, Georgia / ah, The whole day through / Just an old sweet song / Keeps Georgia on my mind* . . . and I just wanted to melt right there in the gym.

Bleaker stood to the right of the door about ten feet down the wall, like some hawk perched in the perfect spot to see her prey as it walked through the open door.

Wes and I moved the other way, steering clear of her by visceral instinct. As we made our way to a far corner, I noticed Donald Wingart standing on the other side of the record table. He had on a bow tie, it was bright pink, and a starched shirt and slacks. His shoes were shined. I could see little glints of lights reflecting from the round toes. I smiled to myself. Little Donald Wingart had come to the dance. I felt a tiny stab of triumph.

Wes and I reached our corner, leaned against the gym wall, and just watched the dancers for a few minutes, more to get our bearings than because we were interested. But there were Daria and Tim. She was dancing rings around him as usual. No one could keep up with Daria on the dance floor. Tim was smart enough not to try. He just let her whirl and every once in a while he put out his arms and she fell into them before turning again, as if she had the music inside her, hair flying, a faraway smile on the lips, eyes half closed, for a few precious moments transported from the view of basketball hoops and the sickly stale scent of sweat and floor wax.

"You read it?" Wes asked.

"Of course."

"And . . ."

"I don't know what to say. I mean, I have no idea what it must be like to have to make that decision." I felt helpless and sounded to myself like I didn't care. Which wasn't the case. But I didn't know how to care about the draft, about war. "I mean, how do you even think about it? We've never had to fight a war. It seems so alien. Like, here we are in school, not even college, and we're supposed to be deciding all this stuff about a future we know nothing about."

"I know. It's bizarre." Wes looked at his shoes. He was wearing jeans and a shirt under a maroon sweatshirt that had the Harvard Veritas logo. He'd applied there. Also Stanford and MIT. I didn't know which one was his safety. It didn't really matter. "I mean, I could register as a CO without any problem. I've been actively going to Meeting my whole life. But from what I hear, they put COs right up front, like with the ambulance corps where you have no protection."

"Where did you hear that?" I always wondered about the guy grapevine. I figured all they did was talk about sports.

"A lot of places. I've read about what happens if you're a CO. Anyway, sometimes I think I'm just a big chicken."

"You don't have to have a gun in your hand to be brave."

"Yeah, but if you're depending on someone else to be brave with their gun on your behalf, then it does seem like you're not taking responsibility for yourself. And you're not much of a team player."

Yeah, that was one of the guy things—being a team player. Girls didn't have to concern themselves so much with that, unless you were on an actual team and even then it sometimes didn't really matter that much.

"Well, if being a team player means killing someone else, then it's really like being a gang member."

"But not in a war. A war is different."

"Are you arguing in favor of war? Here? At this place?"

"No, of course not. I'm just saying, well let's say you and I are married . . ."

He lost me for a second as I fantasized about us being married, a couple, with a baby and a cute little house and our own dishes and a big bed with a feather comforter where we could have sex whenever we wanted.

But he was still talking . . .

". . . and someone breaks into our happy little home, waving a gun and threatening to kill us. Well, if I had a gun I'd probably shoot it at him. I'd protect my family."

"But you wouldn't have a gun."

"No, but the argument still holds up."

From somewhere at the periphery of my vision I felt, rather than directly saw, Moll enter the gym.

"Wes," I said and held up a hand.

"What is it?"

"Moll just showed up."

"So?"

"Well, that's so great."

"Why?"

"Because Donald came to the dance, too."

"You mean Wingart?"

"Yes. Look." I nodded toward the record table.

Donald had moved in front of it. He was looking at the door, at where Moll was standing.

"She looks different, kind of," Wes said.

The melancholy strains of "Mr. Blue" wafted through the gym as couples slow-danced.

I'm Mr. Blue (wah-a-wah-ooh)
When you say you love me (ah, Mr. Blue)
Then prove it by goin' out on the sly
Provin' your love isn't true
Call me Mr. Blue
I'm Mr. Blue (wah-a-wah-ooh)
When you say you're sorry (ah, Mr. Blue)
Then turn around, head for the lights of town
Hurtin' me through and through
Call me Mr. Blue

"She got herself done up. Her hair looks teased. And where did she get that bright red blouse?"

I shook my head. "I doubt Donald will notice anything different. He's pretty oblivious."

Donald had started making his way to the front door. Moll just stood there, looking as if she'd been stopped by a cop, eyes wide, staring across the room. I started saying a little prayer to myself: *Just be cool, Moll. Let him come over to you. Don't get flustered. He wants to make contact. Just let it happen.*

And then he had made it to where she was standing. I saw him say something to her. And she nodded. So far so good. Contact! Moll would be happy tonight. Finally.

"Let's dance," Wes took my arm and led me out to the floor where Mr. Blue was still crooning and we turned away from the front door and slow-danced, drenched in the lovesick feeling that 1960 would soon be over and Wes would face a decision that could affect the rest of his life.

"I wish I could be more helpful," I whispered.

"It's okay. It's enough just to know you're there. Just to have someone to talk to."

"When will you decide?"

"I don't know. I thought about talking to Mr. Brownell about it. Their son was a CO in Korea."

"Really? I didn't know that."

"Yeah, he was with an ambulance corps. His leg got shattered by a land mine."

"That's horrible."

He held me as close as was safe with Bleaker in the gym. I looked around to find her and there she was standing guard by the door, arms crossed, that grim look still on her face. Moll was nowhere nearby. I thought she and Donald must have found a place to talk. I looked over at the record table but he was gone. And then I noticed him under one of the basketball hoops. He looked frozen to the spot. But no Moll.

"Maybe we can meet up by the track—you know at the steps—after study hall?" Wes whispered.

I nodded but my attention was somewhere else, wondering where Moll had disappeared. And then I thought maybe the girls' room, and after that I stopped thinking about Moll because Wes had his arms around me in another slow dance, and even though we had agreed that only desperate couples used it, I started to think that maybe we should try the mattress room some night because by then it had turned too cold to go to the trestle again.

TWENTY-SIX

If the Key Fits

THE USUAL SCHOOL BUZZ DIDN'T START RIGHT AWAY. MORN-
ing bells sounded the same as always. I showered quickly,
brushed my teeth, and dried my hair like I did every morning. The first week after any break was always a bit slow to
get going. People dragged themselves to breakfast. A lot of
the boys didn't bother with a.m. grooming—at least the boys
who never dated. We all looked a bit bleary-eyed as we
slowly settled back into the school routine. Even the teachers
at our tables had a hard time instigating the usual in-depth
conversations they liked to encourage about politics and
where the country was headed. I, for one, was perfectly
happy not to discuss whether Nixon or Kennedy had the better plan for America. By Thursday, we were almost back in
the groove but not quite. There was still a little vacation rus-
tle in the air, like leaves that had half turned but weren't
quite ready to dislodge themselves from the trees.

Just as I was buttering my toast, Daria came flying up to
my table and leaned in so only I could hear her.

"Did you hear?"

I sat back and blinked. "About what?"

"The key," she whispered and then Brady appeared and whispered something to Daria and they ran off, leaving me in a state of bewilderment.

"Miss Greenwood, what's going on?" asked Mr. Fenstermacher, our table's faculty member. He was a youngish man, prematurely bald, wearing a tweed jacket that looked as if he'd slept in it for the past year at least. He taught modern European history and was faculty advisor to both the chess and AV clubs. Not really my type of guy.

"Oh, nothing," I shrugged and concentrated on my toast.

"Seems quite a lot of commotion for nothing."

He looked across to a table where Jan was assigned, not far from us nearer the doorway where Daria and Brady were leaning down, whispering behind their hands and shaking their heads.

What key? I thought and then it hit me.

"Um, Mr. Fenstermacher, may I be excused?" I stood up fully expecting him to say yes.

"For what purpose?"

He looked up at me kind of astonished. I thought fast. It came to me without much strain to my gray matter because, after all, what man wants to know too much about the monthly female cycle, especially at breakfast.

"I . . . um . . . have to change . . . um . . . go to the ladies . . ."

"Of course, go ahead." He waved an arm as if to say, "No more information, please."

So I bolted out of the room by way of the other table and managed to poke Brady in the arm as I sped past toward the dining hall door. Once out in the hall, I did head for the ladies room down at the end of the hall and by the time I hit the door with both open palms, the sound of hurried foot-steps told me the others were on my trail.

"What's this all about?" Jan spoke first.

I put my finger to my lips before leaning down to check for feet inside the stalls, but the bathroom was empty so we leaned against the sink while Daria told us what was going on.

"I went down to the mattress room last night after lights out."

"Yes, what about it?" Brady's voice shook.

"I'm getting to it. Shit, let me talk." Daria glared at Brady so we all shut up.

"Tim was meeting me near the laundry room door." She pointed to the end of the hall outside the bathroom. We all knew what she meant.

"So? I've met someone there before," Brady whispered.

"I know. Let me finish. So I stuck a wad of chewed gum in the back fire door latch, and then when Tim got in and met me in the basement, the key to the mattress room didn't work. It wouldn't fit. And now they're tearing Wilkins Dorm apart."

"Wait a second," Jan said. "I don't understand. What are they looking for?"

Daria turned to her with an expression of total exaspera-tion. "The key. You know to the mattress room."

"But Tim has the key," Jan said, still bewildered.

"No he doesn't. I told him to flush it."

"Why didn't it work?" Jan wouldn't let it go.

Brady broke in, "Someone must have changed the lock."

"That's what we think," Daria nodded. She looked scared.

It was the first time I saw her look anything but in complete control.

"What happened to Tim?" I asked.

"He went back to Wilkins. He didn't get caught, thank God."

"How did they find out?" Jan asked. She had pushed away from the sink and was clutching her hands, folding and unfolding her fingers.

"Someone must have squealed," Brady said. "Are they also searching Dreier?"

Dreier was the other boys' dorm, mostly for freshman and sophomores except for the proctors.

"I don't know. But Tim is in a panic. So are Stocky and the others." She turned to me. "Wes seems to be calm and collected. Didn't you ever use the room?"

I shook my head and could feel the color spread from my neck over my cheeks. Daria just smirked at me.

"The virgin princess," she mocked.

"Well, what's going to happen?" Jan asked. "I mean, are they going to do a full on police state search and seize, make us all rat each other out, toss seniors out before graduating them? They can be really hateful. Oh shit, is Bleaker part of this?"

"Speaking of old bat Bleaker, did you see what she did last night at the dance?" Brady turned to examine her face in the mirror.

"What?" Jan asked. "I knew she'd be a part of this. But how could she be sleuthing in the boys' dorm. I thought she and Mr. Henderson hate each other."

Mr. Henderson was in charge of Wilkins Dorm and he

pretty much let the boys do what they wanted so long as no one smoked or got totally drunk over there. It was the girls who were watched with an eagle eye all the time, so it was surprising that they were searching the boys' dorm for a key.

"Someone must have ratted," Daria said. "Otherwise they'd have no clue about any key anywhere."

"Right," said Brady. "But that's not what Bleaker was on the attack about at the dance."

"Well then, what else is there?" Jan asked.

"She went after Moll big time."

"MOLL?" I was so startled I raised my voice more than I intended. "What did Moll do?"

"Are you talking about that little mouse who always dresses in brown sacks?" Daria was grinning. "What . . . did Bleaker tell her to get a new wardrobe? One that she could be seen in public wearing?" She giggled.

"She sort of did," Brady answered her. "I was standing to one side of the door and Bleaker was down on the other side a little farther away when Moll walked in and stood there."

"I saw her," I said. "She was wearing some bright red dress or blouse. I remember thinking how un-Moll it was. And I was really surprised, like, to see her at the dance at all."

"Well, that's not all she was wearing," Brady nodded. "Bleaker really lit into her."

"What do you mean?" I asked, now more interested in Moll than in the stupid key.

"I heard the whole thing," Brady said. "It happened just as Donald Wingart crossed the gym. He said 'Hi' to Moll and that's when Bleaker appeared next to them from the other side. She took Moll's arm and kind of shook her a little. Like she was some stuffed doll. And then she said—I couldn't believe this, it was so cruel, I mean even to Moll—'What do you think you're doing?' She said it really mean, in a low voice. And then, 'Who told you to put all that disgusting stuff on your face? You look like a tramp. If you wear makeup, it should be applied with a light hand so no one really sees it. You've made yourself look ridiculous and the message you're sending is unacceptable at this school. I don't know what you're trying to accomplish but you should be ashamed of yourself making such a display. Now, go and wash your face and change your clothes.'"

"*What?*" Now I almost screamed. "She said that? Really? Oh God, poor Moll."

"Yes, and just when I had everything set up so perfectly," Daria said.

"What do you mean?" I asked her. "What did you have set up?"

Daria laughed, tossed her hair and turned to the mirror to examine her lipstick.

"Oh, just that I sent her a KOB."

"What do you mean?" Brady asked her this time. "Why would you send her a KOB?"

"I sent it from Donald Wingart—her beloved. I wrote that I had been thinking about her and hoped she would be at the dance. I said, and oh man, this was so much fun, I wrote, 'I really think you're special.'"

I was too dumbfounded to say anything. I couldn't believe Daria would be so cruel, using what I'd told her. At that moment, I didn't know what to think or say or how to feel. The one feeling I did acknowledge was guilt. I shouldn't have told Daria about Donald or anything Moll had told me. I would have to find Moll and make it right somehow.

"Well, she never came back to the dance," Brady said. "And poor little Donald. I thought he was going to melt."

"Wait a sec," Daria held up her hands in a stop-now motion. "I want to know what's going to happen about the key. Do we have to play defense here? Because if we do, we need to stick together. We know absolutely nothing about any key or any room. In fact, except to pick up or drop off our laundry, we never go to the basement. All agreed?"

Everyone nodded, of course. It was Daria speaking.

TWENTY-SEVEN

Disappearances Can Be Deceiving

BY THE TIME THE DINING HALL DOORS OPENED FOR LUNCH, the news had stampeded through the school. There were differing versions. One was that some boys had been using the mattress room for drinking parties. Another was that one or two girls were meeting boys down there. Another was that there were a bunch of keys passed around by numerous students and that they'd been having parties in the mattress room. It was impossible to tell how many teachers or deans were aware of the gossip blazing through the student body but it was certain some of them knew.

The silent minute at lunch felt like the calm before a hurricane moved in. Bowed heads all over the room, but with eyes peeking up at each other, all wondering, who had keys, what did they do in there? I kept trying to pick Moll out of the lunch tables but it was impossible to see beyond a few tables near me. When the minute was over, a general murmur began. Midway through lunch, I got up to fill my water glass at the drink window near the kitchen so I could wander around and look for her. Daria would be in hyper self-protection mode by now so there was nothing I could add to their efforts at eluding capture. Anyway, I figured, how would the faculty ever be able to find one key? Even if they were looking for multiple keys to something, everyone had keys and anyone who had the mattress room key would have ditched it by now. Daria was the last one to have it and she'd given it to Tim. No one really knew if there were duplicates or not. There certainly could have been.

I didn't see Moll anywhere but I did spot her roommate, Eleanor DeLuca, so I stopped at her table with my full glass of water.

"Hey, Eleanor."

I smiled down at her. The faculty member at the head of her table was Miss Alderton, who liked me. She gave me a little wave and went on eating her salad. Miss Alderton was in great shape. Besides swimming, she was a runner and had that healthy look of someone who spent a lot of time outdoors.

"Hi," Eleanor looked up at me, surprised to see me standing there I was sure. I had never spoken one word to her before this.

"Hey, where's Moll?"

Eleanor's eyes got big at that and she dropped a spoon on the floor. She leaned down to get it and when she came up she looked scared.

"Why?" she asked.

"Because I want to talk to her."

"Why?"

"What do you care? I just do."

"I don't know."

That was odd, I thought. If she didn't know, why didn't she say that at first?

"Well, I don't see her here at lunch."

"So?"

"So is she in the infirmary?"

"I don't know."

"Did you see her last night?"

"Yes."

This was really irking me.

"Why don't you just tell me where she is then?" By then my face was right up in hers.

"Because, as I told you before, I don't know." She backed her chair away from me and looked over at Miss Alderton.

The bell rang. With lunch officially over, I slammed my water glass on the table and squeezed my way ahead of everyone through the open doors. I had a free period after lunch, when it had been my intention to translate how Orgetorix died and what Caesar did after that to unite all Gaul under Roman control. But right now I was concerned about Moll.

Bleaker was such a bitch, was all I could think about as I stomped up the fire stairs to the third floor on the west side of Fox. With every clangy step on each flat metal plate, my brain worked through memories like a film winding fast in reverse. *Picking on the small and defenseless, just like my mother,* I thought. *Never would stand up to someone equal to her in power. Easy to make someone who couldn't fight back feel helpless and under your control. You damned bitch.* I pictured Bleaker with her tight-bunned, black hair and her pinched, white face. My mother had black hair, too, but she was a looker who knew how to manage men to get what she wanted. When there was no one around to stop her, that was when she turned off the charm and turned on the fire hose. *I hate her. I hate her. I hate her.*

I reached the first landing and turned the corner fast, continued up, step-by-step, pounding the unforgiving metal of the fire stairs, my anger not blowing itself out with the climb. *What have I done? I encouraged Moll to go to the dance. Even to meet Donald. It was all my fault. No it wasn't . . .* my rational brain kicked in for a second. *It was not my fault that Bleaker was such a bitch. No other teacher would have said anything to her. No one but Bleaker would purposely inflict that kind of shame on a student. What was wrong with her? Didn't she have any feelings at all?*

I reached the third floor finally and pushed open the fire door. Moll's room was all the way at the other end so I rushed down. The door was open, which was unusual so I walked in. Both beds were neatly made. Eleanor's desk had books half open and a few pens lying on them. Moll's desk was clean of anything. Not one piece of paper. Not one pencil or pen. No books, notebooks, nothing.

"What are you doing here?"

I turned around to see Eleanor standing in the doorway.

"Where's her stuff?"

"Look, what is wrong with you? I told you I don't know where she is. She never talks to me. It's like living with a phantom. I don't know where her stuff is. Maybe she's in the library. Maybe she took all her books with her to study."

"She wasn't at lunch, though."

"So, what if she wasn't? Go ask the deans where she is if you want to find her. I have to get ready for my next class. Go back to your upper class friends and leave me alone."

"Thanks, Eleanor. I'll remember this if you're ever the butt of Bleaker's wrath. But don't expect any sympathy."

"What are you talking about?" she asked as she gathered up her books.

"Never mind." She obviously had no idea what Bleaker had done, so it was a waste of energy talking to her anymore.

"And by the way," she said, "I hope they kick all of you out when they find that key."

Now it was my turn. "I have no idea what you're talking about."

"I guess you will when Miss Bleaker calls you in to ask about it."

She started to walk past me but I blocked the doorway. "Just so you know, I'm about to go down to the dean's office and ask if they know where Moll is and the first thing I'm going to tell them is you're acting really strange about her. So if you have anything to tell me, now's the time." I folded my arms across my chest and waited.

Eleanor stepped back. Her shoulders slumped forward and her chin wobbled a little. I noticed that her forehead was broken out and she'd tried to hide it with her hair. Then she said, very softly so I could barely hear her, "I went to bed early. When I got up this morning, her bed was made and it looked like she had gotten up really early. And that's all I know."

She came toward me so I stood aside. When she was right next to me she added, "It seemed like her bed looked the same as yesterday, as if she hadn't slept in it at all." Then she slipped by me and ran down the hall, clutching her books.

TWENTY-EIGHT

Where's Moll?

AT A PLACE LIKE FOXHALL, OR MAYBE ANY PLACE THAT'S monitored for rule breaking or law breaking or infringement of the social code, you tend to keep your head down. You don't want to make waves. At least most of you don't. There are the exceptions, of course. The China's of the community, who are hell-bent on letting everyone know just how pure they are in soul and spirit, the professional do-gooders, who lord their selflessness over the rest of us so that we may see what a shining example they provide. Of course we disdain them for it. And distrusted them utterly.

But Moll's roommate, Eleanor, wasn't one of those. At least, as far as I was aware. After I left their room, it occurred to me that she seemed more than nervous. That lashing out at me was a cover. She was trying to head me off. And then I had one of those A-HA moments. She was scared. But of what? I got that they didn't ever talk. I had no roommate but the other girls did and most of them were buddies and told each other everything. At least the ones who'd chosen to share a room. But Moll was like me, a new girl. She'd been stuck in with Eleanor. And the way Moll was, well, it wasn't hard to imagine her not warming up to her roommate. The idea that she hadn't slept in her bed was ludicrous. Where else would she have spent the night?

I had about thirty minutes left before my class, so back at my room I gathered the books I'd need and headed outside, followed the cement walk around Fox until I got to the part that veered off to the infirmary. The nurse on duty, Mrs. Waller, was reputed to be okay, especially with girls who arrived at the infirmary complaining of bad cramps. They had some pills she'd hand out and sometimes, if a girl was really having a bad time, Mrs. Waller would let her stay in an infirmary bed for the day and she'd supply a heating pad laid under the hips.

"Hi," I said as she looked up from her desk.

"Yes? What's the problem, dear?"

"I'm having a really bad time this month," I lied.

"When did it start?"

"My sheet was bloody this morning. I had to strip it down and make a special trip to the laundry. It's just so heavy my back is aching." I sat down on a wooden chair for emphasis.

"Do you think you can go to classes?"

The look of concern on her face almost made me feel guilty, so I decided not to pour it on too heavy. "I think so. Maybe I just need some medicine."

"All right, dear. What's your name?"

I told her and she wrote it down in a chart before she took a bunch of keys and went to another room. There was a board by the door that led to the infirmary rooms. Everyone who was there at any given time was logged in on that board. Everyone knew it. I stood and quickly glanced at the board. There were only two names. Both boys. One had a broken ankle that I'd heard about. The doctor had set it late the night before and they were waiting to take him for an X-ray this morning. The other boy had strep. No Moll.

Mrs. Waller came back in and handed me a little envelope. "This should last you for a couple of days. It should let up by then but if not, come back to see me. Okay?"

"Sure. Thanks a lot."

So that was that. Where else could she be? Not knowing her class schedule, the only place left to check on her was the dean's office, where they kept track of everyone all the time. If the roll takers hadn't logged her at breakfast, the deans would know. If she hadn't gone to her first class, her teacher might report her missing. If she were in the infirmary, a note would have been sent to the dean's office. In fact, there was no way to escape the system, unless, of course, you or one of your friends was a role taker and she marked you in, but that would have been prearranged and nobody skipped a Monday morning breakfast. If you were going to skip, it would be a Saturday morning or Saturday night. You would have stuffed your bed, made sure your roommate had agreed, or told your roommate you were sleeping in a friend's room for the weekend. But Moll had no roll taker friends and it didn't seem like her roommate, Eleanor, would have lied for her. And then there was bed check every night. Moll couldn't have escaped that. So, the way I figured it, if Moll was MIA, the deans would know about it pretty soon.

The first class period of the day was almost over. I had to get to my Latin test and then I had English but, before lunch, I would stop in at the dean's office on some pretext and nose around. By this time, I was determined to find Moll. I had pretty well convinced myself that she was hiding out somewhere, crying or feeling too ashamed to show her face. In a way, because I had encouraged her, and because I had talked Donald Wingart into going to the dance, which made what must have been an awful scene even worse, I felt responsible. But there was also my own history. I knew what it felt like to be shamed in front of other people. Like the day my mother picked me up from school to take me to the doctor for a checkup. Right there in front of a bunch of kids waiting for the bus, she told me my hair looked "ratty" like I'd slept on it.

"Don't you carry a comb with you?" she asked. She took a comb out of her purse and started messing with my hair while all the other kids stood there watching.

"A lady doesn't ever go out without a comb and a hanky. You should have a hanky in your lunch box at all times."

For the next few weeks until we got off for Thanksgiving break, I would find Kleenex dropped on my desk by the other kids with notes that said: Use your hanky.

So yes, I knew. How many times had I been told to wear my skirt long enough to cover my knees because my knees were ugly, or to wear my hair over my ears because my ears stuck out and didn't look pretty, or what girls I shouldn't be friends with because they were not like "us." Meaning they were not wealthy, educated, of our class, and couldn't possibly do anything to enhance our standing. Once she did this in the car while two of my other friends were sitting in the backseat. To this day I can't remember the name of the condemned girl. But I remember lying to my mother about not having been at the girl's house two days later. And I remember how triumphant I felt when she bought the lie. So it was

TWENTY-NINE

A Search for the Missing

DARIA CAUGHT UP WITH ME BEFORE I COULD EVEN GET OUT of Bedford after my English class. As I was rushing down the hall, she pulled me over by my jacket sleeve, hissing in my ear.

"I have to talk to you," she whispered. "It's all over the school."

I wondered how everyone else could have known about Moll. Before I could say anything she pulled me into an empty classroom and shut the door.

"Someone ratted," she hissed. "Some squeaky, little, pathetic rat who has no life. Now they're searching for anything they can find. It's like some police state. We're all in trouble. The whole junior and senior classes. Pretty soon they'll be making us rat out each other to save our own skins right when everyone's applying to colleges."

It was dumbfounding. For a minute I couldn't find any words.

"Did you hear me?" Daria shook my arm. "They're after all of us. That means you, too. Don't you get it?"

"Not really," I told her. "Where is she anyway?"

"Where's who?"

"Moll."

"What are you talking about?" Daria stepped back and glared at me as if she thought I must be an idiot.

"About Moll. About where she is."

"Who cares about her?"

"I do. After what happened last night, she must be terrified to face anyone."

"Don't you get it? They're determined to find out who's been using the mattress room. They're after all of us."

"I never used it."

"But you knew about it and they're going after anyone and everyone. It's really bad. Tim's been called in for three this afternoon."

"Wait a minute," I said. "How do you know all of this? Maybe he's being called in for something else. I mean, where is all this information coming from?"

"Some rat. I told you. Someone ratted."

"Maybe it's not someone. Do you know who ratted? I mean, maybe one of the little men went down there and saw some stuff left by someone and just changed the lock and handed in the stuff he found. Maybe it's as simple as that and the deans are just asking around. Did you ever leave anything down there?"

The little men were everywhere at Foxhall. There was no telling how many of them there were but they all seemed to be short and bowlegged. So the students called them the little men. Maybe they were all from the same family because they were indistinguishable from each other. They fixed things and tended the grounds, unplugged toilets and changed bulbs and were often seen carrying ladders or toolboxes.

"Everyone leaves stuff in there. You know, like, oh I don't know. Just stuff."

"Well that's not too bright. Sometimes the little men must have to go in there to actually get a mattress for someone's room."

"That's not the point."

"I wouldn't get so upset until you know the whole story. And anyway, Tim or anyone else can just say they don't know anything. If nobody admits anything, they can't prove it. And they'll never find a key. Never. If anyone asked me anything, I'd say I didn't know there was a mattress room or anything else in the basement of Fox except the laundry."

"I hope you're right," she sounded skeptical but calmer. "What if they find Stocky's phone tool? Or they've heard about the pigpen?"

"If they knew about the pigpen they would have come after us a long time ago."

"Yes, you're probably right. They wouldn't have let it go on so long. So what's the thing about your little friend, Moll?"

"I think she's missing."

"That is just ridiculous. She can't be missing. I mean where is there in this place to go missing? She'll turn up for dinner. Maybe she's in the infirmary."

"I checked. She's not. I'm going to nose around the dean's office now before the lunch bell rings, so I've got to go."

"Maybe her body will turn up in the mattress room."

It was a lame joke but at least she still had some sense of humor. We left the classroom together but Daria peeled away from me when she saw Faith at the top of the stairs. Before I turned toward the opposite end of the hall, she ran back and whispered, "Be careful in the dean's office. They can be very snoopy without seeming to be, especially when they're trying to get something on you."

It should have been clear to me at that point that Daria was completely paranoid, but I was thinking about what I could say without making the deans suspicious. Daria's concerns seemed remote, at least as far as they connected to me personally. On the other hand, it would be awful if all my upper class friends were summarily tossed out of school in the first semester. I couldn't imagine the school doing that. I was too young to realize the economic consequences to the school of such a move. Of course, there were stories of kids who'd been expelled from other schools and ended up at Foxhall. It had the reputation of being tolerant of past misbehavior, open to giving a kid a second chance in a supportive environment where personal responsibility was lauded and held as a virtue. Of course if the misbehavior began at Foxhall, it was a different matter, especially for a girl. So if I'd thought about it, I'd have understood why Daria was so worried. But then I'd also have reasoned that no one who'd used the mattress room, or the wire, or gone to the pigpen, or done anything else they weren't allowed to do, would rat out anyone else because that would only get them all in trouble. Co-conspirators have a stake in keeping quiet, at least until they were offered some immunity.

There was a fine art to getting information without giving any away in the process. As I crossed the path leading back to Fox Building, I came up with what seemed a reasonable strategy. Moll and I were in Quaker Life class together. I needed to discuss a paper I was working on with her but I didn't know her whole schedule and I needed to talk with her right away. Could anyone in the dean's office tell me what classes she had and where she'd be after lunch? If she was missing, and they knew about it, they'd tell me. If she wasn't, there was no reason they wouldn't tell me where she was. Maybe she'd gotten sick and her mother had come to pick her up. Or there'd been a death in her family and she had to leave suddenly without telling anyone. *It could be anything,* I was thinking as I pushed at the heavy old door and walked straight down the hall toward the dean's office.

THIRTY

Gone

THE SYSTEM OF STUDENT CHECKS AT FOXHALL BEGAN WITH the roll takers. This first semester they happened to be Brady and Jan, which meant I was lucky. When I reached the dean's office there they were, poring over the pre-lunch lists of what students had been marked in at which classes, at study halls, the free period lists, the infirmary list, the attendance list from breakfast, and the list of any approved absences.

The door to the dean's office was always open. Right away, I noticed papers strewn all over the big desk. With a black pen, Jan marked off student names on a long list laid out flat on the desk.

"Hi." I said it to let them know I was there.

At the same time, Brady was saying to Jan, "So you got Miller and Clausen?"

"Yes, got them both."

They looked up at me.

"What's going on?" I asked. This did not look like the usual pre-meal check.

"Miss Alderton told us to double check the lists before we go in to take roll," Jan said. She wasn't smiling or joking the way she usually did. In fact, she looked grim.

"Is this because of the . . ." I stopped and looked around but didn't see any of the deans. "You know, the key search?" I whispered it.

Brady shook her head. "No." she looked down at Jan's big list again. "Did you get Marston and DeSalvo?"

"Yes," Jan answered. "And that is it. We've accounted for everyone except . . ." She stopped and looked up at me again. "We're not supposed to say anything," she told me.

"About the key?"

"No. It's not about the key. But I can't say anything else."

"Is it about Moll?"

They both looked at me like, *where did she hear that*, but they still stayed silent.

"I've been looking for her all morning. I couldn't find her at breakfast and I checked the infirmary and her roommate. I can't find her anywhere. I don't know her class schedule. What's going on? Did she miss her classes?"

"The deans are in a big meeting with Bleaker. That's all we can say," Brady whispered. "And you'd better keep a lid on this. Bleaker's a wreck I heard."

"She ought to be, after what she did to Moll last night at the dance." At that moment, I was thinking that if only I hadn't been so focused on Wes, maybe I could have followed Moll out and talked her down. Anyone would have been upset but apparently her little chat with Bleaker had sent Moll into hiding. "You saw it," I said to Brady.

"Yeah. It was pretty bad. It would have put me under a bed somewhere. I do feel for Moll, even though what she was trying to do with that get up and makeup is a mystery."

"She just doesn't know anything about that stuff," I said.

"She's all up here," I pointed to my head. "Do you guys think Moll is okay?"

"I have no idea," Jan said. The lunch bell rang and she stood up. "But we have to get to the dining hall."

"Right," Brady echoed.

"What's going to happen?" I asked.

They both gave me a 'who knows?' look and left with their clipboards and pencils and student lists.

———

Arriving in the dining hall late, after the moment of silence had already been observed, I looked over to the head table where Bleaker always sat. No Bleaker there. Then I wandered down one row to Brady's table, where Miss Alderton was the assigned teacher. No Miss Alderton. That meant the deans were still in their meeting. From there I could see Daria's table, two rows over. She was also surveying the hall. She caught my eye by raising her eyebrows, which signaled me to come over her way. When I got there, she stood up.

"Let's get some drinks at the pitchers."

Meals were set up in bowls and platters on each table by the slop workers. Slop was a chore every student had to take on at least once during their time at Foxhall. It was handled in three shifts. Set up, which meant setting the tables with tablecloths, silverware, plates, glasses and napkins. First shift had to show up early, making first shift breakfast slop the school's most hated chore. Second slop shift filled bowls and platters with food—except for dessert—and set it on all the tables. Third slop shift was the worst, though. Everyone carried their plates and glasses to a long ledge where they scraped their debris and leftovers into bins and then stacked their plates and glasses on rotating metal wheel things that the kitchen slop workers spun around to the kitchen side and unloaded them, sprayed them down, and stacked them onto a conveyor belt that fed the dirty dishes through a giant dishwasher, tray after tray, after which they were fed into giant dryers, then unloaded and stacked on shelves.

On one side of this ledge, along the wall there was a table with an assortment of pitchers with milk, juices, and water. This was long before the salad bar became a staple at institutions. When everyone at a table had finished eating and scraped their plates, one person from each table was designated to pick up whatever the dessert was that meal and bring it back to the table. There was a dessert wheel rotating out the bowls of dessert with new ones as they were picked up. There was also a bread wheel with freshly sliced loaves on trays. If your table ran out of bread, there was always more. Rice pudding was a common dessert. As was rhubarb floating in some clear, slimy, pink stuff. Sometimes we had bread pudding or brown betty. And at dinner once a week we got bricks of vanilla ice cream wrapped in thick paper—one to a student—open at both ends, so that you had to slip a knife under the paper to unwrap the ice cream brick before it thawed and turned into ice cream soup. With this, the school always included a bowl of thawed strawberries in syrup. On ice cream nights, there was a lot of fast maneuvering to get extra bricks other kids didn't want.

At lunch that day they'd served up Welsh Rarebit, a soupy cheese concoction that you ladled over slices of bread the school cooks baked fresh on Tuesday and Thursday mornings in the pre-dawn dark. On those days, the sweet, musky scent of fresh bread permeated Fox building and wafted over the campus. The bread wheel was a popular destination on bake days. Also on the tables that day, next to the bowls of Rarebit I saw bowls of pale green lima beans and uncut apples one platter to a table. When I met Daria at the pitcher table, she leaned over to whisper so no one else could hear.

"They're going to start grilling people after lunch, one at a time. They're leaving notes at our tables. Tim got one. So did Stocky and two other boys. No girls so far. Stocky thinks they know a boy had the key so they're starting with the boys."

I nodded and smiled so no one would suspect what we were talking about. "Did he say anything about the wire?"

"He didn't say. I don't think they know about that."

"What about the pigpen?" I was thinking about the train trestle. What if someone had seen Wes and me there?

"Nothing. I think it's all about the key. I don't know what someone left in the mattress room. Whatever it was must have been pretty bad to stir all this up."

"Yeah. Kind of stupid to leave anything behind."

"I'd better get back to my table or Tomlinson will have a fit."

Mrs. Tomlinson was Daria's table head. She taught Spanish and first year French and was known as a stickler for the rules. Daria would be taking roll after Christmas break. She and Faith were the next team, so until then they had to stick it out at tables like the rest of us. I grabbed her wrist before she left.

"What have you heard about Moll?"

"What about her? Except that Bleaker stripped her naked at the dance. God that woman is a bitch."

"Then you haven't heard anything?"

"No. Hey, I have to get back."

With that, she grabbed a milk pitcher and left me standing at the table wondering what to do next.

THIRTY-ONE

The Note

BEING THE LAST ONE TO ARRIVE AT MY ASSIGNED TABLE FOR lunch, there was only one place to sit. I arrived carrying the milk pitcher, thinking that made my late arrival at least look legitimate but it didn't mask what was surely a look of panic when I saw a sealed white envelope at my place. My hand was so shaky some of the milk slopped over the lip when I leaned down to try to see if there was any clue about what was inside the envelope.

"The dean's office left that for you," Mr. Fenstermacher told me.

Everyone stared my way and for a second I felt the panic a criminal caught in the act must feel.

"What is it?" That was Amy Gould, a junior who I knew hated Daria with a passion and, by association, me. My take on it? Pure jealousy. Amy was one of those sweater-set girls from a rich New York family. She had more shoes at Foxhall than anyone else. So many they didn't all fit in her closet so her mother had a special shoe closet constructed for her. It fit under her bed, was on little wheels, and when she pulled it out the top opened automatically and all her extra shoes were neatly arranged by color.

"I'll open it later," I mumbled and reached for an apple. Suddenly my appetite was gone and that Welsh Rarebit looked like crayons that had melted in the sun.

"Scared?" she sneered.

"That's enough," said Mr. Fenstermacher. "I wonder what you students think about the issue of Laos."

Laos was one his favorite topics. Every morning a variety of daily newspapers were laid out on the benches outside the dining hall. Anyone could sit and read them after breakfast and one day before Thanksgiving break, I'd heard one of the senior boys reading an article in the *Times* about how our government was sending advisors into Laos presumably to spy on Vietnam. A couple of the boys got all heated about it saying advisors meant soldiers or CIA and we were getting embroiled in a war we couldn't win and that Laos was in turmoil. That the French had pulled out of Indo China and we were taking over for them.

"What about Berlin and Khrushchev? Don't you see that situation as more dangerous?" Mr. Fenstermacher asked of anyone who would join in.

"I don't think the Soviets want to start another war," one of the boys offered.

"But you think there might be a war in Vietnam?"

"I think the Soviet Union will use proxies to keep nipping at our heels is all. Vietnam. Laos. Cambodia, Berlin. I think it's all part of their strategy to keep us occupied."

"Maybe all they want is assurance that Germany won't attack them again," one of the other boys said.

I was glad Mr. Fenstermacher had brought it up. While they talked, it gave me a chance to slip the envelope onto my lap and surreptitiously try to open it, but the seal was impossible to break without making noise so I sat through the meal, toyed with a piece of bread and some apple, until finally the end of meal bell rang, announcements were made from the head table by a teacher—still no dean in sight—and we could leave.

When dismissed, we rose like a flock of geese from a field that we'd depleted of seeds. I practically ran out the door and headed for the girls' room at the far end of the hall. Once inside, I tore open the envelope and pulled out the paper inside. The note was typed. Unsigned. Plain as starch.

Miss Greenwood, please come to Miss Bleaker's office directly after lunch.

That was it. No explanation. No subject. No rebuke or question or discussion. I had no choice. That was clear. So Daria was wrong and they were rounding up girls, too. I turned and stared at myself in the mirror, practiced my 'I have no idea' look, well perfected after years of interrogations from my mother, squared my shoulders, ruffled my hair and tore up the note. I could handle this. I would know nothing. I would say nothing. I would reveal nothing by word or attitude. I would be stone.

———

"Sit down, please."

Bleaker looked different. It wasn't a total change but it was there. A few strands of hair had escaped her tightly wound bun. A groove had formed between her eyebrows. She held the corner of her lower lip between her teeth and clasped her hands with fingers tightly intertwined, moving them in a circular pattern back and forth as if trying to crush some small particle between her palms. It was an odd gesture that you couldn't help but notice. I wondered if she thought of me as that small particle.

She stood to the side of her desk, which had a number of handwritten notes on it, unlike the last time I'd been summoned to her office, when her desk had been completely barren. Also, she said please this time. I sat in the same chair and waited for the interrogation to begin, imagining as I sat there what a defendant must feel like when the jury comes back to take their seats with a verdict in hand. Just a little slip of paper. Folded, inscrutable, the future foretold in a scrap no bigger than a loose-leaf page from a notebook. Innocuous and plain. Not a scroll, unfolded to the sound of trumpets blaring, with fanfare and pomp. So I waited. Tried to maintain a calm exterior. Ready to lie my teeth out if I had to.

"Miss Greenwood," she began, calmly enough. "I . . . uh . . . I . . . well that is, I understand you've . . ."

She stopped and turned toward the window. The day had begun with gray clouds but now they were breaking up and patches of blue gave the afternoon a bright light, which often happens in the late fall, for brief hours during the shorter days. It was the kind of sky that makes you want to walk in the woods, leaves crunching underfoot, air crisp and clean. I remembered my aunt Judith saying when there was enough blue in a cloudy sky to cut out a pair of britches, it meant the day would turn clear and storms would be over.

"Miss Greenwood," Bleaker began again. "Something has come up."

There it was. She was going to grill me now. She just didn't know how to open the subject. I sat mute, staring at her back and the changing sky beyond the window.

"Something of a serious nature."

Now it seemed she was stalling for some reason. Before, she had started gunning for me right at the outset and never let up. What was all the hemming and hawing about now?

"Something, well, I would characterize it as quite serious."

She stopped and turned to me. Were her eyes wet? I thought I must be mistaken but my eyesight was good and I could swear I saw glistening. She walked to her desk and pulled out a drawer, lifted a tissue, blew her nose slightly, and then dabbed at her eyes.

I was right. Bleaker crying. What the hell?

"I hope it is not serious. I hope it is a tempest in a teapot, so to speak. However I must ask you . . ."

She stopped again. And her hands started that crazy grinding with her fingers laced together. She sat down in her chair and her hands disappeared behind the desk, presumably onto her lap. She sniffed once and looked down at the papers on her desk.

"The deans had a meeting this morning," she tried another tack. "With Mr. Williamson."

A meeting with the headmaster and all the deans? Wow, they really were upset about that key.

"We have searched the school thoroughly. Every inch of it. And we have made inquiries of some other students. And we have come up empty handed at this point."

If I had been anywhere else, I would have cracked up laughing. As if they actually expected to find a key somewhere on the campus, like some prep school Captain Queeg, endlessly searching for a mythical key. It was ludicrous but not really surprising.

"In the process of searching and questioning, your name came up and I have been asked by Mr. Williamson to make note of anything you may know."

She still hadn't asked me anything outright so I kept quiet. There was no reason to proffer any information. Let her sweat.

"As I stated, this is a very serious matter. So I'm asking if you know anything, that you please tell me now before something happens."

Still, I sat mute.

"Does your silence mean you do not know anything?"

"That's right," I said as calmly and quietly as I could, although all I wanted to do was bust her one and then run.

"Because if anything happens to her, and you knew where she was, you would be as responsible as anyone."

That sounded more like the Bleaker I knew. But wait a second.

"What are you talking about?" I asked. And I didn't sound so calm this time.

"Why Moll's disappearance, of course." Her hands came back to her desk and she stacked some of the pieces of paper. This definitely was not the old Bleaker who would have shot back something like: "What else do you know?" so she could nail me with it.

"We're all very worried. I understand from Eleanor De-Luca that you were in their room looking for Moll this morning. Moll wasn't at breakfast and she missed all her morning classes. She never went to the infirmary. She seems to have evaporated. If we can't find her . . ."

There was a curt rap on the door and it swung open. There stood Mr. Williamson.

———————

It was my first encounter with him since I'd arrived at Foxhall.

"We understand," he started, "that you and Moll were friends."

At first I didn't register this as a question. But he followed up with this.

"And that she did not have many friends yet, being new this year, while you seem to have been accepted well and are liked by many of the students. We understand that coming into a school like Foxhall can be quite difficult in the sophomore year. I expect that you and Moll being the only two new sophomores created a bond between you."

As he said this, he raised his eyebrows expectantly and leaned back against Bleaker's desk, his arms folded across his chest. He seemed to be holding himself back. It wasn't a stance that made me feel like opening my heart to him so I kept my mouth shut. But it was beginning to feel less like an interrogation and more like a fishing expedition where they thought I'd swallowed the fish. But what were they looking for from me? I certainly had no idea where to find Moll.

"If Moll shared anything with you that might help us locate her—"*Okay, here it comes,* I thought. *They think I know where she's hiding out—fat chance—*"you would be doing her a great favor. We don't want any of our students in jeopardy."

It finally dawned on me. They were scared. I slipped a glance at Bleaker. Her expression read pain and fear. This was a situation I certainly had never expected to be plugged into, let alone to be the one holding the power cord.

"I wish I could help but I have no idea where she is. I'm worried about her, too." When I said the last part I looked directly at Bleaker. And I had to admit I felt a surge of pleasure to see her squirm, which she did, visibly shrinking back, her brow knit into a contorted version of its implacable norm.

THIRTY-TWO

Sixteen Days Left

ONCE AGAIN IT SEEMED THE ONLY PLACE I WANTED TO GO was Daria's room. I didn't know if she had a free period but I headed up to her hall anyway just in case. Williamson and Bleaker had kept me for half my English class so there was no reason to rush over to Bedford. When I got to Daria's door, it was open. She and Brady and Jan were all in there, as if they'd been waiting for me again.

"So?" Brady shut the door and I sat down on Daria's bed.

"We saw you go down to Bleaker's office. What happened?" Jan asked. "What do they know? Did you tell them anything?"

"It wasn't about the key," I said. "It was about Moll. They're scared to death because they can't find her. Williamson came in, too."

"He never gets involved in disciplinary stuff," Jan said. "That's creepy."

"Did they grill you?" Daria asked.

"Not really. I mean they asked if I knew anything. They knew I went looking for her in the infirmary and that I went to her room and talked to Eleanor. They're totally blindsided. Bleaker was crying."

"What?"

They all yelled at once and it was a moment to savor, a kind of triumph I had not expected, given the circumstances, but I guess at prep school, when you were thoroughly isolated from the real world, whatever that was, you took your notoriety wherever you could get it. So I must admit I was pretty pleased with myself at that moment.

"Tell us everything." Daria moved in closer to me in a way that made me think I had shifted from a subordinate position to equal footing. Strange how pressure in one area pushed at another and I thought briefly that it must be some kind of law of physics but I had no idea which one.

During classes that afternoon, I had trouble concentrating, which was dangerous because we only had the next sixteen days to study, hand in papers, and take tests before the Christmas break. For seniors there was an enormous amount riding on these sixteen days because their college applications were due to mail in January. For the rest of us, it was crunch time, too. Sometimes it was hard to toe the line and concentrate on classes with all the social stuff going on. This was one of those times.

My thoughts kept wandering back to Mr. Williamson. During my classes and afterwards, I reconsidered that scene, and it began to dawn on me that Moll might really be in trouble. During dive practice, Daria sat next to me while we waited for our turns.

"So, I saw Tim before he went to practice." Tim was a

varsity basketball player and pretty good. Although, at six foot three, he was not nearly tall enough to be a contender beyond Foxhall. "They hauled him, Wes, Stocky, and a few others in for guidance. Ha. Guidance."

"Did anyone blab?"

"No one has talked. I mean why would they? But I did find out what happened. See one of the little men had to replace a mattress in the boys' dorm so he went to get one. Someone left a pair of boxers in there. And . . ." she looked around to make sure no one could hear us, "a condom wrapper. I mean, good God, who would be so stupid?"

"Maybe they heard someone and had to get out fast."

"Maybe, but still, now it puts everyone in trouble. I bet it was Stocky. So they've changed the lock to a deadbolt and now no one will be able to get in there."

"I bet you could still get in through one of the windows." It was true. Since the mattress room was more than half underground, there were two window wells that you could climb down into without any trouble since they were only about three feet below the ground. There were shrubs in front of them and the windows opened in. Sometimes if a girl had the key, she would go to the mattress room first then open a window to let a boy in. But what about the girls? It would be harder for them to get into the mattress room from the outside through the window. "I doubt they know that the windows don't lock."

"Oh, you're right. I'll have to get someone to check that out."

Naturally Daria was not going to check it out herself. She'd rope someone else into doing it. Probably Stocky.

"I'll bet no one ever cleans those windows or even looks at them. The little men trim the shrubs but why would they get down into the window wells?"

Miss Alderton motioned to me so I stepped off the bleacher and went for my turn on the board. Surprisingly, even though my mind was a mile away, my dives went well and Miss Alderton was happy.

"You're going to be fine at the meet this weekend," she patted me on the back as I came out of the pool. "Nice work. Good practice today." And then she said something that made me really start to worry. "I know you've spoken to Miss Bleaker and Mr. Williamson." *So it is all over the faculty by now.* "And I just wanted to add how worried we all are. Especially Miss Bleaker. I understand there was some sort of exchange between Moll and her at the Monday night dance. It's very unfortunate. But if you know anything at all—anything—you really must share it with someone. You won't be in any trouble, I can assure you."

I grabbed my towel and dried my face and hands then looked up at her.

"Honestly, I didn't see Miss Bleaker talking to Moll at the dance. But I heard about it later and went to Moll's room to talk to her. I figured she'd be, like, upset. I mean anyone would be, like, you know."

"I know."

She looked sympathetic, so I went on.

"Maybe I shouldn't say anything, but this is really Miss Bleaker's fault. I mean Moll is so sensitive and shy. She came to the dance because I encouraged her to. And she has a little crush on Donald Wingart and Miss Bleaker dressed her down right in front of him. I mean it must have been so humiliating for poor Moll. So I, like, went to her room and spoke to Eleanor DeLuca but she hadn't seen Moll and didn't know anything. She told me it's like living with a phantom. Moll is just very isolated."

She patted my shoulder again. "It's certainly not your fault. Of course we don't know yet what to think. Mr. Williamson has called Moll's mother. Apparently Moll hasn't called home. I can't imagine where she could be."

Not being able to even imagine where someone could be left your mind free to wander into dangerous and scary territory and that was what mine was beginning to do.

"Well, we have to find her soon. With Christmas break coming in less than three weeks, we don't have much time left."

"What happens if no one can find her?"

"I don't know," she said and then added, "but if it were up to me, I'd call the police."

THIRTY-THREE

The City Never Sleeps

THE KEY CRISIS FADED, AND BY THURSDAY WE HADN'T HEARD any more about it. After all, it was only when they caught you in the act that you could be punished and, as long as everyone kept their cool and played dumb, no one could do the time for an unsolved crime. This late in the fall, almost winter now, the nights were too cold to try accessing the mattress room from outside through a window, and with Christmas break approaching we were all focused on tests and papers and just getting through the semester. A kind of bunker mentality set in as the days grew shorter and darkness arrived before the dinner bell. The sky was often gray now, and we wore jackets or coats going between classes.

Our last dive meet was coming up on Saturday, only eleven days before break. My skin was raw from the chlorine and hair dryer and getting in and out of the water, and I was looking forward to getting past Saturday. Although for me, Christmas break was another question mark about where my mother would be and where I would have to spend those two weeks. My father had called a few times, given me updates, but they didn't remove the uncertainty and he sounded sad and lonely. He tried to be upbeat but I could tell he was suffering. Again, no space for me, no shoulder for my tears, no safe haven.

On Thursday night, Wes and I left study hall carrying our load of books and walked slowly along the path that led to all the dorms.

"Hey," he said, twining my fingers in his, "since your father doesn't know what's happening with your mother by the time we leave for break, how about coming out to California with me?"

I stopped walking and turned to face him.

"Are you serious?"

"Of course. I asked my mom about it and she talked to my dad and they both said it would be wonderful."

"Wonderful? They used that word?"

"Yes. Exactly what they said. Wonderful. My mom always does a big Christmas thing with all the relatives and some friends. I mean I know it's California and everything, but we do celebrate the same holidays." He was smiling, teasing me.

"I don't know." I hesitated because I was thinking of my father being alone at Christmas, not that the holiday meant anything particular to him but still . . .

"There would be other people staying at the house. We have a huge house, you know. My mom likes to have lots of people around for holidays. She's really great. You'd like her."

"Would she like me is the question?"

"How could anybody not like you?"

He put his arm around me and we started walking again. This was a dangerous thing to do. Some dean might see us and haul me before a committee for guidance about displays of affection. But I didn't care. When we got closer to Fox building, he took his arm away and whispered, "Gotta be careful. In just thirteen days you'll be off demerit."

"I know. Thanks for meeting me after all the study halls."

"Hey, it's worked out okay. My grades are going to be fine."

"You still hoping for Stanford?"

"Yeah."

"You still worried about the draft?"

"Yeah."

"Next time my father calls I'll ask him if it's okay to go to California with you."

"I wish I could kiss you."

"When we get to California . . ."

———

I got to my hall just as the phone started to ring. At one end of each hall in Fox there was an ancient black phone on a little table. These phones could only receive calls and they all came through Mrs. W.'s switchboard. Each one had a short cord so you never had any privacy, which is why there was so much demand for the pay phone in the public hall downstairs. Whoever had the room nearest the phone table usually ran out to catch it because Mrs. W. would only let it ring five times before hanging up. She had other calls to route through and no patience for halls that would let the phone ring and ring endlessly.

"Hey, Greenwood, it's for you," Jenny Biddle called. Jenny's room was closest to the phone and she was always annoyed to have to answer it. At our weekly hall meetings she complained that just because she'd been assigned that room didn't make her a telephone runner and other people should have to answer it. She suggested a rotation but that never worked and Jenny got more calls than anyone else so she was trapped into answering it most of the time.

She let the phone drop. I heard it clatter to the floor as I tossed my books onto my bed. I walked over to pick it up, thinking it must be my father and collecting my thoughts about how to broach the California subject with him. I didn't know how he'd take it. I thought maybe I'd better let him give me a condition report on my mother first and then lead into it gradually. Maybe he was planning on being away again and would want to send me to my aunt and uncle. There was no soup kitchen to save me from that this time. *Wes was so sweet,* I was thinking when I pulled the phone cord up to get the receiver off the floor so I could hold it to my ear.

"Hello." I said it carefully.

I heard a sharp intake of breath, like a little gasp, and then, "Hello?" It was definitely not my father. The voice was soft and muffled. I could hardly hear it.

And then again, a little louder, "Hello, Greenwood?"

"Yes," I said, trying to figure out who would be calling me on my hall. Students weren't allowed to call each other through Mrs. W. No one from home called me by my last name. And then it hit me.

"MOLL?" I said it too loud, I realized, but no one was around. They were all getting ready for lights out, brushing their teeth and stuff.

"Shhh," she said. "You can't let anyone know I'm calling you. Promise me."

"Okay," I said and thoughts started whirring. "Where are you? Everyone's all upset. I mean the deans and everyone."

"Listen, I can't talk long. Just don't tell anyone I called and don't say anything that anyone could hear. I'll call you again tomorrow after study hall at 9:55. Okay?"

"Wait, listen, don't hang up."

I heard a click and stood there like an idiot, holding it next to my chest as if by hanging onto it I could rouse her again, but the line was dead and I finally had to place it back in its cradle.

The next twenty-four hours dragged like a boring textbook. No matter where I was I wanted to run up to my hall and wait by the phone. I argued endlessly with myself over whether I should tell someone and if so, who. My first thought was Wes.

I can trust Wes. I know I can. He'll stand by me through anything. *But why burden him with this when he already has so much on his mind? But if I don't tell him he might feel hurt that I didn't confide in him.* Like that night we went to the Social Room. *I don't want that to happen again. But if I do tell him, what can he do? He can only tell me to do what I think is right. I don't know what I think is right. I don't even know where Moll is or what she's doing much less what she's thinking. He might tell me to go to Mr. Williamson. I don't know if I can trust Mr. Williamson. I know I can't go to Bleaker. She's the one who started all this. It's all her fault. But when Williamson was in her office he didn't seem to be blaming her. If he knew what she'd done he would have called me into his office not come into hers to see me. And what if I tell*

Wes and then I get into trouble? If he knew then he would get into trouble, too. So I can't tell him because it's important to protect him. So that can't be the right thing to do.

Then I thought about telling Brady or Jan. That seemed a bad idea. If I told either one them and didn't tell Daria, she'd freeze me out for sure. But Faith. Faith would be a good person to tell. And after the soup kitchen, Faith and I had bonded and I trusted her. She always seemed to know what was right. Yes Faith. But then I started to think about it more.

Faith would certainly say to tell the school. I mean Faith is no rebel. She has no axe to grind with the school. She's not like Daria. She's not ever out to prove anything to the powers that be. She'd tell me to do what's best for everyone, meaning best for Moll too I guess. But what if I do tell them, then what happens? Because I don't even know where Moll is. So what good would it do to tell them she called? They would probably want me to make her tell me where she is. And then what? Wherever she is, she might not stay there. And to make her tell me anything she doesn't want to would be manipulating her and that could not be the right thing to do. So what good would telling Faith be anyway?

"Miss Greenwood? How about it? The translation at the top of page thirty-two." My Latin teacher, Mr. D'Amico, had come toward my desk. Apparently I'd been so busy with my own thoughts I hadn't heard him.

"Um, yes," I said and read what I had translated.

"He proves to them that to accomplish their attempts was a thing very easy to be done, because he himself would obtain the government of his own state; that there was no doubt that the Helvetii were the most powerful of the whole of Gaul; he assures them that he will, with his own forces and his own army, acquire the sovereignty for them. Incited by this speech, they give a pledge and oath to one another, and hope that, when they have seized the sovereignty, they will, by means of the three most powerful and valiant nations, be enabled to obtain possession of the whole of Gaul."

"Well done, Miss Greenwood. I hope you'll find our company more engaging for the rest of the class."

He moved on to someone else, and I sank back in my seat. But my thoughts would not be still.

Not Faith. But maybe go straight to Mr. Williamson and drop all of it in his lap. No, I couldn't do that. I have no idea what he would do. What if he thinks I had something to do with Moll's disappearance? Or if he thinks I know more than I'm telling him? If I tell him she called me, he'll think I know more than I do. Why would he believe me? He might make them kick me out. I'm already in trouble. I could get in so deep I couldn't climb out. Daria . . . I should ask her what to do. Oh hell, she'd just tell me to let them all find their own way out of this. She never understood why I was nice to Moll to begin with. Especially after how she'd set Moll up at the dance. No, not Daria. Poor Moll. Where could she be? Maybe she just walked to town and she's staying in a room at one of those old houses owned by some old lady who took pity on her.

I dawdled through meals and managed to get through classes and even sat through study hall with my books open but I couldn't concentrate. Wes had a big term paper to work on so he walked me back to my dorm quickly, all the while I tried to act normal and he didn't notice anything. Once there, I dumped my stuff and waited by the phone so Jenny Biddle wouldn't get it again. I picked it up the second it started to ring so no one else would question who it was for and said, "Hello" as quietly as I could.

"Greenwood?"

"Yes. It's me. Listen don't hang up. No one knows you're calling me. I didn't tell anyone."

"Okay." She spoke softly and I tried to keep my voice down, too. I turned to the wall to get as much privacy as possible.

"Where are you?"

"New York."

"City?" I was amazed. That was the last place I thought she'd go.

"Yes."

"How did you get there?"

"I walked to Newtown and called a cab to take me to a train station and then took a train."

"Are you okay?"

"Sort of." She stopped and I wasn't sure what I should say next. "But I'm never coming back. Not ever."

"I understand how you must feel. Bleaker's a bitch and she should burn in hell. But you didn't do anything wrong."

"I don't care about any of that anymore."

"What do you mean?"

"I mean there must be a higher purpose to life."

"Moll, where are you staying?" She was starting to scare me for real.

"That's why I called."

"Why?"

"I'm running out of money."

"Do you want me to send you some?" Money was never a problem for me. There was always plenty of it. I didn't know if Moll's family had much money but it seemed to me they didn't, with her mom working at some pharmaceutical company as some kind of scientist.

"Well, maybe. But really I need a place to stay. I've been staying at this youth hostel run by a church but I have only one night left and then I have to leave. I only have twenty dollars. I don't know where to go."

I thought quickly. What could I do? And then it hit me.

"Listen, my parents have a big apartment on the east side. You could stay there. My mother's in the hospital and my father's at our house in Connecticut."

"How would I get in?"

"I'll call the doorman. The day guy is Jake. I'll tell him your name and describe you and he has an extra key. He can let you in and once you're in you can use the extra set of keys my parents keep in the apartment. They're hanging on a hook inside one of the kitchen cabinets. You'll find them."

"Are you sure?"

"Of course. But Moll, you really should call your mother. Everyone's worried and they've pressured me to tell them what I know. That was before you called but now that I do know, it'll be hard to keep quiet."

At that moment someone down the hall yelled my name. "Hey, Greenwood. Get off the phone. I'm expecting a call."

"If you tell anyone you talked to me, or tell anyone where I am or tell anyone anything, I'll kill myself." She said it quietly. As if she'd made up her mind. "I already walked on the Brooklyn Bridge yesterday."

A chill ran up the back of my legs to my neck.

"Please, Moll. Just go to my apartment and take it easy. I can call you tomorrow from the pay phone so I'll have some privacy. I won't say anything to anyone. I promise. They're yelling at me to get off the phone." I gave her the address of my family's apartment. "I'll call you at my apartment at this same time tomorrow."

"Okay," she said. "Thank you."

"Moll," I said. "Please take care. Don't do anything, Promise me?"

"We'll see what happens," she said. She hung up and I slumped against the wall for a minute and then the phone rang again. It was for that girl down the hall, which gave me a chance to search my purses and wallet and pockets for whatever loose change I could get my hands on and run down to make a quick call from the pay phone to leave a message for the doorman, Jake, to let Moll Grimes into my parents apartment the next day. The hell with waiting to use the wire.

THIRTY-FOUR

Fighting with Myself

AT FOXHALL, IT WAS ALMOST IMPOSSIBLE TO KEEP ANYTHING secret. Everyone was whispering about the mattress room key, but since no one who had actually used the key was about to rat out anyone else who'd used it, gossip was rampant but unsubstantiated. And since no one who would have spilled the news to the deans actually knew who had the key, the story simply whirled around like an eddy in a stream, never spilling into the stream and never totally fading away either. It was kind of funny to us, the ones who knew about it, to hear the story expanding. One version had some kid who'd been kicked out of another school living down there. Another version had a girl giving birth on one of the mattresses and that's why the school changed the lock. I even heard a version where a male teacher (a lot of conjecture about just who) and a senior girl were having an affair and using the mattress room for their trysts. The word tryst actually floated around for a couple of days.

But once I had spoken to Moll, I no longer paid any attention to the gossip and, after hearing her talk about the Brooklyn Bridge, I knew this could go no further than me. Still, carrying that weight around was like trying to keep a river that had breached its banks from flooding. My sleep that night was interrupted by nightmares and every time they woke me, I found myself twisted around in my sheets like a knotted up piece of string. By morning, I wished I had never agreed to help Moll. Still, what else could I have done? It was too late for second thoughts now.

I caught up with Wes after breakfast. He and some other guys were reading the newspapers on the benches outside the dining hall. I sat down close to him and spoke low so no one else could hear me.

"Hey, can you get the wire from Stocky so I can use it tonight?"

He had the paper opened to double pages so he could see all the OpEds in *The Times* at one time. He lowered the paper a little and turned to me.

"Why don't you ask him? He's right over there." He pointed with his index finger without letting go of the pages.

"Uh-uh. I want you to ask him. You know how he is."

"How is he? I thought he's let you use it before?"

"He has but if I ask him, he'll be insufferable and try to get me, you know . . ."

"Really? Even though you and I are going together?"

"Stocky's kind of a pig, y'know."

"Really? The guys all like him. Huh. I had no idea." He shook his head.

"Well will you?"

"Now?"

"Sure now. But get it later and give it to me at study hall so I can hide it with all my stuff."

"What do you need it for?"

"I've got to call a friend tonight. We agreed on a time after study hall. So I need it before then."

"What friend?"

"Just a friend."

"Yeah. I know a friend. What friend?"

So here it was. Should I tell Wes and possibly get him in trouble if it came out that he knew? Or should I lie and tell him it was a friend from home? I could say it was my friend Melena. But that would mean lying to Wes and eventually he'd probably find out. We'd had that one fight about me being too secretive. I didn't want to have another one. Maybe I should forget about the wire and just pay for the call. But I had no idea how long I'd be on with Moll or how much change I'd need. There was only so much change you could even get at school and nowhere to get it during the week. The wire was my only option. I could call my apartment collect but then my father would see it on the bill and if he asked about who I called collect while he wasn't even home, what would I say? This was a mess that I didn't see any way to escape.

"Wes," I began.

"Present."

He was being silly. That was a good sign.

"Do you trust me?"

"Sure."

"I mean really? I mean if I told you I couldn't tell you something, would you trust that I was doing the right thing and thinking about what was best for you?"

"Like what?"

"If I could tell you what, I wouldn't be asking if you trust me."

"Oh. So you want to tell me there's something you can't tell me but you want me to trust you."

"Yes."

"For how long?"

"I don't know."

"But it has to do with the wire."

"Sort of."

"And you want me to get it for you but you can't tell me who you're calling."

"Right."

He put down the paper and stared straight ahead, then turned to me.

"Is it another guy?"

"No."

"Are you in trouble?"

"No. At least I don't think so. Not yet."

"But if you do get in trouble, will you let me help you?"

"Yes."

"Okay, then I trust you. I'll get the thing from Stocky and give it to you after study hall."

"Thank you." I hadn't realized it but I'd been holding my breath and now I let it out and slumped back against the wall.

"But be careful, okay?"

"I will."

THIRTY-FIVE

Right and Wrong

IT WAS NERVE-WRACKING TRYING TO USE THE WIRE ALONE in the booth with no one standing guard but I got it into the slot and opened a canvas bag on my lap to catch the change when it came back out. The thing worked fine, Moll answered on the first ring and I pulled the booth door shut at the same time as I pulled on it to release my change so I could use it again when the operator came on to say my time was up and so no one walking by could hear me. I reinserted the wire to be ready for later.

"Are you okay?" I asked first.

"Yes. Thank you for letting me stay here."

"No problem."

"I only have sixteen dollars left."

"Well, eat anything in the kitchen. I'm sure there's lots in the freezer, too. Take whatever you want."

"I already had some toast and tea." Her voice was quiet, not like the night before when she'd sounded kind of petulant.

"Moll, we really need to talk about this."

"About what?"

"About you running away. They called your mom. She must be worried sick."

"I'm sure she is. But that's just the way it is."

"I don't understand. I know Bleaker hurt your feelings. She's a bitch. But your mom hasn't done anything." *Look who is defending a mom. As if I know anything about what a supportive mother would feel like.*

"It's not about that."

"Not about what?"

"About what happened at the dance."

"Then what is it about?"

"Everything."

"It may feel like everything is wrong, but if Bleaker hadn't said anything to you, you'd still be here, wouldn't you?"

"I guess. But that was just . . . you know, the last straw. Nothing's been going right anyway."

"But Moll, you're so smart. You're doing well in all your classes aren't you?"

"So what? What does that mean? The world doesn't care about classes and term papers and exams."

"It's supposed to. I mean, that helps you get into college."

"Where it will be more of the same."

"Maybe it won't. Maybe college is different."

"It won't be any different. It's been like this my whole life. I don't fit in anywhere. I just have to accept that."

"Well, but you can't stay at my parents apartment forever. Eventually they'll be back."

"I know."

"So what is your plan?"

At that moment, the operator came on and said I had to put in more money for the next three minutes, so I chucked the same change in again.

"I'm not sure. I'm thinking about it."

"Well, you either have to come back to school or go home to your mom. What else can you do?"

"I don't know."

"Is there anything I can do to help you make up your mind?"

"I'm never going back to Foxhall. Never."

"Okay. Then how about letting me call your mom. Maybe she can come to New York and get you."

"No."

"How about if I at least tell her you're okay?"

"Not now. Maybe later. I'll call you tomorrow at this time on your hall. I have to think about it some more. Bye." With that she hung up and I was left feeling like I'd pushed her too much. It was then I remembered the Fifty-Ninth Street Bridge was two blocks from my parents' apartment. It also spanned the East River, just like the Brooklyn Bridge. And my bedroom window in the apartment looked right at it. My hand shook as I yanked the wire and the last change I'd put in came gushing back out. I slipped it into the bag and slid the door open, looked out at the hall, didn't see anyone, and let myself out.

———

There was a KOB waiting for me back at my room. Someone had tossed it on my bed. It had to be from Wes. I could spot his handwriting when I picked it up. Inside he had drawn a big heart and inside the heart he'd written, "Hope everything went okay. Were you careful?"

I sat down and tears pricked at my eyes. I wanted to tell him everything. Wanted to feel his arm around my shoulders, reassuring me that everything was going to be okay. It was funny that someone else—who couldn't possibly predict what was going to happen any more than you could—telling you everything was going to work out for the best, made you feel like it actually was.

Being too late to send a return KOB, I would have to wait until breakfast to give Wes an answer. It was time to get ready for lights out so I gathered my things to go to the bathroom but just as I was about to leave my room, there was a knock on my door. Figuring it was Brady or maybe Jan I yelled, "Yeah, come in."

But it wasn't Brady or Jan and I nearly fell over when there stood Bleaker. With the bright hall light from behind, her standard black dress looked even darker filling up my doorway. And the look on her face, well, it kind of terrified me. As far as I knew, she had never come to a dorm room, had never even been on a dorm hall, and for her to be here now, especially at night, was creepy and I didn't know what to say.

"I would like to speak with you, Miss Greenwood," she said but took no step forward.

"Here?" It sounded incredibly stupid, but it just popped out.

"Yes." She glanced around as if looking for a place to land. "May I come in?"

"Sure," I said and then almost bit my tongue. *Sure? Sure? Who do I think I am talking to?* I wished fervently that someone—anyone—would show up and interrupt this visit. I saw a few girls skitter past my door, whispering and pointing. That was when my mind started rushing to find an answer to the more obvious question of why she was at my door in the first place. And in the second place, the question of what kind of trouble I was about to be in. My brain went into overdrive. If I could have peered inside my head—maybe through one ear with a tiny piercing flashlight to illuminate its workings—it probably would have looked like a high speed bumper car chase all the cars spinning and whirling, crashing into each other and jerking to a new start.

Was it the wire, not very well concealed at that very moment at the bottom of my closet? Had someone seen me, had someone heard me, had the telephone operator suspected something, would I go to jail, did I need a lawyer, had my father been notified, how would this affect my mother, had someone on the hall overheard me last night, was it that day at the trestle with Wes, had we held hands and been seen by Bleaker walking back from study hall, had someone seen us on the hidden steps by the track, did they think I had the key to the mattress room or worse, were they after Wes, did they know I had set up Donald Wingart to be at the dance to see Moll, was I going to be expelled, what else could they catch me for, how many infractions had I committed, and how bad were they?

I must have looked as guilty as Bonnie and Clyde, blinded by my own thoughts standing there for what seemed like forever.

"May I use this chair?"

Bleaker was talking. She couldn't possibly hear my thoughts. She wanted to sit down. If she were going to throw me out of school, it wouldn't be like this, not right before lights out on a weeknight. No, she wanted to talk to me but maybe, just maybe, I wasn't in trouble.

"Oh. I'm sorry. Of course." I pulled the chair away from the desk and shoved it toward her.

She sat. With her knees pulled tightly together on that old wooden desk chair that had likely never seen the backside of anyone but a student in all the years it had gone from room to room and student to student. It was pitted and scratched and one leg was slightly shorter than the other three, which allowed a student studying or writing a paper to tip the chair to one leg in a kind of tapping that prevented the student from falling asleep. At least that was what I had found. But Bleaker sat as still as a cat on a windowsill.

"I've come to ask for your help," Bleaker began and that hand motion where she appeared to be squashing something between her palms began again.

"It is not normal for me to find myself in this position as I'm sure you can understand. Nor is it a comfortable position that I find myself in."

What in hell is she going on about? I didn't know what to do with myself, standing there holding my bathroom caddy in one hand and a tooth brush in the other. A bell would ring soon signaling fifteen minutes until lights out when we all had to be in bed with no control over the lights and the room would be totally dark. She must have known that. The same way she must have known we only had ten days until Christmas break began and we'd all disappear for three weeks. But she seemed oblivious to everything, especially to me standing there awkwardly looking around for some way to feel normal in this abnormal situation.

It was at that point I noticed her eyes. They were red and swollen as if she'd been crying for a very long time. I knew what that looked like, having spent much of my childhood in tears over one thing or another, precipitated by my mother, extended by my sense of isolation, and never having a satisfactory resolution when the tears were over. They just dried up and life moved on.

It was an odd situation, this being in the middle of something I felt was impossible. When you have a choice between right and wrong or good and evil, you always know which was the choice to make. You might not choose the side of right or good. You might do something you know was wrong. Hadn't I done that many times myself since arriving at Foxhall? The rebellious among us didn't think of those infractions as moral choices. We thought of them as striking a cause for freedom when every waking moment in the ecosystem we inhabited told us we had no freedom of choice. We were opting for neither good nor bad, right nor wrong. We were maintaining a sense that we had some control. Okay it was always clandestine and it came with risks. Still, it gave us a sense of self-determination.

But this was different. I had no loyalty to Bleaker. No, I had a decided antipathy to her. Had I looked deeply into that antipathy, would I have found a layer of payback for all the wrongs done to me by my mother? Probably. Yet the wrongs perpetrated by my mother were interwoven with all sorts of conflicting feelings and loyalties. I needed her, whereas I decidedly did not need Bleaker. If that meant any decision I made now, facing what I could only characterize as begging for my help on her part, was colored by dislike for her and everything she stood for (all right—I did not know every-thing she stood for but at least what I had perceived she stood for), then so be it. Being on the receiving end of my mother's inexplicable emotional meanderings had inured me to the needs of other authority figures, whether or not those figures had needs I could alleviate. In other words, and per-haps I should have begun here, I really didn't give a shit what Bleaker wanted or needed. I would bear that burden later. But standing there in my dorm room, I had no idea what burden I would eventually face. At that moment, the thought of the Fifty-Ninth Street Bridge framed by my bedroom win-dow overlooking the east river in New York City with Moll standing there, staring out at it, possibly contemplating a drop into the icy waters below, was enough to cement my loyalties. I did not move. My shower caddy was my shield, my tooth brush my sword. I would vanquish the intruder.

She was going on about her role at the school, how much she cared for all the girls, how she had been at Foxhall for twenty-five years and nothing like this had ever happened before, how girls must have standards of comportment—she actually used that word—how easy it was for girls to forget themselves in the face of social pressure, how she herself had been tempted when she was young but how she had resisted and how glad she was that she had chosen the path of de-cency, pudency even (Pudency? What was that, I wondered, and made a mental note to look it up later.), how girls must choose their role models with care and how her only aim had been to guide Moll along a path of moral and ethical behavior that would yield her the eventual results she would desire when she had passed through these difficult years.

Finally, she stopped talking at me. I didn't know what to say. But I shouldn't have been concerned because at that point she reached into a side pocket of her black dress and pulled out a folded piece of paper, which she carefully and slowly unfolded. It had been folded three times so this took a few seconds. She held it carefully in front of her at reading distance and stared pointedly at me.

"I want to read you something," she said.

What is this now? A written lecture? Something she found in her archives?

She cleared her throat, took a raspy breath then began to read.

"When a person devotes her whole life to one purpose, that life takes its meaning from that purpose, it upholds the virtues that flow from that purpose and it rests its moral imperative upon that purpose. Such a life, devoid of other, more temporal pursuits, must, by definition, rise above and seek recompense beyond petty deviations from its purpose. It must, if its purpose is worthy, pursue it above all else until its purpose has been fulfilled."

She stopped and looked up at me. I had no idea why she was reading this to me or what it meant. But it sounded to me like she was headed to the nearest convent to splay herself on a cement floor in front of a statue of Mary and beg forgiveness. At least she would have admitted her sin and been out of my life. But she wasn't finished.

She cleared her throat again and continued to read one last sentence.

"What is one to do if she finds that her purpose has been for naught?"

The fifteen-minute bell had rung in the middle of her oration and with only twelve minutes left until my room went dark, it was still not clear what she was doing there—or what she wanted from me. Fear of saying the wrong thing kept my lips shut tight. On the other hand, I couldn't stand there forever and she apparently had said her piece and was not about to go further. She folded her paper with great solemnity and slipped it back into her pocket.

So we had reached an impasse. My feet were reminding me that they were meant to move, the fingers clasped around the shower caddy were turning numb at the tips, and I feared I would soon sink down onto my bed like a sack of sand. And then the most astonishing thing of the whole visit happened.

Bleaker advanced toward me, the look on her face unreadable, as if she was wearing a mask that only looked like her. The eyes were wide, pupils dilated, pale skin taut over the flat cheeks, but it was the mouth that fascinated me as she approached. The lips were moving prayer-like, but no sound emerged. She wore that slash of lipstick but it had become dry and cracked and as her lips moved, she drew them back in a kind of grimace. When she reached me, she took both my wrists in her hands, pulling them to her at the waist, which made the shower caddy bump against her, jiggling its contents. She seemed not to notice there was something between us as her lips moved ceaselessly. Finally, finally a sound emerged.

"You must tell me," she said. "I've seen the call logs at the telephone operator's office. I know you received a call from her. You must tell me where she is. You must, you must, you must."

She clung to my wrists. Just as it seemed she was coming

unhinged, she dropped them and sank back onto my bed and sat staring up at me.

"If you tell me, I won't say a word to Mr. Williamson or anyone else. It will be strictly between us." The look on her face reminded me of a child pleading for a treat, a child who knew no treat would be forthcoming. "I give you my solemn word. You must understand. You girls and Foxhall are my whole life. That is my mission. I can't allow one of you to go astray."

I'll admit it. Right then all I could think was: *Then why, you petrified old biddy, did you treat Moll so shabbily, shame her practically in front of the whole school, take a poor innocent girl who was only trying to fit in and make a boy pay some attention to her, why did you do that? You deserve to suffer for that.* Although I thought of her as old, now that she was up close, it seemed she was only about, maybe, forty-five. At fifteen, anyone over nineteen fell somewhere into that indeterminate category of "older," but not like my sixty-two-year-old gramsy, which was ancient. Now, of course, sixty-two seems relatively young. If I could go back there, Miss Bleaker was probably almost young enough at that age to be my daughter at my current age. Yes, perspective plays tricks on you, especially about age. But that night, to me she was old. And old meant *do not trust.* And especially do not trust at Foxhall because once that ball of twine began to unravel, who knew where the string would lead. So finally, I spoke.

"I don't know what you're talking about, Miss Bleaker." I said it the same way I had lied my way through her interrogation about the wilted dandelion rings. It had worked then, so why not now?

Ahhh, she knew. I could see it on her face and she knew

that I knew she knew. It also seemed clear that I was not about to give up or give in. And this was where the hypocrisy and rigidity shook hands and came out of their respective corners ready to do battle. I knew hypocrisy would win but rigidity wouldn't go down until about the fifth round. So she went on and on, begging in her Bleaker-ish way, pleading as only someone who was used to being in the dominant position can plead, that was, with a superior attitude as if she was doing you a favor by allowing you to give in to her.

She came back to the same points but with each plea, she added another sweetener to her proffers—she would cancel my study hall punishment, she would give me the plum assignment of role taker starting after Christmas break (how she would do that was not clear, but I assumed it meant she would take it away from someone else), she would, if I wanted, give me a single again next year, she would have me excused from Sunday breakfasts for the rest of the year so I could sleep in. The list expanded as her desperation grew until at the end, her hypocrisy had won and I believed she would have sold me her soul had I been the devil.

"Miss Bleaker," I finally answered. "Lights are going out in a few minutes. I have to get to the bathroom before that."

"Don't be concerned about the lights out rule. I can excuse you from that, too."

"Miss Bleaker," I said this as emphatically as I deemed possible in the situation. "I really don't know anything and I have to go."

"Then the consequences will be yours to bear." She said this last in a desperate way; her shoulders sloped down and inward like a U.

She stood up and I figured at last she'd go, but no. She turned to me with one last salvo.

"Foxhall is my life," she said in a tone I'd never heard from her before, her voice cracking a little as if she'd breathed in some dusty air. "I've given the school and the girls who come through here everything I have. If I can't remedy this situation, my life here will be over. And no other school will ever give me a second chance. I know you girls think I'm unreasonable but you don't understand it from my side."

All I could think was: *So Mr. Williamson must know it's because of her Moll ran away. But if she thinks the threat of losing her position here is a reasonable argument for me to help her, she must be completely bats. If helping her find Moll means she'll be here forever and the other girls find out that was because of me . . . that's all I need.*

Later, even years later, these thoughts would come back to me. I don't deny the uncharitable nature of them or the impulse behind my unwaveringly stubborn stance. Nobody liked Bleaker, Nobody liked Moll, but for different reasons. One was disliked because of the power she wielded; the other was disliked because she was easy to victimize. At a Quaker school, the victim came first, theoretically. Bleaker had other choices, other tools at her disposal but she chose shaming and bullying. I wasn't about to give in to her and, it occurred to me, in a less than altruistic vein, that if I told her about where Moll was, she could turn her bullying in my direction. And hadn't I already seen evidence of that? Even at fifteen, I knew that you couldn't make an honest deal with a person whose motives were suspect.

THIRTY-SIX

The Last Call

THREE NIGHTS LATER, THURSDAY, MOLL CALLED ME. I HADN'T expected it so Jenny answered the phone again.

"Greenwood, for you—again." She yelled with impatience as if to say, "Why can't you answer your own damned calls?"

I'd been castigating myself for not setting up another time to phone Moll at my parents' apartment. But then I also told myself that there was so much on my mind at the time, I really wasn't thinking ahead but just trying to manage what was right in front of me. Which, in addition to my visit from Bleaker, included a note from Mr. Williamson, delivered to me the next day at breakfast, to come to his office in my free period after lunch. He knew when I had a free period, of course. "They" knew everything about us, except for whatever secrets of our Foxhall lives we could manage to keep from "them."

I didn't rush to get to the phone this time. With barely a week left before Christmas break and Bleaker already well aware that I had gotten at least one call from Moll, it didn't seem important to hide from it anymore. I vaguely wondered if they could listen in on the line and if they could, was that even legal. I guessed they could argue that the phones on our halls belonged to the school. Anyway, I wasn't worried about it. Just a passing paranoid thought. I knew kids back home whose parents sometimes listened in on their conversations. My parents never did that. If anything they were probably too hands off. They had so many other concerns I was left pretty much to my own devices. But while I recognized that at least Bleaker and Mr. Williamson knew that I had been in contact with Moll, I still couldn't talk about it with any of my friends, as potentially that could put them in the hot seat and they might not feel as protective toward Moll as I did or might not even believe her bridge threat was real. After all, they hadn't heard her. And I figured Bleaker and Headmaster Williamson were too afraid of the consequences if they pushed me too far so they were holding back. In an odd way, it was the most comfortable I'd felt at Foxhall since my arrival. Like I had some kind of amulet protecting me.

I picked up the phone from the little table, and scrunched down into the corner.

"Hello?"

"Is that you?" Moll's voice sounded small and far away.

"Yes. It's me. Where are you?"

"Still in your apartment. Listen I wanted to tell you so you wouldn't worry anymore."

"Tell me what?"

"I've made a decision."

"About what?" I'd heard somewhere that when someone decided to take their own life, they became resolute, even calm. It didn't make sense to me but the hair on my arms prickled and I wished I had gone to New York to be there with Moll.

"Listen, Moll, I know how upset you are but think about what you're doing. There are people who love you and want to see you. The whole school is upset and wants you to come back."

She cut me off before I could think of any more arguments or lies.

"I appreciate what you're trying to do. Really I do. You're about the only person who's ever bothered to try to understand how I feel. I know my mother loves me—in her own way—and that my brother cares about me. But he has his own life and that's fine. My mother will just have to get over this. One day I was bound to leave so she should have known it was coming."

Oh God, I thought, *how do I talk her down now?* But I didn't have a chance because she continued.

"I've thought about this a lot. Being at a Quaker school actually helped me. It wasn't just Miss Bleaker who tipped the scales. She was an aggravating factor, that's true. She made me feel all the worst feelings I've ever felt about myself all at once. I don't believe things will ever get better for me at Foxhall or any other school. It doesn't make any difference where I am. It's the culture that I don't fit into. I'm not pretty and I never will be. I'm not gregarious and I never will be. I'm not funny, or witty, or engaging. I don't have any social grace and I feel embarrassed around other people. I know other girls look at me and think I'm a nobody and a loser. Boys don't look at me at all. I'm nothing but invisible to them. See what happened when you tried to get one boy to talk to me? That was a sign. And now I have to act on that sign. And maybe it's better this way. At least I know I'll be accepted."

What was she talking about? I thought she was finished and was about to ask when she began again.

"I don't want you to blame yourself for any of this. You tried your best, but I'm a losing proposition. You're better off trying to help those people in Philadelphia at that soup kitchen. So this is the last time we'll be talking. I'll try to leave the apartment exactly the way it was when I got here so no one will know and you won't have to explain anything. I want to thank you for all your kindness."

"Moll," I whispered into the phone because I felt I had to interrupt her before she hung up. "What are you going to do? Please, please tell me and talk to me about it."

"I met some people. I met them at the train station when I first got to New York. They're really nice. They said I could join them at any time. They said they're part of a new group started by a great leader. They said everyone is welcome and everyone is equal within the group. They said everyone gets a partner for life and eventually they all marry in a big cere- mony together to affirm their vows and their faith. It's what I have always wanted. To be included and accepted. They were understanding and sympathetic. They didn't try to change me or tell me anything about me was wrong."

"Oh, Moll, what group is this and how do you know they're not dangerous?"

"I know it because I feel it. I'll be happy within the group. I'll be able to lose myself and become one with them. And I'll find a life mate. I know it's not what anyone at Foxhall would understand. Or what my mother would understand. But this is right for me. I feel it deep down inside."

"But what is the group called?" At first I thought she was

going to become a nun, but then I thought maybe she was going to become a Mormon or perhaps a Seventh Day Adventist, or possibly some highly religious Jewish sect. Whatever it was, it sounded like the kind of commitment she wouldn't be able to get out of once she got in.

"It's been started by the Reverend Sun Myung Moon. He's Korean and he's just begun to accept members to the Unification Church here. He's brilliant and I know this is the right thing for me. I finally feel safe. So I wanted to tell you good-bye and thank you for all your kindness. My friends will pick me up at dawn tomorrow which will be the dawn of my new life."

Before I could say anything else, she had hung up the phone. I heard a soft click and that was that.

THIRTY-SEVEN

Bleaker

I'D NEVER SEEN A DEAD BODY BEFORE. AND IF I HAD, IT probably would have been in a satin-lined casket at some fancy funeral home, the deceased dressed to the nines with rouged cheeks and coiffed hair. One thing was sure, it wouldn't have been hanging all alone from a beam in a room that could house six hundred people. Just floating about eight feet off the floor, a ladder kicked over on its side beneath its feet, still in their sensible brown shoes with black stockings stopped just above bony knees below the creamy white flesh of thighs. You could see right up her black dress and that was what I'll always remember. She had on lacy pink panties and a pink garter belt.

I'd told Daria once that Bleaker wouldn't have been a panty hose wearer. That she'd have gone for the clandestine femininity of lace underwear that no one could see but her. So I was right.

That I was the one who found her that Friday morning following Moll's call, added an extra sadistic twist to her death. She must have planned it that way. Later, when the air had cleared and I'd gotten back to what everyone called normal, that was what I thought. She'd have wanted me to know how guilty she felt. And she'd have wanted me to feel guilty, too. Guilty about her and about Moll. I never told anyone that, especially not Daria. She would have laughed at me and sneered at the idea that Bleaker ever thought about me at all. But she'd have been wrong. I came to understand that much later, too, because hanging herself in the Assembly Room where she must have known I would find her first—how could she not have known it was my chore to sweep between the rows of seats early on Friday mornings before assembly since she'd assigned me that chore—was an act of revenge. And later I would remember the paper in her hands, remember her reading it as if we were in class and she was the teacher.

Daria had told me once that Bleaker was subversive just like we were, only she did it to make herself feel like she was the most important part of the system, while we did it to make ourselves feel powerful over the system. So maybe hanging herself like that, in the most public place there was at Foxhall, turned out to be a subversive act for Bleaker. And maybe Daria was right about that part. It was one of the things I would never know.

I didn't scream or do anything dramatic like you see in the movies when people come upon a scene like that. I just stood there inside the double doors a few yards from her dangling feet. I think I even advanced a few steps, which was how I could see up her skirt and that was where I stopped. I mean what could I do?

Thoughts whirled by fast then. I imagined righting the ladder and trying to reach her but I think I shuddered at that prospect. And I imagined a body would be too heavy for me.

Dead weight. That phrase came to me and suddenly I knew precisely what it meant.

I was still holding my broom and dustpan. And just staring up. Then I noticed the neck tilted at a crazy, impossible angle and it hit me that she was dead. Hanged by the neck until dead—that phrase echoed, too. And when it did, I began to shake and the dustpan clattered to the floor because my fingers stopped working properly and then the broom banged down at my feet and still I could not look away. The eyes. The eyes stared out. Not at me, but past me, as if at something behind me, and that was when I lost it and a shriek wanted to escape from my mouth but couldn't. My mouth was open. But no sound emerged. I wanted to run but I could not move either.

I have no idea or memory of how long I stood there like a tree stump. But somehow voices came to me and then a hand grabbed my arm and there were people everywhere and then I remember nothing else until I woke up in the school infirmary, in a room with a narrow bed and white walls and a white glass-domed ceiling light and a window that looked out toward the school kitchen where the black men and women who were the backbone of the school workings came and went every day, laughing and grousing, cooking and cleaning, singing and arguing, keeping us privileged kids nourished three times a day. I could hear them now because the window was open.

"Hey Clyde, you goan ruint dem beans, you put dem in dat pot too lowng."

"Nobody goan gimme no ride home tonight wid all dese heah . . ."

"Getchyoo over to duh plates and pick me up a . . ."

And then I heard one of the boys I knew—one of the ones who'd bet on me in the nipple pool. I knew because Daria had told me he'd be a good one to win it because he was known for his kissing technique, all tongue, she'd said. His voice came in clear, "Jimmy, I heard you could get me some reefer . . ."

"You be gettin' me in foh some big troubles, boy, you come 'roun heah foh dat . . ."

I didn't understand what he wanted from Jimmy but then I drifted out again and woke up and the sun was gone and twilight had come and the school nurse was standing by the bed, holding my wrist looking at her watch and that was when I remembered. And I did scream. Like in some horror movie. When I couldn't stop she slapped me across the face one time and told me it was all over.

"One of the deans called your parents," she said. "I'm sorry but Doctor Grady said I was to slap you if you screamed again. He said the shock would bring you back to your senses."

Screamed again? Had I screamed before? I wanted to punch her. And the last thing I wanted was to see my parents. My parents . . . as if they would both come to get me. Not likely with my mother still in some hospital somewhere, as far as I knew. I had a lot to scream about. Why couldn't they all just let me alone?

"Where's Daria?" I asked.

"You mean Daria McQueen?"

"Yes."

"If you think that would help you, I'll call her hall and see if she can come over."

"Yes, please," I think I tried to smile. Just to convince her I was all right, to get her out of my room. I could feel the sting of her fingers on my left cheek and all I could think was my mother had done that, too.

I must have drifted off again because when I opened my eyes Daria was sitting in a wooden chair next to my bed.

"Hi," she said.

I stared at her. I wasn't sure if I was dreaming or awake. So I tried to say something and it came out kind of croaky.

"Did you see her?"

Daria shook her head.

"It was all over by the time I got there. They blocked off the Assembly Room. But I heard about it. The police came later."

"Who got her down?"

"Oh my God," she said, "it took three of the little men and two ladders."

I nodded, imagining the scene.

"Everyone's talking about it," Daria said. "And about you finding her."

I nodded again.

"She was wearing lacy pink panties and a garter belt," I whispered to Daria. I didn't want the nurse to hear me.

"No shit?" Daria whispered back. "A closet female? Bleaker?"

She grinned and I suddenly felt a whole lot better. Now that I knew how Daria was taking it, I even thought I could face my parents, if by some miracle they actually showed up at Foxhall to help me through this.

And then Daria looked serious.

"What about Moll?" she asked.

Before I could say anything else, the nurse came back in and told Daria it was time to leave and she could come back later for another visit.

Before she left, Daria leaned down as if to give me a kiss on the cheek or something and whispered in my ear, "Headmaster's doing a special assembly about it tomorrow morning and then there's a special meeting for worship that the whole school has to attend. Lucky you, get to miss all the maudlin hysteria. Sleep well."

And then she was gone.

THIRTY-EIGHT

A Visit from Wes

DARIA WAS WRONG. I WANTED TO GO TO THAT MEETING for Worship. Because there was nothing wrong with me physically, the nurse couldn't prevent me from leaving. I just didn't want to walk in there alone, so I waited a little while after Daria left and when Mrs. Waller came in to check me again, I asked her if I could call someone else.

"Not yet, dear," she told me. "But if you want me to call or get a message to someone else for you I can do that. Meantime would you like some tea or maybe a snack? I can ask the kitchen to send something over for you."

"Can you ask Wes Ritter to come over?"

"Do you know where he would be now?"

"What time is it?" I had completely lost track. "I should be in class now."

"You're allowed to be resting so don't worry about your classes. I'm sure your teachers will give you extensions. Let's see," she looked at her nurse type watch, worn around her left wrist with the face on the inside so she turned her hand up to see it. "It's almost two. That makes it the end of—what —fifth period?"

"Yes," I said. "He should be leaving physics when the period's over. I think his next class is calc with Mr. Benning."

"I'll get a note to him for you. Do you want him to visit after class or after sports?"

"After class," I said.

All of a sudden I felt simply exhausted, like I couldn't keep my eyes open or speak anymore. I must have fallen off to sleep. Later, when I would awaken as if from a long absence, the last thing I would remember thinking was that Mrs. Waller would have been a nice mom to have. I didn't dream or even turn over. I knew that because when I did wake up, with Wes sitting in a chair pulled over to my bedside, I was in exactly the same spot and position in the bed and nothing came to my mind about my sleep. It was as blank as if I'd never existed before I woke up. But I had existed. And there was Wes to prove it.

"Hi." He smiled down at me.

He seemed a million miles away until my eyes focused and I slowly came awake.

"How you doing?" He reached out and laid his hand on mine.

My hand felt heavy, and as if it was not attached to anything, like a brick left on my bed in the white room with nothing on the walls, this sterile, comforting room, like a little chapel.

"Mrs. Waller's nice." *Why did I say that?*

"Yeah," Wes said. "She is."

I took a deep breath. Images started coming to me. Disturbing images. I shut my eyes tight to hold them back but they came cascading in anyway. My shoulders began to shiver. I was cold. Or no . . . I was not cold. I was shaking. But I couldn't move. How could I be shaking and completely still at the same time? I could feel the weight on my hand, feel Wes squeezing it, feel his energy and that was what made me open my eyes and turn to look at him.

"I'm here," he said.

"I want to go to Meeting For Worship."

"You're not ready," he whispered. "You need to stay here. Take it easy."

"I want to go. Help me go. Please."

"Mrs. Waller won't sign you out. She says you're not to leave the infirmary."

"Please . . ."

"How?" he asked.

"I don't know." My voice was shaky. Somewhere I knew I should stay put. But somewhere else, I knew I had to go to Meeting, had to tell everyone what I thought, why I did what I did, had to explain to the whole school so they heard it from me. No rumors. No wild stories. No making things up to suit their purposes. I began to feel stronger, thinking about what I wanted to say at Meeting.

"By tomorrow morning, I could get out of here," I said. "Could you ask Daria to bring me some new clothes to wear? She could come over after dinner."

"What will you say tomorrow?"

I stared at the ceiling. It was so hard to collect my thoughts. I wondered where Moll was right then.

"Have they called my parents?" I asked and then added, "Because it won't do any good. I guess my mother's still in the hospital. I don't know where my father is right now."

"I don't know about that. I haven't talked to any faculty or deans."

"The deans. Oh God. Who's taking over for Bleaker?"

"I heard Miss Alderton but it may be only a rumor."

I moved my legs slightly, vaguely aware that I was starting to feel stiff from lying in the same position so long.

"What are kids saying?" I asked, and turned to see his face. Wes was lousy at hiding his emotions so it would be easy to see if he was covering anything.

"Well, you know how it is."

"How?"

"Oh, some stupid jokes and stuff. Nothing to get upset over."

"Like what?"

"Are you sure you want to talk about this now?"

"What jokes?"

"Well, there's this one. 'Guess who got caught hanging around Greenwood?'"

"Nice," I muttered. "Any others?"

"Yeah. 'The Assembly Room's the new spot for just hanging around.'"

"So I'm the school joke now?"

"Not exactly. A lot of kids are just wandering around looking for someone to tell them why it happened. And rumors are flying. You know how that is."

"What kind of rumors?"

"Weird ones. Like about Moll. That she's dead somewhere and it was a suicide pact with Bleaker. That's the most outrageous one. Nobody really knows what happened except the story about Bleaker chastising Moll at the dance over something. I mean that's what's really weird. Nobody even knew who Moll was before this and no one can figure out why Bleaker singled her out at the dance. What happened anyway?"

My thoughts began churning again.

Wes doesn't know. He might think I'm hiding something again. Something else to worry about. I can't take one more thing. Not now. How much should I tell him? This makes me look really bad, like I didn't tell Bleaker and then this is all my fault. But how was I to know what would happen? I couldn't have known Bleaker would do this or Moll would run away or anything else. But maybe I should have seen how Bleaker was cracking. I've seen it with my mother. But she never tried to kill herself. She just fell apart and went away. Then came back and was sort of normal for a while and then fell apart again. How could I tell with Bleaker? Except for that weird letter she read to me.

Wes fidgeted in the scratched-up wooden school chair next to my bed.

"If you don't want to tell me, that's okay," he said. "But I bet you're going to have to tell somebody. I mean the school can't just let this go."

"Oh," I said. "I hadn't thought about that."

"What are you thinking about?"

I rolled over onto my side to face him. I pulled the top sheet up and tucked it under my chin. The sheets felt buttery soft from being washed over and over for years. The white room with no adornments was comforting in a spiritual kind of way. There was one window, fairly large, that looked out to the woods behind the infirmary. The trees were bare by then, the branches made lacy patterns against the clear afternoon sky. Soon it would be dark. The shorter days of winter were here. Very soon now we would once again scatter for the school break. At that moment, I wondered if Wes still wanted me to come to Carmel for Christmas.

"Christmas break. Where I'll end up. What's going to happen now. What kind of trouble I'll be in."

"Can't you tell me what happened?" He leaned toward the bed. "I won't judge you or tell anyone."

So I told him. Told him the whole story. He listened quietly, nodded once or twice, but didn't say anything until I finished. Then I waited. And even then, even with all that had happened, my biggest concern was that Wes might want to break up with me.

"Wow," he finally said. "I feel bad that you had to carry all this around by yourself."

Before he even finished what he had to say I was thinking: *So he doesn't want to break up. He's being supportive. Why do I keep misjudging him? Why can't I accept what a really good guy he is? What's wrong with me?*

"I don't know what you could have done," he was saying. "I mean I think you were put into an impossible situation between Moll and Bleaker. It wasn't fair. I mean the school is responsible for how they treat students and for what happens to students. They're kind of like surrogate parents while we're all here. They should have watched more closely."

I interrupted him. Even though I was arguing against myself, I had to say something.

"But you know they don't know half the stuff that really goes on. I mean like the mattress room and the wire. Even us at the trestle."

I glanced at him and he smiled that little intimate smile of his.

"Yeah," he said. "I'm glad they don't monitor some stuff. That's one of them."

Mrs. Waller poked her head in the door. "Time for you to go, Wes," she said. "And you need to rest now." She pointed at me and turned from the doorway. We could hear her nurse's shoes squishing against the floor tiles.

"Listen," he said as he stood up. "I'll get Daria to bring you some clothes for tomorrow morning. And I'll come over and get you out of here somehow. Maybe by then they'll let you out anyway. Just be really careful about what you plan to say at Meeting."

"I know," I told him. "And Wes . . ."

"Yeah?" He was heading for the door but turned back.

"About coming to Carmel?"

"My mom says she can't wait to meet you."

THIRTY-NINE

By the Book

I DIDN'T KNOW IT, BUT WHILE I WAS LYING IN BED IN THE infirmary, a boy named Linden Houghtling was working overtime in the photo lab down in Wetherall, which was the art center. Linden was president of the photography club so he spent a lot of time in the dark room, which was why no one questioned him about being there at odd times.

The week after Thanksgiving break, the girls had a scheduled swim and dive meet. I'd been practicing my double forward somersault in preparation for it. Our practices were restricted to the girls team so, during practice, we were alone in the gym. Daria was doing a more complicated dive routine than I was. Naturally, I was in awe of her control and discipline. She'd been a state champion from Connecticut twice before she came to Foxhall, but downplayed her ability saying she'd never be good enough to go to the Olympics. Well, who would be?

The day of the meet, a group of boys streamed into the gym and took their places on the metal bleachers. There was a good amount of shoving and pointing and laughing until one of the coaches gave them a dirty look and they settled down.

"Look," Daria nudged me in the rib cage, "the Nipple Brigade has been put in its place."

"Why can't they just stay away?" I held up my hand to whisper it to her as if I thought there might be a lip reader among them, which was idiotic.

"Are you kidding? For them the sport is not the diving. You know that. Just ignore them. Or do what I do."

"What's that?"

"Play to the crowd, honey lamb. Flaunt what God gave you."

But I was not like Daria. And, although Miss Alderton had warned me I had to use the pool ladder at meets I tried to ignore the brigade, in fact tried to ignore everything to better concentrate on my routine, going over and over in my mind the double forward, exactly where I would place my feet, how high I had to spring on the board, how close to come to the edge without tripping myself by going too far and catching the top lip of the board, when to tuck, how hard to pull in, when to extend, how close to the water to enter, all the details step-by-step in my dive mind, still I couldn't completely erase the images of boy after boy settling in to watch. And I didn't notice Linden Houghtling with a new and very tiny camera. Looking back on it, I doubt that anyone saw that camera. And even if anyone had noticed what he was holding, after the meet was over, no one heard anything about it. And, because of photography club, he was always snapping pictures of students and teachers and buildings and random cats and dogs wandering around the campus.

———

I ate dinner in the infirmary again. One of the students who had early kitchen slop brought it over and Mrs. Waller let her bring it to my room. Her name was Anna Sue. Most of the students were from the northeast or New Jersey or Pennsylvania but Anna Sue was from Georgia. A certain group of boys—Stocky for one—called her Magnolia Peachtree. She didn't seem to mind because it got her noticed. She was a sweet girl, a little awkward and didn't seem to get it when the boys teased her.

"Hi," she said. She seemed kind of embarrassed.

"Hi."

"Here's your dinner." She shrugged one shoulder. "It's what they gave me. I guess it's what everyone's having."

"Thanks. Hey, Anna Sue, um, could you tell me something?"

"Sure." She laid the tray down on the little table by my bed. Whatever was under there didn't smell too good. "What is it?"

"What are people saying? About . . . you know . . . Miss Bleaker and everything."

"They've kind of stopped talking about it now that . . ."

She stopped abruptly.

"Now that what?"

"Just some stupid stuff some of the boys are doing."

"What are they doing?"

"Oh, I don't know. Listen I've got to get back, okay? So, y'all get better." Anna Sue's drawl was somehow comforting to hear at that moment.

I picked at the food until Mrs. Waller came in.

"Your father is calling you. We don't have phones in the rooms so you'll have to take it at my desk."

I looked at the clock. Six fifteen. Daria would be coming over soon with my clothes. I was still wearing my clothes from yesterday. I needed a shower and wanted to get out of that bed anyway.

Mrs. Waller left the room so I'd have some privacy to talk. Her board showed I was the only one in the infirmary.

"Hello."

"Hi, angel face. How's my girl?"

"I'm okay."

"I spoke to Mr. Williamson. He said the whole school's in shock. They're worried about you."

"Why?"

"Come on, sweetheart, it must have been awful for you."

"Not really. I mean, it was at first but I'm okay now."

"You're a strong girl. I'm proud of you."

"I don't know why. I didn't do anything. Where are you anyway?"

"I'm up in Rochester, researching a company."

"Rochester, New York or Minnesota?"

"New York."

It was incredible how we could talk and not say anything.

"Your mother's doing better. Her doctor says he's hopeful she could start taking a weekend outside soon."

"Oh, that's really good."

"I'm afraid you'll have to go to your aunt and uncle's this Christmas, though. I have to work straight through. I really won't be home except for Christmas Eve and Christmas Day.

I was thinking I could spend that time at your aunt and uncle's, too. At least we'd get to visit a bit."

"Well, a friend invited me to spend Christmas break in Carmel. Out in California. So I was going to ask you if that would be okay with you."

"Sure. I guess so. Would you need plane tickets?"

"Don't worry. I can get them. I have plenty of money in my school bank account still. I didn't have time to spend any money over Thanksgiving. You know, with the soup kitchen and all."

"But you're okay now? I mean about that dean and everything."

"Yeah, Dad, I'm fine. I'll be out of the infirmary tomorrow and back in classes. I really don't need to be here now anyway."

At that moment I saw Daria at the door. She waved and pushed the door open.

"Dad, I have to go. Someone's here to see me."

"Okay, sweetheart. Will you call me from California? You can always call my secretary and give her the number where you are."

"Sure. Um, can you call the dean's office and tell them it's okay if I go out there for Christmas break? I need permission to go anywhere but home. And say 'Hi' to Mom when you see her. Bye."

I made a swipe across my forehead to let Daria know I'd escaped yet another confrontation with an adult. She raised her eyebrows and when I hung up the phone, I said, "My dad."

"Oh. Right. Parents just don't get it."

We went back to my room where I climbed into bed again.

"I brought your stuff. Is there a shower here?"

"Yeah, there's one down the hall. I really want to get out of here. I'm going to see if Mrs. Waller will let me go tonight. What's going on out there?"

"Oh, nothing. Except the Nipple Brigade has struck."

"Oh God, what did they do?"

"That guy Linden made a nipple yearbook."

"A what?"

"He blew up all the pictures he's taken at the meets of the dive team's nipples and then pasted them all into a book he made up. He numbered them and then pasted pictures of all the girls on the team and gave them different numbers. The guy who matches up all the nipples to the right girls first wins. He gets his name written into the first page of the book as a dedication. And he gets some plaque they've made in shop class that says Nipple King 1960-61."

"That's sick."

"Yeah, but the guys are, like, going crazy trying to match them up. Linden made a master list from numbers he assigned all the photographs. He's the only one who knows the match ups. His room was ransacked trying to find the list. Guys are bribing him. It's a real scene."

"It's mortifying. Can't anyone stop them?"

"I don't think so. Unless they get caught. And, you know, who's going to turn them in? They never could find the mattress room key. They'll never find this either."

FORTY

Meeting for Worship

MEETING FOR WORSHIP WAS PACKED. I'D NEVER SEEN THE Assembly Room so full. Even the balcony rows were overflowing so that people were sitting on the aisle steps. Wes met me outside the Social Room after Mrs. Waller let me leave the infirmary. I was officially better, I guess. I'd spent much of the night writing and rewriting what I wanted to say at Meeting.

"Are you sure you want to go?" Wes asked.

"I'm sure. I have to get all this off my chest." I waved the papers at him.

"You could just let me read what you've written."

"No. I don't care what happens anymore. I want to have my say."

"Your day in court?"

"Maybe. At least my day without anyone influencing me. At least these are my thoughts and feelings."

"Okay. I'll stand with you if you want."

I took his hand and squeezed it. "Thank you. But I don't want anyone else's future on my conscience. I'll stand alone."

It was a surprising new me. I should have been terrified. In shock. Withdrawn. Tentative about what to do next. I should have felt guilty. Yet that was not happening. For the first time since I'd left home and arrived at Foxhall, I just didn't care what anyone else thought. It was like I was itching for a fight. Maybe not a fight. Not even a confrontation. No, I wanted to let everyone know what I thought. Not what I thought would make me look cool. Not what would get me accepted. And that was another thing. This wasn't really about me. It was about one girl who was so unsure of herself that one authority saying one cruel thing to her sent her over the edge. I was not going to let Bleaker off the hook. Even after what had happened.

So I took the hand Wes offered, glad he was there with me, but not about to let him stand as a shield between me and my fate, and walked into the Assembly Room to say my piece at Meeting For Worship.

We took two seats on an aisle about halfway between the stage and the back doors. Up on stage the facing bench was full. Ten chairs. Six faculty members, one dean, three students. Mr. Williamson sat in one of two middle chairs. Next to him, the president of the student council, a smarmy senior named Garret Holyfield, elected because the one person who ran against him was accused of stealing his roommate's watch after said watch was found at the back of his closet in an old sock. Jan told me she thought it was a Holyfield plant.

The elected senior was what was known at Foxhall as a credit collector—kids who would sign up for just about anything so they could add it as an extracurricular interest to their college admissions forms. The two other students were on the student conduct committee and one of them was also on the faculty-student rules committee. Foxhall was rife with committees. An integral part of life at the school was to serve on at least one committee. Miss Alderton was up there in one of the chairs, as was Mr. Henderson. I was surprised to see my Latin teacher, Mr. D'Amico, on the facing bench along with Mr. Brownell, who I thought looked like he was in pain. At the last minute, Mrs. Doyle, who had taught Moll Greek, ran in and took the last facing bench seat at one end. Moll once told me that was the one class where she felt comfortable because she was the only student. She told me that after our Quaker Life class. I thought she felt safe there, included and listened to, but I'd been wrong because that day, after class, when she told me about being the only student in Mrs. Doyle's Greek class, she also said, "If you weren't in Quaker Life class, I'd never say a word." I didn't understand then, and never did understand, why Moll had attached herself to me like moss to a tree or why she felt she could unburden herself to me.

So there they were, staring out at us from the facing bench. And then, as it always did, the room began to settle down on its own as if a fog had descended to muffle all the sounds and a subdued quiet replaced the chatter and mumbling that always preceded Meeting. It was my plan to stand up right at the beginning and say what I had to say and then sit through the rest of Meeting with my head down. To that end, I'd brought a Bible I'd plundered from the infirmary.

Some of the kids hid other books inside their Bibles. But mostly, we came into Meeting clean, sat for the allotted time, thought our thoughts, and left the way we'd entered—neither worse nor better for the time elapsed. I wish I could say we were all uplifted because of our meditations. Some probably were. But most of us likely were not.

I didn't get the chance to speak first because China popped up like a bean sprout. I should have seen that coming. As soon as she stood up you could hear a general soft shuffling sound spread through the Assembly Room. But she didn't notice, it seemed, and began to do her usual "My parents are missionaries" thing. But then she veered off and talked about how once when a village elder died, how the villagers had celebrated his life with singing and chanting and dancing for two days and nights. She was surprised by that and found it quite uplifting, she said. Uplifting, as if the elder's spirit had been truly uplifted to heaven. She sat down abruptly. Her voice had a tremor in it at the end.

My fingers were having trouble holding the paper where I'd written out what I wanted to say. I was struggling to get control of my hands when from the stage came Mr. Brownell's soft voice.

"It is at times like these, rare as they may be, that we search within the community of spirit to ease our shock and calm our grief."

As he began, I looked across the row to where Daria, Tim, Brady, Faith, Jan, and Stocky were all sitting. I expected Daria and Jan to have those slightly cynical expressions they usually had but was surprised to see Daria, especially Daria, with tears glistening on her cheeks. Jan's head was bowed. Faith looked straight ahead and Brady looked as if she had been wounded somehow and was trying not to show the pain.

"For we are a community," Mr. Brownell was continuing. "A community in more than spirit but no less than spirit. For the spirit that resides in each of us has its own voice, its own purpose, its own dimension, immeasurable by any standards and complete within itself. We are here to support each other and when one of us falls outside the circle of spirit, we mourn for all our spirits. We might feel we failed our spirit sister. I caution especially the young people in our community not to despair even as we say farewell to one of the spirits among us. Life is a long road and at the same time a short one. Young people must look to the future while learning within the present. It is our mission—our mission undertaken together here at Foxhall—to always aspire to a more centered space within the spirit of community and the life of individuality. Rely on each other, confide in each other, trust each other as a community of one collective spirit out of many singular ones."

Before I could stand, Mr. Williamson began to speak.

"I am reminded today of the difficulty in knowing what is right."

He means me. He's speaking right to me. So they all think it's my fault. That I did the wrong thing. That I screwed up the whole school, upset the equilibrium.

"The right thing is not always the easy thing or the clear thing. At times we are faced with choices in life that are not clear-cut. That's when we must look to the inner light to guide us on the path of right. We have all faced a shocking situation here at Foxhall. We are all part of it. No one person is responsible. Perhaps it is a lesson for all of us that we never know what is in the heart of another and therefore we must tread carefully lest we do damage, even without realizing it beforehand. The human heart can be fragile. The human soul can be bruised. The human mind can be distorted. So we must find it within ourselves to always allow the dignity of the human spirit to shine through.

"I want to read a note that was found in Miss Bleaker's possession after her death. Perhaps it will explain, at least in some small measure, the events we have all experienced."

He read the same note that Bleaker had read in my room. And I realized it had not been about some abstract concept but about her and how she viewed her life—and ultimately her death.

When he stopped, silence once again filled the vast Assembly Room with its tall windows and row upon row of old wooden seats, each held to the next by a network of iron fittings, each seat with a hymnal in its holder beneath the seat. This was my chance and I stood and looked over the rows I could see from my position on the main floor midway between the doors and the stage. I held the paper tightly in front of me and cleared my throat. Then, something came over me. I couldn't say what. It was like the spirit that was supposed to move you to speak at Meeting For Worship actually found its voice from somewhere inside me, or perhaps around me, or even from the air I breathed in at that moment. All I can say was I felt untethered for a few seconds, maybe less, maybe more, but certainly for some indeterminate time, as if an updraft had lifted me and separated me from myself—or at least from the self that monitored my own feelings and doubts and fears. In that moment, I also felt a wave of something unseen hovering there with me, a benign yet powerful sense that I was not alone, that all the people in that great room, there with me, were part of this feeling that I was not alone and this sense of well-being felt like a blessing of some kind.

Maybe it was simply adrenaline. Or the feeling a runner gets during a race. Endorphins maybe or some other surge of energy. I had no need to examine it then. I simply felt it and, from that place, I began to speak.

"This is all new to me," I began. My own voice sounded hollow to me, as if from inside a giant tin can that made the sound reverberate.

"I've only been coming to Quaker Meeting for three months, so I've never been moved to speak before. I know we're supposed to voice some spiritual concern but I guess that leaves a lot open to interpretation."

By now my voice didn't have the hollow sound in my ears anymore. But I noticed something else. A lack of sound, or rather a lack of the sound of anything but my voice. I'd become used to the sounds of shuffling, coughing, throat clearing, even muffled whispers during Meeting. But I'd never heard the sound of absolute quiet before. The sun had risen high enough by then to cast a glowing light through the tall windows, a light that spread across the room making everything look softer. I looked up then, up to the beam where Bleaker's body had hung.

"I don't know if the spirit is moving me or if it's events that have made me stand here today. Maybe you could argue that the spirit is always operating while events are transitory. I'm not smart enough or educated enough to know how to interpret a spiritual awakening. I'm only left with questions. Like, was it her spirit that made Miss Bleaker hang herself in this very room?"

There, I had said it out loud. She hanged herself. I waited for the gasp but it didn't come. In that few seconds, I knew that nobody was going to stop me or make me sit down.

"It seems like an awful way to die. I hope when I die, I just drift off to sleep and enter another dimension. I hope it's not painful or violent. I hope it's like coming home. To a spiritual home. I can't believe it was that way for Miss Bleaker. I think she must have been very unhappy and tortured about her life. I can't say I thought about that when she was here. I've only thought about it after. Because before, when she was someone who had power over me, I thought of her as an enemy, as someone who was only there to thwart me. I wasn't the only one who thought that. It was probably cruel and thoughtless of me to think that way. I can say that now but I never would have admitted it to anyone, especially myself, before."

I hadn't looked down at the paper in my hand yet but now my glance fell on the word Moll. I looked up again, at the light streaming through the windows, streams that glared a little, no longer soft, early-morning light, but mid-morning rays soon to reach their most piercing.

"There's really not much more I can say about that. Except no one has talked about Moll Grimes. And she's the person who really suffered because of all this. She doesn't know what happened here and, if I could speak to her, I would never tell her about it because it would just make her feel worse about herself. So what's the point of making a person feel worse? Poor Moll. So unsure of herself. I mean, I think we're all unsure of ourselves in some way but Moll was unsure in almost every way. She was only trying to feel pretty. What's wrong with that? Is that unQuakerly? Is that against some sort of rulebook? Moll wanted to fit in, at least to try. And she got squashed the first time out of the gate. And that makes me angry, on her behalf.

"In Quaker Life class we learned about how Friends side with the abused and disenfranchised of this world through everyday activities and on a global political level, through work camps and the American Friends Service Committee. Sit-ins and soup kitchens and working for political refugees and those without any power.

"Maybe I'll get in trouble for saying these things. I guess I don't really care much about that anymore. But what about a girl like poor Moll, who never hurt anyone? What kind of a place is it where students ostracize and ignore the weaker ones? What about the Miss Bleakers of this world, who misuse their power and authority without understanding how it hurts the ones they're supposed to be helping?

"I'll never see Moll again. She ran away to join some group where she feels wanted and accepted. I don't know if it's a better group than a Quaker group was for her. I sure hope so. I hope she finds some contentment. And a place to use her brain, which is exceptional. Better than mine, certainly. Why can't we be prized for the gifts we do bring instead of chastised for those we don't? I can't answer that. But it's something I'm going to strive for from now on. It's something I hope to be able to develop. I want to accept people for who they are and what they offer. Isn't that what Foxhall is supposed to be about?"

When I sat down, there was not one sound in the room. I looked down at my hands, holding the papers that I hadn't even read. They were not shaking anymore. Wes reached over and squeezed my arm.

FORTY-ONE

Christmas Break

So what was it all about after all? Sometimes life seemed like a conspiracy theory. Nobody really knew the totality of what happened, so everyone felt free to weave stories out of bits and pieces that didn't necessarily fit together. The old saying that truth was stranger than fiction may be the closest I would ever come to untangling the threads of my first sophomore semester at Foxhall School.

One truth I knew: power would always seek to increase its strength in whatever way it could. It was like one of those infernal black holes whirling out there in space, pulling every bit of matter into itself until it would be crushed by its own pressure. But power could never operate on all fronts at all times. It was in power's unattended gaps where the meek might make their move. Would they truly inherit the earth? To be honest, I didn't think anyone would inherit anything. We were all so temporary. One direct hit by a big asteroid and we could all be gone, leaving the earth to re-imagine itself over the next few millennia.

What happened to Moll and Bleaker would fade from collective memory at Foxhall. Today, I'm sure no one knows what happened back in that first semester of 1960. Today, things are radically different at Foxhall. The students there now would look back at my first semester and wonder what the fuss was about. And today, the cult started by Sung Myung Moon owns newspapers, multinational corporations, and banks and still adheres to the ideology of its founder. I have no idea if joining what became known years later as the Moonies was good or bad for Moll, probably some of both. But here is what I believe: she finally felt accepted otherwise she wouldn't have followed them.

Continuity. Plants know about that. Trees lose their leaves and the next season start all over, pushing out the green buds with fervor and certainty in the future. People are like that, too. Resilient, always looking for a recovery, a new start, often giving birth under awful circumstances but doing it anyway. While we continue the paths that have been laid before us, we look over the hill at new vistas, turn corners, and meet new possibilities.

I never did get to California for Christmas. I was interviewed at length by Mr. Williamson, Miss Alderton, and Mr. Brownell, who turned out to be incredibly understanding and kind. They asked countless questions about Moll. I told them everything I knew. I never did meet her mom and I guess that was the way they wanted it—or someone did anyway.

As it turned out, the doctor let my mother go home for Christmas, so my parents drove to Foxhall and told me we were all going to some fancy resort in the Caribbean for the holiday. Someplace nice and warm where we could all relax. It was a funny idea, I thought at the time. Relaxing was about the furthest thing from my mind. I tossed some clothes in a suitcase and met them at the front porch of Fox Dorm. Wes was waiting to say good-bye. I never saw him look so sad.

"Don't worry," I said. "It won't be long. We'll be back in three weeks."

"You'll be all tan and gorgeous," he told me.

"Yeah," I smiled at him and noticed my father getting out of the car and opening the trunk. "Don't let any of those California girls snap you up."

"Not likely," he touched my cheek with one finger. "You really okay? I mean after everything?"

"I think so. I'm not really sure. I'll write you a long letter from whatever beach they throw me onto."

I saw my father waving me to get in the car and gave Wes a peck on the cheek and ran down the steps to the car and my waiting parents.

My mother sat in the back with me, which was unusual. As we drove along the paved road out of Foxhall, I felt something I hadn't felt since I'd arrived. A kind of nostalgia for Foxhall. Now that I was driving away, I realized I'd become a part of the school or maybe it had become a part of me.

My mother put her arm around me. I rested my head against her shoulder and started to cry softly.

"Poor Suzi," she said softly, which was unlike her, or at least unlike the way I thought of her. "You've been through a lot. You'll have to tell me all about it now that I feel better."

She wrapped her arms around me there in the back seat and stroked my hair. I trusted her no more then than I had before. It was certain she'd get sick again because the quiet times never lasted for long. But on that day at least, I could cry and let her comfort me, which was all I ever really wanted.

"Right after you were born, I asked the nurse for a baby hairbrush. You had thick dark curls that needed brushing right away. You were a beautiful baby with big hazel eyes. I'm sorry I've been sick so much. I know it's been difficult for you. I'm trying very hard to be better."

———————

So, about my grandson. Remember him? Born after a thirty-two hour labor, he did not enter this world easily. The last few minutes were accompanied by the wailing blare of a hospital code, immediately followed by waves of staff, white paper bags over their shoes, stampeding past me in a blur of hospital-scrub pale blue.

I couldn't imagine wanting my own mother anywhere near me while giving birth, but then I've been a very different kind of mother to my children and was grateful that my daughter had wanted me there. At the finale, there were fifteen people plus the husband in her room, all stationed around the mother-to-be, everyone on high alert, so no one noticed when I retired to the hall outside the door. That's the hardest part. When you feel like yelling commands and taking over but you can't. And you know it.

Two female obstetricians—one of them herself a tiny thing—inserted their hands up my daughter's birth canal and literally turned the baby so they could ease him into this world. What was keeping him from sliding out on his own? Something called shoulder dystocia, when the baby's shoulder gets stuck behind the mother's pelvic bone. How come they didn't notice this—oh, like twelve or so hours earlier—and rush her to a nice, sterile OR and, with a neat, little incision, lift him out with no drama? Who knows? Things don't always go the way you think they should, even when you have the best intentions and make decisions with a good heart. I learned that long ago at Foxhall and never forgot it.

When I entered again, after the drama had played itself out, what greeted me was that bright, red patch in the middle of the washable floor. Although someone had swabbed the floor dry, the faded brick color remained a gruesome reminder of the struggle for life. My daughter was still lying in the middle of Heinz 57 blood-red sheets with a nurse fussing around her, checking tubes and vitals. But she was smiling, my daughter, smiling like an angel had just visited and blessed her. So it was going to be all right. Another nurse wheeled in a new bed and the transfer was made, the criminal clues hustled away in a plastic bag, and in came the little, swaddled newborn in his own Tupperware bed on wheels followed by a beaming, exhausted dad and that was a scene I'll never forget. It was five a.m. and I hung around the hospital, everyone glowing, me included, until my daughter finally drifted off to sleep with newborn James cradled in her arms.

It was after that traumatic night that ended so happily that I ran into Daria on a steep hill on a windy morning. In my memory, she will always be beautiful Daria aged sixteen. But the reality is different. She aged the way we all have. She wears her life on her face and you can see the pain there.

Well, we were just kids after all, trying to do our best and often succeeding. I wouldn't want to leave the impression that, after all these years, I look back at my time at Foxhall as anything but enriching, even the bad stuff. What would have been better, you might wonder, for the teen years are not real anyway? Not real in the sense that they are a way station on the path of a life that is becoming. The teen years are a dress rehearsal. But they feel real. That's for sure. We reside in the teen years for such a short time, and the paths we take during those years diverge and take us off course in such a variety of ways that we only know we came out of a maze and into a world we inherited.

Was it better for me that I went away to school instead of staying home at that girls' school? Probably. But no matter where you go, you can't escape crazy. It's everywhere. In people, in politics. In wars and religions. I don't know where it comes from in people. You don't see crazy in animals or insects or birds. They do their thing—eat, bathe, drink, procreate, care for their young. When it's time to die, they go quietly.

So there was crazy at Foxhall just like at home. It stayed with me for life but you can get used to anything. I got used to crazy. I expected it. It got me down for a long time. I felt responsible for it, like I had to do something about it but I didn't know what or how. The thing is, I'm not at its mercy anymore. If we are all joined in some cosmic way, I no longer need to see the threads or to pull at them or even know where they come from. The cycle of life will spin on its own. I accept that with all its imperfections. For me, that's aging gracefully.

The Nipple Yearbook was discovered and confiscated by one of the boys' dorm teachers. Linden Houghtling blabbed the minute he got caught and the whole Nipple Brigade was given study hall for the first month after Christmas break, which hardly seemed fair given what I'd suffered at the hands of Bleaker. All the kids knew that no one was as much of a hard ass as Bleaker and it bestowed on me an infamous status, not only to have withstood her punishment, but to have exacted some sort of revenge on behalf of all of us.

The mattress room key was never found and I heard that some kids started using the room again by going through the window well. I never went down there, and as far as I knew Wes never did either. Over the summer, the trees that Bleaker had pruned to the nub were dug up and replaced with some really pretty crape myrtles that did not lend themselves to climbing.

Tim Payton wasn't the only boy from Foxhall who was sent to Vietnam. Stocky went as an Army draftee. He got a Purple Heart for being wounded while saving five of his platoon that were trapped in a swamp. When he got back, he called every girl he had ever known looking for someone who would have sex with him, including me. Daria told me he'd become a trial lawyer in Denver.

Wes and I dated the rest of my sophomore year, and then he graduated and went off to Stanford. He registered for the draft and, at the physical, they discovered a problem with one of his heart valves. It kept him out of the service but, since it couldn't be fixed, it eventually made him a semi-invalid.

Jan was diagnosed with a very aggressive breast cancer and died in her mid-thirties. Faith went to medical school and became a child psychiatrist. Brady, who'd always been what they used to call a free spirit, a euphemism for sleeping around, became a nurse and also went to Vietnam where she oversaw a MASH unit nursing staff. When the war was over, she took on the job of director of nursing at a VA hospital where she managed the nurses looking after the boys who came back from war.

After Daria and I parted on that morning in San Francisco, I thought a lot about what happened back then and where I ended up. It was true that I was happy with my life. I wondered, off and on, what happened to Moll. Daria said she kept in touch with some of the others on social media. She was hoping to start a new job working for a photographer who did a lot of fashion and travel work. She visited Tim's grave once a year to lay flowers on it and tell him she misses him still. I hoped Moll found acceptance wherever she landed. I hoped she learned to accept herself. Maybe I would find out one day.

Forgiveness takes a whole piñata of mental twists and turns. I forgave my mother a long time ago. I forgave Miss Bleaker. I forgave Daria, but I'm still not sure for what. Now I think I can finally forgive myself for what happened to Moll. I'll never see her again and I'll never see Daria again. But we carry with us the composite of all the relationships we've ever had. We can no more rid ourselves of them than we can harness the glow of the moon. If it's true that the spirit is within each of us, maybe God resides in all the bits and pieces of others that we've incorporated into ourselves.

Reader and Book Club
Discussion Guide

1. At age fifteen, Susannah Greenwood arrives for her first semester at a Quaker prep school and says at the end of the prologue that she is "both happy and unhappy to be there." Why do you think she is both happy and unhappy? Discuss how—and under what circumstances—it is possible to feel two opposing emotions at the same time.

2. Throughout the book, Greenwood questions, and even flaunts, authority. What do you think the connection is between her unwillingness to obey authority and her experiences with her own mother at home? Discuss how and why some people seem to need a strong authority telling them exactly where the boundaries are, while others demand freedom to decide for themselves what course to follow? What are some examples of this in the book and beyond?

3. Greenwood's need to feel accepted at her new prep school leads her into direct conflict with the school's rules and the strict dean of girls and, at the same time, puts her at risk of severe punishments, even expulsion. Was she justified in choosing acceptance over compliance? What do you see in adults where the same struggle may be played out?

4. Greenwood's conflict between loyalty and responsibility leads to stark consequences. Do you think she did the right thing by not divulging where Moll went? Who was at fault when Moll disappeared? Do you think Greenwood should have been more attentive to what was going on around her the night of the dance?

5. Moll insists that Greenwood keep her secret. How do secrets lead to dire consequences? What other kinds of secrets do you find people keeping and what are the consequences for them and others? Should Greenwood have helped Moll stay away from the school? What would you have done?

6. One of the themes underlying the story is faith as practiced by Quakers. Discuss the roles of organized religion vs. individual faith vs. moral conviction. When do they diverge and how are they different or the same?

Acknowledgments

When I first began writing seriously, I was naïve enough to wonder about all those writers whose books opened with a page or more of thanks to dozens of people for help in making their books a reality. After all, I reasoned, one of the elements of writing I most prized was that you could accomplish it all alone, without having to rely on anyone else. What I failed to understand was that it would take many years of help from others before my writing felt accomplished, professional, or cogent. That help came from writers who taught and writers who became friends.

So I thank them all, beginning with Fred Leebron whose writing workshops and critiques were invaluable both for his lessons on fiction writing in general and his insights into my own works-in-progress. His book, *Creating Fiction A Writer's Companion* http://amzn.to/2lbldcd, is an invaluable resource.

Next, thanks to Sue Levine and Lary Bloom, who I met in Praiano, Italy, for the first time where I absorbed their wisdom and extensive comments on this book in particular. Their later critical suggestions provided enormous help in shaping the finished work.

Finally, I thank Wally Lamb, for his generous spirit and decades of teaching the craft of writing. He is both a mentor and a model for using writing as a tool for growth and redemption.

To the writers whose paths I've crossed over the years—Kim Wiley, Karen Cantwell, Dawn Clifton Tripp, Allison Smith, Priscilla Cutler Bourgoine, Eileen Dougharty, Emily Miranda, Nicky Wheeler Nicholson, Catherine Michele Adams, Dorette Snover, Jane Wells, Malcolm Campbell, Michael Neff—thank you for all the readings, musings, suggestions, corrections, and encouragement.

I thank Brooke, Lauren, Julie, Crystal, Morgan, and all the She Writers.

Of course my husband and daughters, who always encourage the very best I can give, to them I blow kisses of gratitude.

About the Author

LB GSCHWANDTNER is the author of four adult novels, one middle grade novel, and one collection of quirky short stories. She has attended numerous fiction writing workshops—the Iowa Writers Workshop and others—and studied with Wally Lamb, Lary Bloom, and Suzanne Levine in Praiano, Italy and Fred Leebron and Bob Bausch in the US. She has won writing awards, *Writers Digest* and Lorian Hemingway fiction competitions, and been published in literary digests and magazines. She lives on a tidal creek in Virginia with her husband of forty-five years, with whom she cofounded the multimedia company Selling Power Inc. LB has been the editor of *Selling Power* magazine for more than thirty years. She and her husband have three adult daughters and two grandchildren.

Books by LB Gschwandtner

The Naked Gardener
http://amzn.to/2kCrW06

Artist Katelyn Cross loves Greg Mazur and he loves her. He wants to be married but a previous relationship that went sour has made Katelyn overly cautious about any permanent commitment. And what about Greg's first wife? He lost her to cancer and Katelyn worries that he's only looking for a replacement. What's a girl to do? Canoe down a river with five gal pals, camp out, catch fish, talk about life and men.

Shelly's Second Chance
http://amzn.to/2kCjUnM

Shelly Wagner is in trouble but her fiancé, Ben, doesn't know it. Broke and ready to gamble her last dollar on a Super Lotto ticket, she really needs some help. It arrives in the form of Joe and Alanna—Wish Granters from another world. One problem: it's their very first assignment and they're fairly clueless about their new wish granting powers and how to best use them. Plus they have a few things to work out in their own lives—if only they were still among the living. They want to return to earth, but can only get back by helping Shelly first.

Carla's Secret
http://amzn.to/2mcLYdK

A long time ago, something terrible happened to Carla Patterson. She locked that terrible thing away in a secret place and moved on with her life. Now the Wish Granters mysteriously arrive, offering her one wish that could change her life . . . or leave her brokenhearted. Will Carla wish for a new beginning, or turn the Wish Granters away and deny the love she might have had?

Page Truly and The Journey to Nearandfar
A Middle Grade Novel
http://amzn.to/2kXr8Py

What if . . . a girl and her tooth fairy flew away to the realm called Nearandfar and the girl discovered she had more power than the fairies?

Page Truly is on a mission. It won't be easy. There will be danger. Page will have to be very brave and very smart.

It all happens one night when a sassy tooth fairy brings a borrowed wand and a big attitude to Page's bedroom. She makes it look like a wand can do anything. That is until Page has to save Nearandfar, and discovers that a magic wand is only as powerful as the gifted one who knows how to unlock its secrets and use it wisely.

Maybelle's Revenge
http://amzn.to/2kXMiNm

A short story collection with an edge. Paranormal events, vengeful attacks, payback for past pain, and lots of other quirky tidbits are the stuff of this collection, including a love-stricken parrot and a town that takes on an electric glow. It's all in here but, to start, there's Maybelle's Revenge. And she is out to get some payback.

Foxy's Tale (with Karen Cantwell)
http://amzn.to/2kCxHLd

Former beauty queen Foxy Anders has fallen on hard times.

Her new tenant, mysterious, bumbling Myron Standlish carries wads of cash and hoards vials of blood. Her new assistant, Knot Knudsen, loves shoes and conservative politicians, but man can he sell Foxy's antiques. Amanda, Foxy's teenage daughter, thinks they're all crazy. But, when she hooks up with Nick, a cute guy at school, she's in for some crazy of her own. Ultimately, they're all in for some romance with a dash of suspense and a sprinkle of supernatural. And laughs . . . as an added bonus.

SELECTED TITLES FROM SHE WRITES PRESS

She Writes Press is an independent publishing company
founded to serve women writers everywhere.
Visit us at www.shewritespress.com.

How to Grow an Addict by J.A. Wright. $16.95, 978-1-63152-991-7.
Raised by an abusive father, a detached mother, and a loving aunt
and uncle, Randall Grange is built for addiction. By twenty-three,
she knows that together, pills and booze have the power to cure
just about any problem she could possibly have . . . right?

Magic Flute by Patricia Minger. $16.95, 978-1-63152-093-8. When
a car accident puts an end to ambitious flutist Liz Morgan's dreams,
she returns to her childhood hometown in Wales in an effort to
reinvent her path.

Cleans Up Nicely by Linda Dahl. $16.95, 978-1-938314-38-4. The
story of one gifted young woman's path from self-destruction to
self-knowledge, set in mid-1970s Manhattan.

In a Silent Way by Mary Jo Hetzel. $16.95, 978-1-63152-135-5.
When Jeanna Kendall—a young white teacher at a progressive urban
school—becomes involved with a community activist group, she
finds herself grappling with issues of racism, sexism, and oppres-
sion of various shades in both her professional and personal life.

Keep Her by Leora Krygier. $16.95, 978-1-63152-143-0. When a
water main bursts in rain-starved Los Angeles, seventeen-year-old
artist Maddie and filmmaker Aiden's worlds collide in a whirlpool
of love and loss. Is it meant to be?

Beautiful Garbage by Jill DiDonato. $16.95, 978-1-938314-01-8.
Talented but troubled young artist Jodi Plum leaves suburbia for
the excitement of the city—and is soon swept up in the sexual
politics and downtown art scene of 1980s New York.